NANTUCKET SUMMER HOUSE

PAMELA M. KELLEY

ISBN 978-1-953060-53-2

DESCRIPTION

Lauren is up for the opportunity of a life-time, to be the lead producer for a new reality show set in Nantucket. Nantucket Influence will follow a group of young influencers as they spend the summer at a gorgeous waterfront home. It's a concept that Lauren has worked on successfully before and the job is hers—as long as she doesn't mind that one of the influencer's is Billy—the ex that she caught cheating on her. Does she really want to spend the summer working with him every day? This is her first chance to run a show, though,—and she can't pass it up.

Hudson, runs a Nantucket based production company, with the famous actress and new Nantucket resident, Cami Carmichael. Hudson is good friends with Billy, but Lauren finds herself drawn to him, though they can't be more than friends since they are working together—and since Lauren will be heading back to LA when filming ends.

Meanwhile Angela is thrilled to see her college friend Lauren and has some exciting news to share. And Lisa discovers that her nemesis, Violet, who runs a competing inn is ready to declare herself as the top lobster quiche maker on the island. But not if Lisa has anything to say about it—she signs up for the local food festival as well and will let the people decide who makes the best quiche.

CAST OF CHARACTERS

Hodges family and friends, followed by the cast of the reality show that is filming near the inn!

Lisa Hodges—fifty-something mother and owner of Beach Plum Cove Inn. Now married to **Rhett.**

Kate Hodges—thirty-something twin daughter of Lisa, married to **Jack.**

Kristen Hodges—Kate's twin sister, an artist engaged to **Tyler** a bestselling thriller writer.

Chase Hodges—Lisa's only son, runs a construction business and is married to **Beth,** his office manager/partner.

Abby Hodges—the youngest daughter, married to her high school sweetheart, **Jeff.**

Angela—thirty-something, runs a cleaning company, friend of the Hodges, married to Philippe.

Taylor and Victoria—friends of Hodges, both are reporters with local paper.

Mia and Izzy—sisters and friends of Hodges, Mia is

a wedding planner and Izzy owns a clothing shop on the wharf.

Cami/Bella—thirty-something actress also owns a production company, engaged to **Nick**, chef at Whitley hotel

Kay—Seventy-something friend of Lisa's and now dating next-door neighbor, **Walter** also 70's and a widower.

Marley—Lisa's friend, also fifty-something.

The Nantucket Influence Reality Show cast/crew

Lauren—Lead Producer, thirty-something

Eloise—Producer

Hudson—Lead camera man and partner in the production company with Cami. Assisted by **Mike and Tom.**

Billy—30's one of the influencers and also Lauren's most recent ex-boyfriend.

Katy—youngest in the house at 24, short and curvy, makeup influencer

Anna—26, lifestyle influencer, tall blonde, cute dog, Smith

Honey and Brett, 30, married, she's a food influencer, he's in finance, live in Charleston, cat Simon also influencer

Sami—28, health influencer, yoga instructor

Noah—early 30's, comedian

Jason—33, former NFL receiver, now famous for funny fitness videos, huge online following

Suzanne—29, lifestyle and entertainment influencer

CHAPTER ONE

The best thing about Lauren Singer's Hollywood Hills apartment was the panoramic views of Los Angeles. It almost made up for the high rent and hideous rush hour traffic to get to the film studios. The apartment was small, just one bedroom, but the ceilings were high with big windows and French doors that let in lots of natural light.

Lauren made herself a cup of vanilla coffee and tried to relax and read the novel she'd been so excited about when it arrived in the mail that morning. It was hard to focus, though. She kept getting up and pacing around the room, glancing at the clock on the wall. It was Friday and as the time inched closer to five, she grew more tense. If she didn't hear today, she likely wouldn't hear anything until Monday and the stress of not knowing would drive her crazy all weekend.

She took a deep breath and had just resigned herself that the call wasn't going to come, when her iWatch started vibrating and a second later her phone rang and it was the studio.

"Hi Andrea," she said, trying to sound calm and collected. Andrea was the decision maker for the new show that the studio was developing. The show that could be a huge opportunity for Lauren and a chance to get back to the East Coast for a few months. She had stiff competition, though. Lauren knew that it was down to her and Toby and they were equally qualified.

"Hi Lauren, I have some exciting news for you. You got it! We'd like you to be the lead producer on *Nantucket Influence*. Can you leave next Thursday?"

Lauren's last show had wrapped over a month ago, and she was more than ready to go. She'd been feeling stir-crazy just sitting around waiting.

"Yes! Thank you. I'm so excited about doing this. And it's been ages since I've been to Nantucket. I only get home to the Cape once or twice a year, usually around the holidays."

"To be honest, that gave you an edge, that you know the area. There's one other thing you should know though, before accepting..." Andrea paused, and Lauren wondered what she thought could make Lauren hesitate.

"What is it?"

"So you know, like the other shows we've done, we'll be putting an interesting friend group in a share house for a few months."

Lauren knew that 'interesting' also meant attractive. The formula had worked very well in other locations.

"So, this will be a little different," Andrea continued.

"Instead of people who are already friends, this group will be influencers. Some of them know each other, of course, but it's more acquaintance level, if that makes sense."

Lauren smiled. It actually seemed smart to add a new hook, an additional twist that would cause people to watch.

"I like that idea and if they are influencers, some of them might already be familiar to viewers and they'll bring their followers along, which will help boost ratings," Lauren said.

"Exactly! I'm so glad you like the idea." She paused for so long that Lauren wondered if she'd dropped the call. But then Andrea spoke again. "One of the influencers is someone you know. He just signed on today—Billy Winston will be in the house."

Lauren instantly felt sick to her stomach.

"Billy's going to be there? I'll have to produce him?"

There was another long silence. Andrea sounded overly cheerful as she said,

"Yes, though you'll have help, of course. I know that might be uncomfortable for you. If it's too much, I'll understand and we'll go with Toby."

Lauren felt a rush of anger. They'd only broken up a little over a month ago, and it didn't end well. But she was not going to lose this opportunity because of Billy. She'd find a way to deal with it.

"It's okay. I'm still in."

"Excellent! Marissa will be in touch on Monday once she has all your travel details confirmed. We are all so excited about this, and I know you're going to do a great job."

When the call ended, Lauren felt a mix of emotions. She was thrilled to get the job, but was apprehensive about seeing Billy and having to deal with him on a daily basis. She was looking forward to seeing Angela, though. At least she'd have one good friend nearby. They'd gone to college together and had kept in touch after Angela had moved to Nantucket permanently. It would be nice to see her old friend again and catch up in person.

CHAPTER TWO

A stunning bouquet of roses arrived the next day. Lauren assumed they were from Andrea to congratulate her as they were a brightly colored mix of mostly pale-yellow roses with a splash of pink, red, and orange. But when she read the card, she shook her head and sighed.

"Heard you got the job! Excited to see you and work together, Lauren. Cheers to a fun Nantucket summer. Love always, Billy."

The flowers were beautiful and her first thought was that maybe it was a nice gesture and that Billy was going to make an effort to behave. But she knew Billy better than that. When they'd first started dating, he'd love bombed her, sending flowers in between every date and they'd always been red or pink roses, never yellow. Yellow meant friendship. And even now, Billy couldn't commit to that either. There were a few pink and red ones mixed in, which Lauren knew was Billy's way of saying he'd love to pick up where they left off, if she was open to it.

And that was not going to happen. Billy was like a high energy, adorable puppy—hard to resist but after a while the charm wore off when it became apparent that he simply couldn't be faithful. Billy loved women and as much as he'd told Lauren he loved her and that she was 'the one', after a few months, when the love bombing slowed, she started getting a sense that something was off. But she couldn't explain why. Until she stumbled across a pretty blonde actress on TikTok raving about her newest crush and showing off the red roses he'd just sent her. They'd only had one date, but he'd told her that he was falling fast and that she might be 'the one'. The girl was thrilled, just as Lauren had been when Billy had told her the exact same thing.

She'd ended it the next day when Billy stopped by when she wouldn't answer his calls. She'd needed time to cool off before having a conversation with him. But he'd sensed she was upset and rushed over. So she let him in and wordlessly handed him her phone with the TikTok of the blonde girl. His big smile faded as he saw that he'd been caught. And he instantly started to backpedal.

"Okay, I screwed up, but it's not what you think. My manager wanted me to meet her as we might be working together on an upcoming movie. It will be my first lead role." Billy had fallen into being an influencer. He'd started out chronicling his efforts to land his first acting jobs and quickly built a following on social media. He was funny and not afraid to make fun of himself. And he was very good-looking. It didn't take long before Hollywood took notice.

"Well, that's perfect then. I'm happy for you, Billy. You should go. I have things to do." She could barely get the words out. She'd believed Billy, and she'd been falling fast for the first time in ages. Billy had been fun to spend time with. He always found the humor in any situation and when they were together, he always gave her his full attention. He was charismatic and when those blue-gray eyes were focused on her, he was hard to resist. She was going to miss him.

"Lauren, don't do this. We were so good together. Don't you want to see if we can keep it going?" His eyes pleaded with hers, and she didn't doubt that he meant it —in the moment.

"Billy, I really cared for you. But I can't trust you. I can't get past this. I deserve better. And I'm not changing my mind." She spoke as firmly as possible and hated the wobble in her voice that gave away how shaken she was by it all.

Billy heard it too and sighed. "I'm so sorry, Lauren. I never meant to hurt you. This is all new to me and I don't always handle things well. I wish I could turn back time."

Lauren knew that he meant it. And she knew that having this level of attention was sometimes over-whelming for him. Billy had told her that it was only in the past few years that he'd grown into his looks and after discovering the gym, had gone from a tall, scrawny guy to filled out with washboard abs and he'd also learned that leaving a five o'clock shadow transformed his face and made his jaw look square and sculpted and his lips that he'd thought were too full, were actually irresistible to

7

women. Billy turned heads, and once he took off on social media with his funny skits and witty observations, his following exploded and women began throwing themselves at him.

When Lauren first started dating him, his looks were actually a concern. She'd met Billy at a Hollywood party and he'd made her laugh immediately. He'd been introduced by her colleague Toby and while she'd felt a spark that night, she'd ignored it. Billy was too good-looking for her to take seriously. She was well aware of the type, as there were many of them in LA and she knew he'd have his pick of beautiful women. Still, when she went home, she looked him up and laughed at some of his funny videos. She also caught her breath at the ones where he was in the gym, working out without his shirt. That was her first glimpse of his abs and it was impressive. She quickly put it out of her mind, though. He hadn't asked for her number, so she assumed she might not ever see Billy again.

But he'd called the next day. Toby had given him her number and texted her to let her know, but Lauren didn't see the text until after Billy called. So it took her by surprise and when he'd asked her to dinner, she was so shocked that she just said yes.

She knew now that love bombing behavior was a red flag in a relationship. But she'd never experienced that kind of intensity or received so many flowers and she gave into it and enjoyed every minute. Until she felt his attention fading and saw the video. And she realized that she'd expected the moment to come, eventually. She'd researched Billy online and learned this was a pattern he repeated over and over with the women he dated. No one had a bad thing to say about him, except that he couldn't seem to stay faithful. And that was a deal-breaker for most.

She glanced at the flowers and sighed again. It would be rude not to thank him. But she wasn't eager to reach out to Billy. She didn't want to give him the wrong idea that she might be open to reconciling. She'd noticed online that his fling with the pretty blonde girl was over and there didn't seem to be a replacement. As she was debating texting him, her phone dinged with a text message from Billy.

Hope you like the flowers. Excited to see you soon.

She smiled. Typical Billy, like a puppy, anxious for approval.

She texted back.

Thank you. They just arrived and they're beautiful.

He replied immediately.

Great! When do you leave for Nantucket?

Her heart sank. She hadn't thought of that—that they might be on the same flight.

I'm not sure, I don't have my tickets yet. When are you going?

I fly out Friday morning. Hopefully, we're on the same flight.

Lauren did not hope for that. She thought Andrea had said Thursday, and she was going to call Marissa first thing Monday and make sure they were on different flights. It was a good six hours to Boston, at least another hour or so before she'd touch down on Nantucket as she would likely have a layover and change planes first. She wasn't ready to spend that much time with Billy.

Billy have to go, have a call coming in.

No worries. See you soon.

CHAPTER THREE

"You really think it's a good idea? I'm not sure I'm thrilled about the thought of sharing a house with a bunch of strangers for a few months...or about being that public with my private life." Anna was on her cell, sitting on her Manhattan terrace, her fluffy, white Maltese dog, Smith, on her lap while she talked to Susan, her talent manager. Susan was twice her age—in her late fifties, and usually knew what was best.

"Anna, you already share most of your life online as it is," Susan said reasonably. "This will just take it to the next level. It could be a really good thing for your career. And you'll be paid to spend the summer on Nantucket. Most people would kill for an opportunity like this."

Anna laughed. "You make it sound like a no-brainer. I know it would be good for my brand. I'm just a little nervous about the idea of it. Will they let me bring Smith? I can't leave him for two months."

"If they say yes, can I tell them you're in?"

Anna took a deep breath and gazed out at the Manhattan skyline and a cruise ship going by on the East River. "Yes, if they let me bring Smith, I'll do it."

CHAPTER FOUR

L isa Hodges surveyed the breakfast offerings and debated what to add to her plate. She knew that fresh fruit and oatmeal would be the sensible choice, but the ham and cheddar quiche she'd made smelled so amazing and the tray of brown-sugar crusted crispy bacon was tempting, too. She compromised by adding a sliver of quiche, two slices of bacon and a big bowl of cut cantaloupe and honeydew melon. She added a splash of coffee to her mug and headed to the table where Angela and Kay had just sat down with their breakfasts.

As she did every morning, Lisa rose early, usually by five, and started preparing the meal that was included for guests of The Beach Plum Cove Inn. Several years ago, her son Chase had helped her to transform her waterfront home into a bed-and-breakfast. That income allowed her to remain on Nantucket, close to her four adult children and friends.

Her quiches were so popular that she'd expanded and

started an ecommerce company to initially sell the lobster quiches and other items online. It grew so fast that she quickly outgrew her home kitchen and hired a commercial one off-island to help produce and ship. It all kept her very busy, but she still had time to have breakfast occasionally with friends.

And this morning she had two visitors. Angela was a young woman in her thirties that had once stayed at the inn after inheriting her grandmother's cottage. Her initial plan had been to fix it up and sell, but Angela, who was alone in the world, grew to love Nantucket and the sense of family and community she'd found. She'd also fallen in love with one of the many island celebrities. She'd married Philippe, a bestselling local author, who also spent time on the West Coast as many of his books had been turned into film or TV series.

Since moving to the island, Angela continued to grow her cleaning business. She'd started out cleaning houses while in college and found she enjoyed the work. Now she mostly managed a busy team, but also pitched in as needed if someone was out. The regular cleaner for the inn sprained her ankle, so Angela would be taking over for the next week or so. Lisa adored her and was eager to catch up over coffee.

She'd already invited Kay to stop in as well. They saw each other often, as Kay had been a family friend for years. She was in her early seventies and had been a dear friend of Lisa's mother. She hadn't been able to make it to Lisa and Rhett's wedding, as she'd been traveling in Europe with friends. But she came for an extended visit, initially meant to be two months, but Kay was at a cross-roads in her life and found what she didn't know she was looking for when she met Lisa's neighbor Walter, who was also recently widowed. They clicked instantly, but first as friends, and it slowly turned to more. Now they were inseparable.

"Walter and I sat outside yesterday for an hour or so, having our coffee and watching the cars come and go at the house next door. We're not really sure what's going on over there. Have you heard anything?" Kay asked.

Lisa nodded at Angela. "Do you want to explain about the show they are filming?" Lisa knew Angela could explain it to Kay far better than she could.

Angela smiled and set her coffee cup down. "They are filming a reality show. My friend Lauren is a producer on the show and is on her way to Nantucket. Nine influencers will be spending two months together, working from the house and enjoying the island."

"What is an influencer?" Kay looked thoroughly confused, and Lisa knew it was a strange concept, one she was just learning about herself.

"These people have turned themselves into a brand. They post content on social media—could be TikTok or Instagram or YouTube or all of the above. They have hundreds of thousands of followers—some even have millions—of people that watch everything they post. When these influencers mention a product, their followers rush out and buy it. They get paid a lot of money to promote products."

"Like a commercial?" Kay asked, trying to make sense of it.

"Sort of. So, to give you an example, there are lots of beauty and makeup influencers. They post videos where they are putting on makeup and trying different products and then their followers will often want to buy those products."

"Videos on makeup? And these people make money from that? How interesting," Kay said.

Angela nodded. "They also make money from people watching their videos. Some just put up really entertaining content that people watch until the end and they sometimes sell products directly from shops online. It's all a pretty big business, actually."

"Is it all young people?" Kay asked.

Angela thought for a moment. "Not necessarily. It started out that way, but all ages are on social media and watch videos now, so there are some really popular older creators, too."

"I'll have to watch some of these videos and see what all the fuss is about," Kay said.

Lisa thought about what Angela had said and what Lauren briefly mentioned when she booked a room at the inn. "So a bunch of these young influencers will be staying in the house next to Walter? How does that become a TV show? Especially if they don't know each other?"

"The magic happens in production and editing. From what I understand, the whole house will be wired with cameras so they will be filmed around the clock. Which means they will quickly become comfortable being filmed and we'll get more authentic content."

"I still don't see how that will be all that interesting." It didn't sound appealing to Lisa.

Angela smiled. "There's always drama that comes from these situations. These people will be in close quarters and there will be catered parties and alcohol, which will lower inhibitions and these influencers aren't shy to begin with. There will likely be friendships that form and possibly romances and rivalries. Possibly jealousy and love triangles and other drama."

And now Lisa understood. "That sounds messy."

"But very interesting," Kay said.

"Exactly," Angela agreed. "It's like a train wreck. You know it's going to be a disaster but it's hard not to watch."

CHAPTER FIVE

L auren arrived on Nantucket a little after five on
   Thursday. She'd talked to Andrea's assistant first
thing on Monday and made sure she flew out a day
before Billy. The plane coming to the island had been
completely full and the small airport was bustling. Lauren
couldn't help but notice the row of impressive private
planes—there were so many of them. She knew that
there was a lot of money on Nantucket. She also knew
from prior visits that many of the biggest waterfront
estates were summer homes that sat empty most of the
year.

Marissa took care of reserving a rental car, so when
her small plane touched down at the Nantucket airport,
Lauren stopped by the rental agency and there was a
white Jeep waiting for her. She loaded her suitcase and
carryon bag into the back of the Jeep and put the address
of the Beach Plum Cove Inn into her phone's GPS.

The studio had given her the option of living in a

house with the production team, or having a private room. As much as she liked her colleagues, Lauren didn't particularly want to live with them for two months. She valued her privacy.

Angela had also offered for her to stay at her place, and if it had just been for a week or so, Lauren would have happily accepted, but two months felt like an imposition. Angela insisted that it wasn't, but understood Lauren's hesitation and finally suggested the Beach Plum Cove Inn.

"That's where I stayed when I first came to the island. Lisa and her kids feel like family now. I actually met Philippe through her daughter Kate and we're all good friends. You'll like Lisa. It's also just two houses away from the show house, so you'll be able to walk to work."

Lauren liked the idea of being so close, yet having her own place. And when she'd called to book, Lisa was happy to hear that she was a friend of Angela's.

"A TV show, how exciting! Just knock on the door when you arrive, and I'll come right out and get you settled," Lisa had said.

It was a clear and sunny day, but a bit windy and cool compared to California. Lauren zipped up her jacket, then hopped into the Jeep. About twelve minutes later, she pulled into the driveway of the Beach Plum Cove Inn. There were only two other cars there, and she guessed that one of them was probably Lisa's. Lisa had told her that June was the beginning of the summer season, but it was more weekends than weekly rentals. From July on, they'd be fully booked until September.

"I had a cancellation just yesterday, which opened up your room. And they were going to spend two full months too. Funny how things work out sometimes."

Lauren couldn't agree more. She had a good feeling about the inn. It was a big, beautiful house, with a white picket fence and pink roses climbing over it and along the front of the house. It was right on the ocean, set up a slight hill, with a path to the beach. She looked forward to early morning or evening walks.

She parked and brought her luggage to the house, then knocked on the door. Lisa opened a moment later with a smile.

"Lauren? Come on in." She held the door open and Lauren stepped inside. She was in the foyer and while Lisa went to a roll-top desk by the front door, Lauren glanced through the living room to the kitchen and huge windows that overlooked the ocean. The views were breathtaking. Lisa rummaged in a drawer and pulled out a key on a navy tag.

"I've put you in a room on the top floor. It's a corner room and nice and quiet. It used to be my daughter Abby's room." Lauren grabbed her luggage and then followed Lisa up the stairs to where the guest rooms were. Lisa unlocked her room and held the door open wide so Lauren could step in first. She did and instantly felt a wave of calm and peace wash over her. The views of the ocean and beach were stunning. She could hear the soothing sound of the white-tipped waves as they crashed against the sand and knew she'd sleep well there. She turned to face Lisa.

"It's gorgeous, thanks so much." The bed looked inviting with its pale-yellow comforter and royal-blue pillows. Lauren was tempted to lie down for just a minute, but knew she'd likely fall asleep for hours.

"I hope you'll be comfortable. There's a small microwave and a mini-refrigerator. Stop and Shop is just a few miles up the road if you want to stock up on groceries. Breakfast is included every morning from eight to ten in the main dining room."

Lauren nodded. "That sounds great. Maybe I will run up to Stop and Shop now and pick up a few things."

"If you need anything, here's my cell number." Lisa handed her a business card and Lauren put it into her wallet. "See you at breakfast!"

Lisa shut the door behind her and Lauren sat on the bed. It was soft and cozy, and she yawned. The day of traveling and time difference had caught up with her. She stood and unzipped her suitcase. She needed to keep busy and unpack. If she gave into a nap, it would be that much harder to adjust to East Coast time. After she put things away, she'd head to the store and then settle in and get a good night's sleep. She wanted to head over to the share house right after breakfast and get a feel for the place before Billy and the others arrived.

CHAPTER SIX

Once Lisa got Lauren settled, she headed back downstairs to the kitchen where her husband Rhett was sitting at the island, reading the paper.

"Did you open the wine?" Lisa asked. She'd handed Rhett a bottle before going to meet Lauren.

He nodded at the counter, where the opened bottle of Duckhorn cabernet stood next to two wine glasses. "It's a good bottle. I figured I'd let it breathe a little before we poured."

Lisa smiled. "It's been about fifteen minutes. I think I'll risk it." She poured a little for both of them and handed a glass to Rhett. He stuck his nose in the glass and inhaled deeply before taking a sip. Lisa watched as he swallowed and then gave her the thumbs up.

"I haven't had this in a long time. It is a treat. Are we celebrating something?" Rhett asked.

Lisa took a small sip before answering. She and Rhett usually drank less expensive wine. When she'd stopped at

Bradford's liquor store earlier to pick up a few bottles, she'd chatted with Peter, the owner, who was also dating her best friend, Paige. He was a wine lover and always had good recommendations. She'd asked for something that would be a good wine to celebrate with.

"If you like a rich, chewy cabernet with a lot of depth and smoothness, you can't go wrong with Duckhorn. I brought a bottle home last week for Paige's birthday and she loved it."

Lisa tapped her glass against Rhett's and grinned. "Today is the date when my very first guest arrived at the inn. The one that came and never left," she teased him. Rhett had been her first guest, and neither of them expected the friendship and romance that developed. Rhett had been on the island to open a new restaurant. He'd assumed that he'd get it up and running with a good manager in place and then he'd head off-island to oversee his other restaurants in the Boston area.

"Time flies," Rhett said softly. "I didn't realize it was today. I'm so glad that you remembered."

"Imagine if you'd stayed at Violet's bed-and-breakfast instead? We might never have met."

Rhett laughed. "That would have been horrible."

Violet also owned a bed-and-breakfast and had given Lisa a hard time when she first opened, as she wasn't pleased about the competition.

Rhett took her hand and pulled her in for a quick kiss. "Something smells incredible. What are we having for dinner?"

Lisa loved to cook, and she'd made one of their

favorite meals.

"Braised short ribs over mashed potatoes with sautéed spinach on the side. And I picked up a couple of mini-cannoli for dessert."

"I love your short ribs. Though anything you make is good."

Over dinner, Lisa told him what Angela had shared with her and Kay at breakfast. Rhett looked intrigued.

"First Cami Carmichael's studio and now a TV show. This is good for Nantucket. My restaurant is the closest one. Maybe they will want to venture out—could be a win-win," he said.

"Oh, I didn't even think of that. I can mention it to Lauren. She's one of the producers in charge. That would be nice publicity for the restaurant," Lisa agreed.

"Or if they want anything catered, lunch or dinners brought in, we can do that too," he said.

Lisa nodded. "I'll see what I can find out. I don't really know how it works. Maybe I'll watch one of the other reality shows Lauren has done to get a feel for it. The only thing I've seen reality-wise is *The Bachelor*."

Rhett groaned. "I don't really understand why these shows are so popular, especially that one."

Lisa laughed. "It's just fun. The girls all watch, too, and we chat about it."

"Next year we really should check out some of the films during the Film Festival. Nate, one of my newer bartenders, told me he entered a screenplay into the competition and got an honorable mention. He's all fired up now to get an agent and try to sell it."

"We just missed the Film Festival. Definitely next year. I always mean to go and then remember when it's too late."

"Speaking of screenplays. What's the latest on Kate's potential film deal?" Rhett asked.

Lisa took a big sip of wine before answering. "It's a bit of a sore subject. They were full steam ahead, and we thought it was going to happen. There was a screenwriter attached, and they were talking about casting and it all fell apart. The option just ran out, and they didn't renew it. Kate's so disappointed."

"So, that's it then? Back to square one?" Rhett looked surprised.

Lisa nodded. "Yes. Philippe told her he's going to ask around though. He knows a lot of people. So maybe something will come of it, eventually. He told her this is common, unfortunately. Lots of things get optioned but never actually get made."

"Are they coming for Sunday dinner?" Rhett asked. On most Sundays, Lisa had whichever kids were available over for a midday meal. Everyone's schedules were so busy that it was rare that they were all available on the same day, but now and then, it worked out. And it looked like this Sunday might be good for all of them.

"Yes. It looks like everyone can make it. Fingers crossed that nothing comes up between now and then."

Lisa topped her glass off and looked at Rhett's. He nodded, and she added more to his, too.

"Did you save room for a cannoli?" she asked.

Rhett grinned. "There's always room."

CHAPTER SEVEN

Angela stopped by The Thai House on her way home from work. It was already after five and she didn't feel like cooking. Her husband, Philippe, was usually good about it, but she knew he was deep into writing a book and when he was at this stage, he often lost all track of time. She made a stop at the pharmacy, too. She didn't want to get her hopes up. She knew better now. But still, there was a glimmer of hope that maybe they might finally have good news.

She paused for a moment after getting out of the car. Their waterfront view of the ocean always filled her with awe. Especially on days like this, when a thick fog hovered over the water, which was like glass at the moment, much calmer than usual. A storm was on the way—a Nor' easter was predicted and there was an eerie stillness in the air as well.

She grabbed the mail and headed inside. The view from inside was even more spectacular, as the wall facing the ocean was all glass. They'd watched many a storm from their living room sofa. The house was up high enough on the bluff that they didn't have to worry about flooding.

Angela set her bags on the kitchen counter and listened for a moment. Normally, when she walked in, Philippe came out a moment later to greet her. The room was so quiet that she knew he was still working. She grabbed the paper bag from the pharmacy and went into her bedroom bathroom and followed the instructions on the box. She set her phone timer for three minutes and went back to the kitchen and got plates out of the cupboard and serving spoons, knives and forks from the drawer. That took less than a minute.

She went back to her bedroom and checked messages on her phone until the timer went off and she went to the sink where the test stick waited.

And it was positive! She felt like screaming, but she also didn't quite believe it. There were two tests in the box and she pulled the other one out and waited three more minutes—pacing around her room in a state of nervous excitement.

When the second test was positive, Angela exhaled and felt a rush of joy bigger than she'd ever imagined she could feel. It had finally happened for them. She and Philippe had been trying to have a baby for over a year. And for the past few months, they'd had help with IVF. Their first attempt didn't work, so both Angela and Philippe tried to keep their expectations low this second time. They knew that it could take three or four tries to have a successful pregnancy.

Angela didn't normally interrupt Philippe when he was writing, but he didn't usually work this late and she knew he wouldn't mind. She headed toward his office and just as she reached it, the door opened and Philippe stepped into the hallway. He smiled when he saw her, and her heart felt even fuller. She couldn't wait to tell him the good news. He ran a hand through his hair.

"I should go wash up. I'm sure I look a mess. I haven't left that room all afternoon." He did look a bit disheveled, with his wavy hair all tousled. It was in need of a cut, but he usually let it go until he finished a project. And Angela didn't care. She liked it long on him.

"You look fine. I brought Thai home for dinner. Let's eat while it's hot." She grinned and held out the test stick. "Guess I'll pour some sparkling apple cider to celebrate. Want some?"

A range of emotions flashed across Philippe's face. Confusion, disbelief, joy. He picked her up and twirled around the room, laughing as they went in circles. He finally set her down and stared at her in wonder. "We're having a baby."

Angela nodded, and the emotions spilled over as her eyes watered. "I can't believe it. I want to tell everyone. But I know we should probably wait."

"Probably. What do they suggest, three months? It will be hard to keep quiet, but I don't want to jinx anything."

"I don't either."

"I'll open that sparkling cider," Philippe said and dug deep into the refrigerator to find it.

"You can have the real thing!" Angela laughed.

"Tonight, I'll celebrate your way. We're in this together." He got two champagne flutes out of the cupboard and filled them both. Angela started helping herself to some of the pad thai and tofu Massaman curry over white rice. Philippe did the same, and they took their dinners to a round glass table by the window. It was still light enough that they could watch the fog rolling in.

"Lauren should be here by now. She's staying at the Beach Plum Cove Inn. I'll probably see her at breakfast there tomorrow. I was thinking of having the girls over tomorrow night for drinks and appetizers. I want Lauren to meet everyone and once filming starts, I'm not sure how many free evenings she'll have. You don't mind, do you?"

Philippe shook his head. "Not at all. I'll give Jack a call and see if he wants to grab a beer downtown. Or if he can't get a sitter, maybe we'll just watch the game at his place."

"Thanks, honey."

Philippe took a sip of his cider. "It's going to be hard for you to keep quiet about this with the girls."

"I know. I really want to tell them. But I know it's too soon. I can wait. Three months will go by fast."

CHAPTER EIGHT

Lauren found the local supermarket, Stop and Shop, and stocked up on groceries for her room. By the time she got back to the inn, it was almost dark and foggy and it felt like a storm was on the way. She made herself a turkey sandwich and a cup of hot chamomile tea with honey. She felt grimy from the long day of traveling and took a hot shower after she ate, and climbed into her pajamas. She watched TV in bed and it wasn't long before her eyes grew heavy and she fell fast asleep.

When she woke, the sun was shining and at a few minutes past eight, there were already people walking on the beach. The time difference didn't bother her like it usually did because she'd gone to bed so early. She dressed and headed downstairs for breakfast.

Lisa and Angela were already there, and sitting at a round table with an older man about Lisa's age. Angela jumped up and gave Lauren a welcome hug and Lisa introduced her to Rhett, her husband. It looked like they'd just filled their plates and sat down. Except for Rhett, who only had a mug of black coffee in front of him.

"Help yourself," Lisa encouraged her.

Lauren walked to the side table where all the food was lined up. She helped herself to some fresh cantaloupe slices, hash brown potatoes and a slice of lobster quiche. That was something she'd never had before. She poured herself a black coffee and joined the others at the table.

"How was your trip?" Angela asked.

"Not bad, just long, but smooth and clear. I got here last night before dark."

"Did you hear the storm last night? It was a wild one. Our lights flickered a few times," Angela said.

"They did here, too," Lisa said. "I woke up around three and the lightning and thunder kept me up for a while."

"I slept through it all," Rhett said as he lifted his coffee mug.

Lauren laughed. "I didn't hear a thing, either," she admitted. "I crashed hard last night and early. Traveling always does that to me."

Angela smiled. "That's good though. It always takes me a few days to adjust to the time difference. You're ahead of it now. What do you have planned for the rest of the day?"

"I thought I'd drive into town and poke around in some of the shops. It has been years since I've been here."

"Do you have any plans for tonight?"

"Nothing." Lauren had the whole day to herself.

"Good. I've invited some friends over for a girls' night. I'd love for you to meet everyone and we can catch up over drinks and appetizers."

"I'd love that. What can I bring? I'll be downtown and I bet they have a good cheese shop and maybe wine?"

"Some cheese would be great. Everyone is bringing an appetizer, so that will be perfect."

"What kind of wine do you like these days?" Lauren asked. She knew Angela loved wine, but it had been a few years since she'd seen her.

Angela hesitated for a moment. "Oh, anything is fine. Whatever you like."

"If you stop into Bradford's Liquors, ask Peter, the owner, for a recommendation. He always has good ones," Lisa suggested.

"I'll do that."

#

After breakfast, Angela headed off to start cleaning and Lauren grabbed a sweater and put her sneakers on, then went to the beach. She walked for about a half hour or so toward a lighthouse about a half mile or so down the beach and back. She took pictures with her phone as she walked and stopped in front of the house that just a few doors down. The share house. The house next to it, the one closest to the inn, was an older, more modest Cape Cod style home, with weathered gray shingles and a small deck overlooking the beach. Lauren noticed an older couple sitting there, drinking their coffee. They waved at Lauren and she waved back. She knew they were just being neighborly.

The share house was easily three times the size of the smaller house. It had a huge wraparound farmer's porch and the area facing the ocean extended out further into a large deck. It looked like either a newly built or renovated home, as the shingles looked new, not weathered yet by the wind and water. Lauren looked forward to seeing the interior of the house and thought she might pop in on her way back from going downtown. It didn't look like anyone was there at the moment. And Marissa had left instructions to stop by the real estate office near the wharf to pick up a key.

Lauren headed back to her room and relaxed for a while, checking email and reading a new novel. It was still early, and she knew most of the shops didn't open until around ten or so. She got caught up in her book and lost track of time. It was almost eleven when she stopped to check the time and decided to head downtown.

The last time she'd been to Nantucket, she'd gone there on a day trip with friends. They'd taken the fast ferry out of Hyannis and spent the afternoon shopping and having lunch and dinner before taking the last boat back. She'd never actually driven downtown and needed her GPS to guide her. She knew parking was limited, and she drove around the quaint cobblestone streets until she found an empty spot by the wharf, where there was a smaller Stop and Shop grocery store.

She wandered along the wharf, browsing through the gift shops, looking at the many t-shirts and sweatshirts. She remembered that Angela had mentioned a shop she should check out, owned by her friend, Izzy, called Nantucket Threads.

It was right there at the end of the wharf, and she paused for a moment, admiring the window display. One mannequin was wearing a Bohemian style floral dress with soft brown leather boots and the other was dressed more casually in tan shorts and a thick sweatshirt in a pretty pinkish red color. It said Nantucket across the front.

She stepped inside and was greeted with a warm smile by a petite woman behind the register. "Are you Izzy, by any chance?" Lauren asked.

The woman's smile grew bigger. "That's me!"

"I'm Lauren. A friend of Angela's. She told me to be sure to stop in. She raved about your store."

Izzy looked pleased to hear it. "That's so nice of her. Is there anything you're looking for?"

"Not really. I'm just browsing. But I do love that sweatshirt in the window. The dress too. Could I try them on?" Lauren asked impulsively. She didn't need a thing, but she also hadn't gone shopping in ages.

"Of course. Follow me." Izzy grabbed a few sizes of each item and led Lauren to a dressing room in the back of the store. "Let me know if you need any other sizes. I guessed you were either a small or medium."

"Thanks." Lauren tried on the medium sweatshirt first and instantly loved it. She liked her sweatshirts roomy, and this was just right and soft. She tried the dress next, and it ran big. The small looked best, and it was more flattering than she'd expected. You never knew until you tried something on. She brought both to the register.

"How'd you do?" Izzy asked.

"Great. I'll take them both."

Izzy wrapped them in tissue paper and ran Lauren's credit card. A few minutes later, Lauren left with her bag and dropped it off at her car before continuing to explore the downtown.

She window shopped for another hour, going in and out of stores. She was tempted a few more times, but she definitely didn't need to buy any more clothes. And except for Izzy's store, most of the prices were on the high side. There were some great shops for browsing, though, and several art galleries. When she grew hungry for lunch, she stopped into The Corner Table, another place Angela had recommended. She had a cup of Jamaican Chicken Stew and a fresh cookie for dessert. Then got a caramel latte as a splurge and sipped it as she made her way to the real estate office to pick up the key for the house.

Marissa had told her to ask for Kevin, and he was the only person in the office. He looked to be in his late thirties and hesitated as he handed her the house keys. "I told Marissa this already, but she said you're the person to talk to for any issues here. I should let you know that not everyone on the island is happy about this show filming here. We've had quite a few calls this week, now that word has gotten out. I don't expect that you'll have any serious issues, but just thought I'd let you know, as sometimes people can get nasty and vocal."

Lauren frowned as she took the keys and put them in her purse. "Vocal, how exactly?" She wasn't sure what they should be prepared for.

"Well, so far, it's mostly been people calling the office to complain. There's a possibility you might get some showing up to protest at the house, too."

Lauren sighed. She knew that had happened on a few of the other reality shows, as some towns were worried that filming would bring traffic and noise. And truthfully, sometimes it did.

"I would just suggest that you try to keep the noise down as much as possible. Late nights, loud parties are what could cause problems."

Lauren nodded. "We'll do our best to be good neighbors."

He grinned. "Good, that's all we can ask for."

Lauren left and made her way toward a cheese shop she'd spotted earlier. She hoped that there weren't going to be issues. It was inevitable that there would be a few loud parties. Hopefully, it wouldn't upset the neighbors too much. She'd be in the background for all of it, so would try her best to keep things from getting out of control.

She stepped into the cheese shop and breathed in. It

smelled amazing. The store was busy, and they were handing out samples at the counter. Lauren tried a taste of an aged gouda and a creamy goat. She grabbed the gouda, a sharp cheddar and a buttery wedge of Saint Andre, a triple creme that she knew Angela liked. She added a box of crackers and once she paid, she headed to Bradford's Liquors to get a bottle of wine.

The store had a huge selection of wine and Lauren roamed the aisles reading the descriptions. She had her favorites but wanted to try something new.

"Can I help you find something?" A man about Lisa's age, who Lauren guessed was Peter Bradford, walked over to her.

She smiled. "Lisa Hodges suggested I stop in here. She said you always have the best wine suggestions."

He chuckled. "We do our best. What's the occasion?"

"A girls' night, wine and appetizers."

He thought for a moment. "White or red?"

"Red I think."

He reached for a bottle and held it out. "This is a fantastic cabernet that is only $19 and tastes like a much more expensive wine. I just tried it last night at dinner and we were blown away. If you like cabernet, you might love this one."

Lauren's first choice was usually a cabernet. "Perfect, I'll take it."

She paid for the wine and headed to her car. She'd had her fill of shopping and wanted to stop by the house. Eloise, one of the junior producers, was already on the island and Lauren knew she was planning to head to the house around four to be there as people started to arrive and get them settled. Lauren didn't expect that anyone would be at the house when she stopped by and she was looking forward to doing a walk-through and seeing what the interior looked like and how much space they had to work with.

CHAPTER NINE

There was a car in the driveway when Lauren reached the share house. It was a big black van with East Coast Productions painted in gold on the side. She knew that was the name of the production company that was partnering with the reality show. They'd almost ruled out shooting on Nantucket, because of the difficulty and expense of transporting film equipment there.

This production company was based on the island and co-owned by the actress Cami Carmichael. Lauren knew that Cami made her home in Nantucket now that she was engaged to the chef from The Whitley, the luxurious waterfront hotel where Cami had stayed for several months.

Lauren's contact at East Coast Productions was Hudson Winters. They'd traded a few emails. Hudson was an equal owner in the production company with Cami Carmichael. She'd looked him up online and saw that he brought years of experience on both drama and reality shows as a cameraman, producer and director. He was leading the project from the production side and would be there daily with the three main cameras they'd have onsite, in addition to the tiny cameras in each room that would film around the clock.

The front door was slightly ajar when Lauren reached it, so she didn't need her key. She stepped inside and closed it tightly behind her and put the key back in her purse. She stood in a bright, sunny foyer with a twenty-foot cathedral ceiling and a dramatic curved staircase to the second floor. She stepped across gleaming light hardwood floors and walked toward a gorgeous kitchen on the right. On the left was a big family room with a wall of windows that had stunning views of the water. The surf was bigger than usual today, because of the storm the night before and the waves were tipped with white.

She walked into the kitchen and sighed. It was pretty much her dream kitchen. There was a massive center island with eight stools along one side and two on the end. The countertops were honed marble, with a luxurious and almost velvety feel as she ran her fingers across it.

What made the kitchen even more dramatic was that the floors were made from the same marble, but polished instead of honed. Seafoam green subway titles made up the backsplash, and the appliances were all the high-end brand, Miele—the gas stove had six burners and the refrigerator was hidden behind creamy white wood that matched the cabinets.

Lauren walked into the family room and stood by the

window for a moment, gazing out at the ocean before turning her attention back to the room itself. She was glad to see that it was plenty big enough for the cameras and for the producers to sit back out of the way. She and Eloise would be there in the background for the better part of the day and most evenings—whenever they had any kind of events planned.

She was about to explore the rest of the house when she heard footsteps coming down the hall. A dark-haired man of average height, maybe five-ten or so, walked into the room and stopped short when he saw her. His eyes were a deep brown, just a little lighter than his hair, which was a bit long. He brushed it out of his eyes and nodded. "You must be Lauren? Or Eloise? I'm Hudson."

"I'm Lauren. Eloise will be here soon to help get everyone settled in. I just wanted to stop in first and get a look at the place before they all get here."

Hudson nodded. "I was just testing all the fixed cameras to make sure they're all working as they should be. They are and they're on now. I was just about to bring the main cameras in and get set up to film their entrances and first reactions."

Hudson seemed focused and businesslike. Lauren's initial reaction was that he would be easy to work with. Which was a relief.

"Sounds good. I'm going to check out the rest of the house quickly, then head home and drop some stuff off. I'll be back around four to help Eloise and watch everyone arrive. I think they're mostly due around the same time, between four and six."

Hudson grinned. "I'd be willing to bet at least one of them will have a late arrival."

Lauren laughed. "I haven't heard anything yet, but you're probably right." She looked at him curiously. "Do you have family here on the island? I read that you did a lot of work on the West Coast for a while."

"I do. And I was in LA for twelve years. I hated it there, but it's where the work was. Until Cami decided to move here. We'd worked together on a few projects and she knew I grew up here. She asked if I might be interested in moving home and I jumped at the chance." He smiled, and she noticed two deep dimples appear on either side of his mouth. "My mom is still here. She's a widow now, and the timing was good for me to move home."

"That's awesome. I wish there were more opportunities on the East Coast," Lauren said wistfully.

"Do you have family in New England?" Hudson asked.

"Cape Cod actually. I grew up in West Yarmouth. My parents still live there." She smiled. "They are hoping to get here for a long weekend soon."

Hudson's phone vibrated, and he glanced at it. Then quickly typed a text response. "I should probably get a move on and get these cameras in. See you in a bit." He headed out the front door and Lauren did a quick walk-through of the rest of the house. There were eight bedrooms in total. Several of the rooms had two beds, so some people would have to share. They'd let the cast know that it was to their advantage to arrive early, as the rooms were unassigned.

The house was lovely, light, and spacious. There was also a hot tub on the side porch. And it was an easy walk down to the beach. It was a dream vacation house, and these influencers were all being paid well to stay there for the summer. Lauren felt lucky too that she was also being paid to enjoy a summer on Nantucket.

Lauren passed Hudson on her way out and headed back to the inn to drop everything off and put her cheese in the refrigerator until she was ready to head to Angela's later that evening. They were meeting at seven, so she planned to join Eloise at four and would stay until about six thirty. Eloise would remain until the others arrived.

Lauren headed back to the share house at a few minutes before four. She walked over and when she reached the house, she saw that there were several cars in the driveway. When she stepped inside, she saw that Eloise had arrived and Mike and Tom, her mid-twenties cameramen, were talking to Hudson.

Lauren had worked with Eloise before and was glad to see her. Eloise was tall, blonde, bubbly and full of energy. And she was very good at her job. People tended to instantly find her likable and easy to talk to. Eloise usually handled the side interviews where they got the

PAMELA M. KELLEY

cast members' perspectives and she was able to easily get them to open up. It made for fascinating TV.

Eloise walked over and gave Lauren a hug. "Nantucket is even more gorgeous than I imagined. I can't believe we're here all summer."

Lauren agreed. "I know. I've always loved it here. How's your cottage?" Eloise and the rest of the production team were in a summer rental nearby.

"Oh, it's great. Not as new as this place, but it's really nice and just a short walk to the beach."

Melissa, the catering manager, was bustling around the kitchen, setting out platters of tuna salad and roast beef sandwiches on the huge island. She also put out a big salad and a selection of snacks—including potato chips, salsa, guacamole and tortilla chips and a bowl of peanut M&M's. Since they weren't sure exactly what time people would be arriving, it seemed like a good mix of easy snacks.

They chatted with Melissa for a bit. Eloise helped herself to a sandwich, but Lauren just had a handful of M&M's. She didn't want to ruin her appetite. At a quarter past four, they heard the first car pull into the driveway. Melissa stepped out of the kitchen so she wouldn't be filmed, while Lauren and Eloise went to sit in the back of the room near the cameras. They all wanted to be out of the way, so that Hudson and the guys would get good shots of the influencers as they entered the house and to capture their first reactions to the house and each other.

CHAPTER TEN

Katy was the only influencer going to Nantucket that Anna actually knew in real life. They weren't close friends, more business acquaintances, as they were both beauty influencers and had gone on a few of the same brand trips. Those were nice perks of the job—big beauty brands would invite top influencers to fly out to exotic destinations where they would wine and dine them for several days and stock their hotel rooms with all the newest products. The hope, of course, was that the influencers would then share all the details on social media.

During one of those trips, Anna and Katy discovered over cocktails and appetizers that they lived in the same area of the city—the West Village. A week before they headed off to Nantucket, they met up for dinner and strategized about what to expect from the reality show.

"Realistically, I don't expect to find romance," Katy said. "And I'm not even sure I'd want to be that under the microscope even if I was tempted. But I am excited to pick up new followers. Ultimately, this should help both of us bring in more brand deals, and at higher prices."

Anna agreed. "That's the only reason I agreed to do it. I told my manager no initially. But she laughed at me and said my life is already public."

Katy smiled. "She has a good point. Especially since you did those dating posts."

"That's true. I've slowed down a bit on that, though. Guys get a little weird about it. I don't suppose that I blame them." For a while, Anna had run a series of posts detailing various first dates she'd gone on. She never filmed the men, out of respect for their privacy, but with their permission, she filmed their drinks and dinners and, of course, the outfits that she wore. Her followers loved it. And they especially seemed to relate to her string of first and second dates that fizzled out and never turned into anything serious. For Anna, it had been fun to go out and meet these different men, with no expectations.

"Did you really not like any of them?" Katy asked.

Anna sighed. "Most of them were fine, nice guys. But there just wasn't a spark. It could be that I'm just not really ready to date yet. My last breakup was tough." She'd thought that Ryan was the one. They'd dated since her senior year of college and had been engaged for over two years. She'd just started to plan the wedding when he broke things off.

And he admitted that he'd only gotten engaged because of pressure from everyone that it was expected, the obvious next step. But it turned out that he wasn't in love with her anymore. Anna assumed that there was someone else, but he insisted that there wasn't. She wasn't sure if that made her feel better or worse—to think that he'd rather be alone than with her. He'd been a little distant, but she'd assumed it was just work pressure. It really shook her self-esteem, and she wondered how she could have thought things were fine when they were anything but?

She'd thrown herself into work after that. Going to as many events as possible and filming twice the amount of content. It kept her busy, and it grew her business, which was a good thing, even though she felt kind of numb to it all.

"Maybe spending the summer on Nantucket will be good for me. I've never been there and I hear that it's beautiful. Better than the heat of the city."

"It will be fun," Katy assured her. "We'll relax on the beach, go shopping, eat great food and make fun content, too."

They decided to travel together and shared a car to the airport for the flight to the island. And there was a rental car waiting for them at the tiny Nantucket airport. It was a pretty baby blue Jeep and Katy squealed when she saw it.

"I used to have a Jeep just like this. I miss it living in the city. Do you mind if I drive?"

"Sure." They loaded their bags in the back of the Jeep and then set out to find the rental house. The Jeep had GPS and Katy loaded the address into it. It was a gorgeous, sunny afternoon, warm enough that they didn't need a jacket, and there was a slight breeze.

Both of them were impressed when they pulled up to the house. It was massive, especially compared to the small house immediately to its left. There were a few cars in the driveway already, and Anna guessed it was the production staff. Lauren, the producer, had told them that they would likely be the first to arrive. She glanced up at the two-story house. It was in the classic Cape Cod style, with wood shingles, white shutters and flower boxes. It looked brand new, and she was sure it was beautiful inside. She took a deep breath as they opened the front door, knowing that their entrance and reaction would likely be filmed and hoped it would be a good summer.

CHAPTER ELEVEN

Lauren knew that a few of the beauty influencers had met before, at other events, but that the rest only knew what they'd seen online. Lauren had spent the last week following the influencers across all social media —TikTok, Instagram, YouTube and more. Some of them were so engaging and shared so much of their personal lives on camera that by the end of the week, Lauren felt like she knew them somewhat. She wondered if they would be like their online personas or if some of that was just performing for the cameras.

"It's Katy and Anna," Eloise whispered as two gorgeous girls walked in, pulling giant suitcases and carryon bags. They were both beauty influencers. Katy was barely five feet tall and very curvy. She had auburn hair that was shoulder length and framed her heart-shaped face in long layers. Her best feature was her eyes, which were pale green—her expertly applied shadow, liner and false lashes made them pop.

Katy was also the youngest of the group at just twenty-four and her influencing career had blown up in the past year. She'd gone from working at one of the big makeup stores to having over ten million followers that tuned in several times a day to see her apply makeup and gossip about her life in her thick Southern drawl.

Anna was her opposite in looks—she was twenty-six and about five-eight, very thin, with delicate features and long, fine blonde hair and blue-gray eyes. She had a more natural, understated look and focused on perfume and fashion. She lived in a fabulous Manhattan apartment with a huge terrace and shot many of her videos there, with Smith, her adorable Maltese. Smith was with her, and Anna had an elegant way about her and often hosted glamorous catered dinner parties—where everyone was beautifully dressed and drank gorgeous cocktails and expensive wines.

"This place is awesome," Katy said as she stepped into the family room and saw the stunning water views.

"I think we're the first ones here," Anna said as she looked around the room.

"That means we get first dibs on the best rooms," Katy said. "Let's go find the primary bedroom. It will probably have the most closet space."

The girls disappeared upstairs and returned a few minutes later. As soon as they reentered the room, Katy looked Lauren and Eloise's way and grinned. "Is it okay to talk to you guys now?"

Lauren glanced at Hudson and he nodded. "We're good. We got plenty of film of their entrance."

Lauren introduced herself, Eloise and the camera guys, and Hudson to the two influencers.

"Is it okay if we take the primary bedroom? It's huge and has two queen beds and the walk-in closet is to-die-for," Anna asked.

Lauren nodded. "Totally fine."

Mike and Tom helped the girls get their heavy suitcases upstairs. While they were unpacking, Lauren and Eloise waited for the others to arrive. They didn't have to wait long. Twenty minutes later, a taxi arrived with the one married couple, Brett and Honey Sinclair. They were about thirty and lived in the historic district of Charleston. Brett's family went back several generations there. His grandfather had been a senator and his father was a successful real estate developer. Brett worked for his father's company, though it wasn't clear what he actually did there. He was fond of posting videos on social media and proclaiming himself a Southern gentleman and bourbon aficionado.

Honey was a food influencer. She and Brett dined out at least three or four times a week and documented all of it. On the nights they didn't go out, she often cooked at home and sometimes had elaborate dinner parties and would often invite her guests to help make homemade pasta. She also regularly tried to recreate restaurant dishes she'd loved. Lauren got hungry watching her videos. Since she wasn't much of a cook, though, she usually ended up ordering takeout. Honey's videos made it all look easy, though, and once she was home again, maybe she would try some of those recipes.

They also had their cat, Simon, with them. Simon actually had more followers than anyone else in the house. He was a small orange cat with so much personality. He loved music and often swayed to the beat and when he was really feeling it, he would meow along. People would request their favorite songs for Simon to consider—and no one knew which ones he'd want to groove along to until he heard the music. He liked country, pop, rock.

He was also very smart. He was able to open doors and actually climbed right into cupboards to drag out his favorite treats. He'd carry the bag right over to Honey and drop it at her feet. And then wait expectantly for praise and a handful of treats. He was in a soft, blue cat carrier with a clear window along one side and he was looking around the room with interest.

"It's as beautiful here as Larkin said it would be," Honey said as she looked around the room and out the window.

"Larkin's been to Nantucket?" Brett sounded surprised. His accent was uniquely Southern—a charming slow drawl that somehow gave off big money vibes.

Honey laughed. "She's your sister. I'm surprised you didn't know. She said she came during spring break one year with a bunch of her college friends."

"I don't know the half of what she did in college." Brett picked up Honey's oversized suitcase. We should get our stuff up to our room. I'm assuming we have the primary?" he asked.

Honey frowned. "I think they said the rooms were unassigned. Let's head up and check."

Lauren was tempted to tell them that the room was taken, but she stayed silent. The cameras would capture everything as they discovered Anna and Katy had already moved into the main bedroom. There were plenty of others, though, and they were all spacious. They just didn't have the same huge walk-in closet.

Ten minutes later, they heard another car pull into the driveway. Three people walked in, Sami was a beautiful, twenty-eight-year-old health and wellness influencer. She was about five-seven, brunette, and had an enviable figure, toned from Pilates and yoga. She was most famous for her free yoga videos, where she earned millions from the ads that played before the classes began. She also posted the occasional smoothie or other healthy recipe. And she had a popular dating diaries feature—where every week she'd post a recap of her dates. And Sami dated a lot.

The two guys that walked in with her were about the same age. Noah was in his early thirties and unusually good-looking for a comedian. His career was exploding after a few clips from his comedy shows went viral. He was average height, maybe five-nine or so, with dark brown hair, a strong nose and jaw and a charming smile. His humor reminded Lauren of Jerry Seinfeld, with his ability to find humor in ordinary and relatable everyday things.

Towering over him was a former NFL starting tight end. Jason had back-to-back tendon injuries that killed his career. In the past two years, he'd built a huge following on social media with his funny fitness videos where he gave tips and interviewed popular sports figures. He was six-five with rock solid biceps and washboard abs. He also had a reputation as a ladies' man, always dating different gorgeous women, but never seriously. He was a good-looking guy, thirty-three, and had a mischievous smile that was hard to resist. Lauren expected that the single girls in the house would be drawn to him, Noah, and probably to Billy, too.

Which was fine with her. She hoped that Billy would fall for one of the women in the house. It would be good TV and would be easier for her if he wasn't still trying to convince her to take him back.

"So the only ones left to arrive are Billy and Suzanne?" Eloise whispered.

Lauren nodded as Katy and Anna came downstairs and stopped short when they saw the new arrivals.

Jason flashed his famous smile and Lauren saw Katy and Anna instantly fall under his spell. "Ladies. I'm Jason, this is Noah and Sami." He introduced himself and the others.

Katy's voice squeaked a bit as she spoke, "I'm Katy, and this is Anna. We're both beauty influencers."

Sami stepped forward and smiled. "I watch both of you." She glanced at Katy. "I love your makeup tips. I never knew what primer was until I saw one of your videos."

"And I do your yoga classes almost every day," Anna said.

They all chatted a bit, and when the conversation slowed, Eloise spoke up and introduced the new arrivals to the production team. Honey and Brett walked into the room as she told everyone to help themselves to sandwiches and snacks in the kitchen. They made their way over to the island and everyone helped themselves.

"There's beer and wine in the refrigerator," Eloise added.

Within moments, Jason found the beer and put a six-pack on the island. The guys helped themselves while Katy opened a bottle of chardonnay and poured glasses for all the girls except Sami, who went for a beer.

"So, what's everyone's status?" Katy asked as she looked around the room.

"Well, obviously, we're married," Honey said. Brett responded by pulling his wife in and giving her a quick kiss.

"I'm single, and I know Anna is," Katy said.

"Totally single," Sami said. "I actually just ended a relationship last week."

"Oh! I didn't know. How are you doing?" Katy asked sympathetically.

"Well, this past week has been rough," Sami admitted. "But it's a good thing. I don't think I'm ready to dive back into dating anytime soon. I'm looking forward to chilling on the beach."

"That sounds perfect," Anna said.

"Well, I'm single, too," Noah said.

Jason took a sip of his beer and stayed quiet. Katy pushed through. "What about you, Jason? *Page Six* had a mention that you might be getting serious with someone. Is that true?"

Jason hesitated. "I've been dating someone, but it's not serious, and not exclusive by any means." He grinned. "So, yeah, you could say I'm single too…and ready to mingle."

Katy laughed and lifted her glass. "Cheers to that!" They all clinked glasses and Lauren almost didn't hear the sound of a car door. It was a quarter past six. They were missing the last two influencers, Suzanne and Billy.

The front door flew open and Suzanne walked in and scanned the room. When she saw that everyone was in the kitchen, eating and drinking, she set her suitcase down, reached into her carry-on bag and pulled out a big bottle of tequila and held it high.

"Who wants a shot!"

Lauren and Eloise watched in amusement as she pulled two limes out of her bag and went right to the counter and started slicing limes and looking in several cupboards until she found shot glasses. Suzanne was a party-girl. She was average height, maybe five-five or so and was fit from spin classes and always wore snug tops that showed off her impressive implants. Her hair was long and bleached blonde, cut in long layers that gave a tousled beach wave look.

Suzanne had one of the biggest social media followings. She was twenty-nine and lived in Brooklyn, and she shared everything about her life online. She went out four or five nights a week and filmed it all, restaurants, clubs, sometimes even dates, though she never showed their faces, just the drinks and dishes. She had a way of telling a story that drew you in and kept your attention. She went on lots of dates, many of them awful, and shared it all. So, Lauren knew that Suzanne had just broken up with a guy she'd been sure was the one, until she learned on date six that he was actually married!

The only one missing now was Billy, and Lauren wasn't shocked to get a text update from him.

Missed my flight. Traffic was nuts in LA. Got on a later one, just landed at Logan. Will get on flight to Nantucket ASAP. See you soon.

"Billy is running late. He'll be here in an hour or so," Lauren told Eloise.

"I'll get him settled. No worries," Eloise said.

"Thank you. I'll see you around nine tomorrow."

Lauren stood to go, and Hudson raised an eyebrow. "You sure you want to go? Things usually get interesting on night one."

Lauren laughed. "No doubt. I'll check the film tomorrow morning to see what I missed. Eloise can hold down the fort."

The noise level was already getting loud as Lauren headed to the door. Suzanne and the rest of the group were on their second round of tequila shots. Jason pulled off his shirt, revealing six-pack abs that made her stop short for a moment. Jason looked around the room at all the women. "Who's up for a tequila shot off these abs?"

Suzanne didn't hesitate. "Me!"

Lauren smiled as she walked through the door. Hudson was right. They were going to get some great stuff filmed if this was how the night began.

CHAPTER TWELVE

Lauren felt both somewhat disappointed and relieved that Billy didn't arrive with the others. She hadn't seen him since they'd broken up and part of her was dreading it, but she also wanted to get it over with, so they could both just move on and do their jobs.

She pushed Billy out of her thoughts as she reached the inn and went inside to grab the cheese, crackers, and wine. She ran a brush through her hair and freshened up her lipstick. She didn't want to look a mess when she met Angela's friends.

And she was looking forward to seeing Angela. It had been much too long, well over a year, since they'd met up for dinner when Angela and Philippe were in town when one of his books was being made into a TV series.

Lauren put the address in her car's GPS and fifteen minutes later, pulled onto Angela's street. She'd seen pictures of her house, but it was so much more impressive in-person. The driveway was long and there were several cars already parked. She pulled up behind the last one, a navy BMW.

The house was on a bluff and there was still enough sunlight that she could see the deep blue of the water as the waves rolled in and crashed on the shore. Lauren stood, admiring the view for a moment before heading to the house.

Immediately after Lauren knocked, Angela opened the front door and pulled her in for a hug. "It's so good to see you. I'm looking forward to showing you around Nantucket and just relaxing on the beach."

Lauren looked forward to it, too. "I can't wait. I poked around a bit downtown earlier today. I went to your friend Izzy's place."

"Oh good! Did you get anything?"

Lauren nodded and told her about what she'd bought. And about stopping at The Corner Table for lunch.

"We'll have to drive out to Millie's one day for some Mexican. It's California style and reminds me of home. Though I don't remember seeing scallops and bacon tacos anywhere on the West Coast." Angela laughed.

"That sounds amazing." Lauren's stomach rumbled at the mention of food.

"Come on in. The only one missing is Kristen. She should be here any minute. Can I get you something to drink? Chardonnay or cabernet?" Angela offered.

"Chardonnay sounds good. I brought some wine too, and cheese and crackers."

"Oh, thank you. Let's get a plate for that."

Lauren followed Angela into a gorgeous kitchen. It

had a huge island with white quartz counters and the base was painted a pale blue-gray that was so pretty.

Angela poured her a glass of wine and got a plate from a cupboard. Lauren unwrapped the cheeses and arranged them on the plate with some crackers. They took everything into the living room where several women sat on sofas and chairs, drinking wine and snacking on chips and dips. Angela set the plate of cheese and crackers on the coffee table next to the other food and introduced Lauren to everyone.

"Lauren and I went to college together. I'm so excited that she's here for the summer! Lauren, meet Kate she's one of Lisa's daughters, Mia is Izzy's sister, the one whose shop you went to, Taylor and Victoria both work at the newspaper, and Bella." Angela's eyes twinkled as she glanced at Bella, who looked so familiar to Lauren. "You may know her by another name, though," Angela said.

Lauren realized why she looked so familiar—it was Cami Carmichael. She knew that Angela had met her, but she didn't realize they were actually friends.

"It's nice to meet you," Bella said. And Lauren would recognize that voice anywhere. "Angela said you're working on the show that's filming here. You've probably met my partner, Hudson?"

"Yes. I met him earlier today. It's worked out so well that we could use your equipment. We probably would have ended up filming on the Cape. Which would have made my parents happy. But I'm glad we're here." Lauren felt like she was babbling as the words came out in a rush.

"You're from the Cape?" Kate asked.

Lauren nodded. "I grew up there. I've been on the West Coast since college, though. That's where most of the work in the film business is."

"I'm sorry I'm late." A slender woman with long wavy brown hair rushed into the room, holding a square pan.

"Did you make brownies?" Kate asked.

"Yes, with a swirl of peanut butter in them," Kristen said.

Angela jumped up and took the pan from her. "They look great. Come get a glass of wine. You're not late. We're just getting started."

They returned a few minutes later with Kristen holding a big glass of red wine. A timer went off and Angela turned to go back to the kitchen, but Kate stood. "Have a seat and relax. I'll get the dip."

A few minutes later, Kate brought a bubbling casserole dish to the table. The smell was intoxicating—garlic, cheese, spinach, and artichoke.

"Dig in everyone," Angela said. Besides the cheese and dips, and a bowl of mixed nuts, there were also stuffed mushrooms, and sliced chicken, cheddar and broccoli calzones. While they ate, Lauren listened as everyone shared what was going on in their lives.

"Kate, has filming started yet?" Bella asked.

Kate made a face. "It actually all fell apart. We're back to square one," she said.

Bella looked like she felt awful for asking the question. "I'm so sorry. That's the downside of this industry. Everything takes forever and then this happens way too often."

"Philippe is asking around. And I'm sure Kate's agent will start to shop it again," Angela said.

Bella smiled. "I loved the book. I bet it will get picked up soon."

"That would be nice," Kate said. "I'm not getting my hopes up, though. I've learned that it's more common for things not to get made. So, I'm just focusing on what I can control—writing the books."

"And her new one is so good," Kristen said. "I just finished it a few days ago."

"I didn't know you have a new release." Angela sounded surprised.

Kate laughed. "I don't. But it will be out in a few weeks. Kristen is always my first reader, and Mom and Abby. I get good feedback from all of them."

"Where is Abby tonight?" Kristen asked. "I thought she was coming."

"She was, but both she and Jeff woke up with a bug this morning. She didn't want to get anyone sick," Kate said.

Lauren knew from Angela that Kate and Kristen were twins and Abby was the youngest in the family. They also had a brother, Chase.

"Kristen, did I hear you have an art show coming up soon? I thought I saw something online about it, but I don't remember the date," Angela said.

"I do. A week from today, actually. One of the galleries downtown will be hosting a new collection. This one is all seascapes," Kristen said. "There's an opening reception at six on Saturday." She glanced around the group. "It's open to all, so if you're looking for something to do, please stop by." Kristen spoke quietly and Lauren sensed that she wasn't comfortable being the center of attention.

"We'll definitely try to come to the reception," Angela said. She looked at Lauren. "Maybe you can join us if you don't have to film?"

"I'd love to." Lauren didn't know if she'd be able to sneak away yet. It would depend on what was going on at the share house and if they were home that evening or filming in town.

"I watch all those reality shows," Victoria said. "I can't wait to see how it will turn out. Has filming started yet?"

Lauren nodded. "We started this afternoon actually, as everyone arrived."

"Are there really hidden cameras all over the house?" Taylor asked.

Lauren laughed. "They're not hidden. But they are all over the house and film around the clock. We have several bigger cameras as well that cover the bigger areas where everyone spends most of their time, and then if they go anywhere, the cameras go along."

"Do they forget they are on camera? Or are they always aware?" Victoria asked. Lauren had wondered the same thing on her first reality show.

"It's hard to imagine, but they get used to the cameras pretty fast and especially when the team isn't there and they have the place to themselves. That's when we get some of our best footage," Lauren said.

Lauren had been a little nervous about going to a girls' night where the only person she knew was Angela, but her friends were all welcoming and after an hour or so, Lauren felt like she'd known them all longer.

Once they'd all eaten their fill. Lauren and Kate helped Angela carry the food back to the kitchen, where Angela quickly put the leftovers in the refrigerator and stacked the dirty dishes in the sink to be dealt with later. Kate carried Kristen's pan of brownies into the living room and set them on the coffee table. Angela returned a moment later with bottles of red and white wine and told everyone to help themselves to more wine. Lauren noticed that Angela's glass was empty.

"Are you drinking the chardonnay too? It's really good," she said.

Angela shook her head. "No, I'm just having water."

Everyone looked as surprised as Lauren felt. Angela always had wine when she had people over. She didn't recall her ever being much of a water drinker. But she wasn't going to ask her about it.

Kate wasn't shy, though. She smiled. "Is there something you're not telling us?"

Angela hesitated a long moment before a matching smile slowly spread across her face and she leaned forward in her chair, a decision made. "I'm not supposed to say anything, but I'm not going to lie about it. Not to all of you. I just tested positive yesterday. We're not saying anything for a few months, though, just to be safe."

The room erupted in cheers and congratulations.

Lauren stood and gave Angela a hug. "I'm so happy for you."

Angela brushed away happy tears. "Thank you. It doesn't quite seem real yet. But we're both really excited. Enough about me, though. Bella, how is the wedding planning coming along?"

Bella smiled. "Good, thanks to Mia. She's making it all look easy. We're on track for New Year's Eve."

"Oh, how fun," Kate said. "Are you doing it at The Whitley?"

Bella nodded. "We didn't really consider having it anywhere else, since that's where Nick and I met."

Angela had told Lauren the story of how Bella had been staying at the hotel and tried to go unnoticed. She'd cut and dyed her hair and wore dark sunglasses. She hadn't been looking to meet anyone, just to relax and recharge for a few months on the beach. But then she met Nick, and they both fell fast. And now Bella lived full time on Nantucket. Lauren thought it was so romantic.

Everyone headed home a little before ten, and Lauren promised to let Angela know about the following Saturday and the art gallery reception.

"I think it should work, as long as we aren't going anywhere to film that night. I'll keep you posted," she said before giving Angela a hug goodbye. She walked out with the others and hoped that she'd see them again soon.

CHAPTER THIRTEEN

Anna reminded herself that she was used to being filmed for the many videos she made and uploaded on social media. So, a reality show shouldn't be all that different. But with her own content, she was always in complete control. She could redo a video a million times if she wasn't happy with it and she often filmed multiple times before she captured the feel she was going for.

Having cameras following her every move was definitely strange to get used to. Especially when she'd glance over and see one of the camera guys shifting position to better capture what they were doing. It made her somewhat self-conscious because she didn't want to say anything stupid and look bad on TV.

Lauren and Eloise, the show's producers, had introduced themselves and encouraged them to try to act normally, to forget that the cameras were there.

"Don't worry about looking ridiculous. We'll be

editing out any bloopers and we want you all to look as good as possible," Lauren assured them.

Anna knew that only went so far, though. If she got too comfortable and said something that didn't come across well, it could be used.

"You're getting in your head too much," Katy whispered to her. "Just try to have fun. Let's refill our wine glasses. We're both running low." She went to the kitchen to get the bottle of La Crema chardonnay and topped off both of their glasses.

The others had all arrived by then. Even Billy, who apparently missed his earlier flight. Suzanne got everyone into the party mood with her shots. Anna and Katy both had one, but Anna refused a second. She mostly stuck to wine and didn't want to be hung over on her first full day on Nantucket.

Smith had already settled in nicely. He was a typical Maltese, which meant he was a small, fluffy, adorable white dog and everyone immediately loved him and gave him tons of attention. Which he adored. He made the rounds, going from person to person, sitting on laps and lifting his head for behind the ear scratches.

She knew of most of the influencers already, just from seeing them online. And in the past week, she'd spent time looking over all of their social media to try to get to know them better. She was already a follower of Brett and Honey and their cat, Simon. Like many of their followers, she was fascinated by what seemed like the perfect relationship. Brett was successful, handsome, and thought his wife was the most beautiful woman in the world. It was sweet to see how crazy he was about her.

And Honey was likable too and such a foodie. Anna often got hungry watching what she was making or eating at a restaurant. She made delicious-sounding dishes and somehow made it look easy. Anna wasn't much of a cook, but she had tried one of Honey's recipes, a lemon chicken pasta dish and it really had been easy.

Brett and Honey brought their cat, Simon, to the house. Anna had been a little concerned at first, when Smith ran right up to Simon, but after a tense moment where both animals stared at each other, Simon made the first move and sniffed Smith, then turned and walked off, completely unbothered. It left Smith perplexed, and he ran back to Anna, looking for reassurance.

"Sorry about that," Anna said.

Honey just laughed. "Oh, it's fine. We have two dogs at home and Simon is used to it. They all get along fine. My sister is staying with them while we're here. I'm sure he and Smith will be fast friends in another day or two."

As the night went on, and more cocktails were consumed, everyone, even Anna, relaxed and pretty much forgot about the cameras or at least weren't as bothered by them.

"So, are you a football fan?" Jason asked her at one point. They were all standing around the kitchen island and Anna had just reached for a few grapes from a big bowl. Jason had just opened a new beer and stood nearby, watching her curiously. Anna knew that Jason had been a star player before his career-ending injury.

She smiled. "I am. I'm a Patriots fan though. Are you sure you still want to talk to me?" she teased. He'd played for the Jets, one of the main rivals in the league.

He laughed. "Where are you from, Boston?"

She nodded. "Just outside the city, Arlington. I moved to Manhattan years ago, though. I consider myself a New Yorker now. What about you?"

"Grew up in Brooklyn, and am still there. Just moved into a new condo, though. Great skyline and river views. I can't imagine living anywhere else. I keep trying to talk Noah into moving there, but he's a West Coaster. Someday, maybe."

"I did have fun the last time I visited," Noah said. "New York is growing on me. But it doesn't hold a candle to San Diego. You gotta come my way and I'll show you around. Then you'll understand."

Jason nodded. "Yeah, I do need to get out there one of these days."

Billy walked over, grabbed a new beer, and added his two cents. "LA is pretty awesome. Always good weather. None of this cold you get back east." He shivered dramatically and Anna laughed.

"I don't mind the cold," Jason said. "I kind of like the four seasons." He glanced at Sami, who was leaning against the island, sipping a wine spritzer. "You're down South, aren't you? Georgia or Texas?" he asked.

She nodded. "Galveston. By the beach. Nice and warm."

"You probably like doing your yoga outside, then?" Billy asked. Anna almost laughed at his expression. His eyes twinkled, and he made the simple question sound almost naughty.

"As a matter of fact, I do. We film outside often," Sami said.

"Suzanne lives in Brooklyn, too," Jason said. He glanced her way and Suzanne walked over. "Did I hear my name?"

"I was just saying you live near me."

"Just a few streets away." Suzanne confirmed. "Jason and I actually dated...for a minute. I think we went out for two or three weeks, if that."

He nodded. "Until she dumped me."

She laughed. "I didn't dump you. We just realized we were better as friends. We hang out every so often. We like the same bars in Brooklyn."

Anna thought that was interesting. There was a familiarity between Suzanne and Jason, but it seemed exactly as Suzanne said, a good friendship.

"Katy's in New York too, right around the corner from me in the West Village," Anna said.

"I'm from a tiny town in rural Kentucky, though. New York was a bit of a culture shock at first," Katy said.

"Do you miss the South?" Honey asked. "We really love Charleston."

Katy laughed. "I miss my family. But I get home for the holidays and a few times a year. I don't miss that small town, though. It is very different from Charleston. That is a great city."

Anna noticed that Katy seemed very interested in talking to Billy. She asked him a few questions, and he was excited to tell her all about what he was working on and he asked about her role as an influencer too. He was quite the charmer. But Anna had also seen the online breakup when the girl he'd been dating posted on TikTok and was furious that Billy hadn't ended things with Lauren before he started love bombing her. She felt for Lauren, too. It couldn't be easy having to work with him now, as the breakup was pretty recent. She wondered if Katy was aware of this.

She wasn't sure that Billy was all that interested in Katy, not romantically. He flirted with her, but he also flirted with Anna and Sami and Suzanne and even Honey. It seemed as though it was just in his nature. It would be hard to take him seriously. She just hoped that Katy could see it.

Noah seemed nice enough, but he was so breathtakingly handsome that it was a little unsettling. His features were so chiseled, with a strong jaw, high cheekbones, piercing blue eyes, a cleft chin, full lips, and eyelashes that were so long and dark, it was just unfair. She knew that women regularly threw themselves at him and she could understand it. Noah was upfront with all of them, though, and made it clear he wasn't looking for anything serious—which only made them all the more interested. They all wanted to be the one to change his mind about that. He would be much safer as a friend than any kind of romantic fling. Anna didn't really do flings.

So that ruled out two of the guys immediately. And Jason seemed nice enough, but he definitely wasn't her type. She'd never gone for the big jock guys. Anna was tall at almost five-eight and Jason towered over her. She guessed he was at least six-four, maybe six-five. She also knew he'd had his share of female attention. He was always being photographed with different women. But he'd had longer-term relationships, too. She'd read online that he'd been dumped earlier in the year by his girlfriend of four years. She'd reconnected with her high school boyfriend and they got engaged a month after she and Jason broke up.

Anna imagined that must have been rough. It seemed like he'd gone on a few dates recently—every time he was seen out with a woman, his picture ended up online. She guessed that he might welcome a relaxing summer on Nantucket, too. So, even though she didn't see romantic potential with any of the guys in the house, they all seemed like people she could be friends with. Which could mean a fun summer.

CHAPTER FOURTEEN

"Something smells good," Rhett said as he walked into the kitchen and headed to the Nespresso machine for another dark roast coffee.

Lisa smiled. Rhett was always so appreciative of her cooking. "Thanks. It's a new recipe for a chocolate bread pudding." It did smell amazing. Lisa was hopeful it would be delicious.

Rhett brought his coffee to the island and settled onto one of the chairs. He flipped open the Sunday paper, which Lisa hadn't even touched yet. She'd been too busy with setting up breakfast for her guests and then getting ready for the kids to come for Sunday dinner.

Rhett watched her for a moment as she bustled around the kitchen, stirring the gravy on the stove and checking the rib roast that was resting under a blanket of tin foil. Lisa never got flustered in the kitchen, no matter how many were coming to dinner. It was her happy place.

"You're in an usually good mood. Are all the kids still

coming today?" Rhett asked. It was rare that all four of her children and their partners were available on the same Sunday, but now and then, it happened.

Lisa smiled. "Yes, all of them are coming." She dipped a spoon in the gravy and handed it to Rhett to taste. "What do you think? Does it need anything? More salt maybe?"

Rhett shook his head. "It doesn't need a thing. It's perfect."

Lisa glanced at the time. It was a few minutes before noon. "They should be here any minute. Everything's just about ready."

The timer for the bread pudding went off as the front door opened and her son Chase and his wife Beth walked in. Lisa grabbed two potholders and carefully took the dessert out of the oven and set it on the counter.

She went to welcome Chase and Beth. Ten minutes later, everyone had arrived and Rhett poured mimosas all around. Kate and Abby settled their children at the kids' table and once they were happily eating, they joined everyone else. Rhett carved the beef and everyone helped themselves to mashed potatoes, gravy, carrots, and roasted asparagus.

"I'm so glad you and Jeff are feeling better," Lisa said as Abby, her youngest daughter, reached for a second helping of mashed potatoes. They'd been struck with a stomach bug, and Lisa was surprised they hadn't cancelled.

"It turned out to be one of those twenty-four-hour things, thankfully," Abby said.

"We missed you last night," Kate said to Abby.

"Was it fun? I hated to miss it," Abby said.

"It was. We met Angela's friend, Lauren. She's actually staying here, I think?"

Lisa nodded. "She is. She seems like a lovely girl. Though I'm not surprised since she is Angela's friend."

"I hear that some people aren't thrilled about that show filming here," Chase said as he reached for the butter. "One of my buddies said the neighbors are worried about noise."

"Sometimes I think people just like to complain," Rhett said.

"They definitely do," Lisa agreed. "If anyone has the right to complain, it's Walter and Kay as they live right next door. But they don't seem worried about it. I think they are actually spending more time on their deck, curious about the filming."

"I would be too," Beth said. "I've often wondered how real those shows are. If they actually tell them what to do, you know?"

"I think they are mostly real," Kate said. "Angela and I were chatting about it with Philippe and he knows some reality show producers. He said that truth is stranger than fiction—especially after a few cocktails. Emotions are heightened and drama just happens."

Once they finished the main course, the girls helped Lisa clear the plates and bring out the dessert. She set a bowl of freshly whipped cream on the side so people could help themselves.

The cold whipped cream on the still-warm bread

pudding was decadent. It oozed warm chocolate and rich custard and turned out better than she'd hoped.

"Speaking of drama," Kristen said. "I was getting a coffee downtown yesterday and was behind Violet in line. I overheard her bragging to her friend that everyone has been telling her that her lobster quiche is the best on Nantucket and she's decided to enter it into the food festival. Her evil plan is that when she wins, she will advertise it everywhere."

Lisa frowned. Violet lived in the neighborhood and also ran a small inn. She was less than happy when Lisa opened the Beach Plum Cove Inn—especially since Violet's inn isn't waterfront. She complained that Lisa didn't have the proper permits—which it turned out that Lisa didn't, so she had to fix that fast. This was a bit much, though.

"Lobster quiche? Really? That's something new. And I thought the food festival was for restaurants?" The Whitley Hotel organized a big food festival each June where local restaurants offered sample tastings of their food and people voted on their favorites.

"When I got home, I looked it up online and it seems that they've added a category for inns to participate," Kristen said. "It's probably not too late to enter. You'll win easily. You can enter a savory and a sweet dish."

"You should totally enter," Kate encouraged her.

"I think it's a great idea, too," Rhett said. "It will be good advertising and you can borrow any of my equipment to keep food warm."

"I think you should do it too, Mom. I can help out," Kristen said.

"We can help too," Chase added.

Lisa took a sip of her mimosa. There really wasn't anything to think about. "I'll do it. I'll sign up tomorrow. It will be fun. I'll just have to figure out what else to make for a sweet dish."

Rhett reached for a second helping of the bread pudding. "I vote for this. It's the best dessert I think you've ever made."

Kate reached for seconds, too. "I think he's right. I'm going to need to get the recipe for this."

Lisa smiled. "Thank you. Alright, that's settled then."

CHAPTER FIFTEEN

"Do you know if Hudson is single?" Eloise asked quietly when Lauren handed her a cup of coffee. They'd both just arrived at the share house Sunday morning. It was early, a few minutes before eight, and the house was quiet—everyone was still asleep. Hudson had just arrived as well and was in the kitchen adding cream to his coffee. His hair was still damp from a recent shower and his dark curls glistened in the sunlight streaming through the windows.

"I'm not sure. I don't know much about him. Why, are you interested?" Lauren asked.

Eloise laughed. "Not at all. Things are getting more serious with Jim. I was just curious. I thought you might know, since he's one of Billy's best friends."

Lauren took a sip of her coffee and watched as Hudson spread cream cheese on a toasted bagel. "Billy and I only dated for a few months. I didn't meet Hudson before this."

"Oh! I didn't realize that." Eloise sounded surprised.

"Speaking of Billy, what time did he show up yesterday?"

Eloise thought for a moment. "Maybe a half hour or so after you left. He seemed disappointed that you weren't here. Do you think you might get back together?"

Lauren almost spit her coffee out. "No! What would make you think that?"

"He talked about you a lot. Asked where you were, how you were doing. I think if you wanted to get back together, he'd be up for it. He seems really nice."

Lauren sighed. Everyone loved Billy. He was really nice. He just wasn't a very good boyfriend. "Eloise, I think it's safe to say we are never, ever getting back together."

Eloise laughed. "I didn't realize you were a Taylor Swift fan."

"Who isn't?" Lauren grinned as she felt something soft brush against her leg. It was Simon, purring loudly.

"Do you think he's hungry?" Eloise asked.

Lauren reached down and scratched Simon behind his ears. The purring grew louder, and the cat paced back and forth, flicking his tail and looking toward the kitchen.

"Probably." Lauren got up and looked around the kitchen for Simon's food. She found it in a cupboard and spooned some wet food into a bowl and set it on the floor. Simon dove in happily.

Lauren returned to her seat. Eloise had her laptop open and pulled up a video of film from the night before. "What time did they all stay up till last night? Do you know if it was a late night?" Lauren asked.

"I stayed til about ten and left when Hudson and the guys did. The cast had quite a party in the kitchen, doing shots and drinking and eating pizza they'd ordered. They were all still up when we left, but it was starting to slow a bit." Eloise scrolled through the footage and it looked like no one went to bed before midnight and most were up until almost two. There was lots of laughing and drinking. Lauren imagined that some of them might not be feeling so well today.

"I reviewed most of the footage this morning," Hudson said from across the room where he was sitting with his laptop open. "It looks like they've bonded. They are getting along pretty well, so far."

Lauren chuckled. "Hopefully not too well. We need some drama."

"A few of the girls seem interested in Billy. That could be interesting." Hudson looked Lauren's way. "Especially if he's ignoring it. That will drive them crazy and make them try harder. Could be some good TV."

Lauren felt her cheeks flush. She knew Hudson was implying that Billy was ignoring the girls because he hoped to rekindle things with Lauren. She thought she'd made it clear that wasn't going to happen. But Billy did like the chase. And maybe he thought that he could get his way if they were working together. It only made her more resolved to move on.

Lauren and Eloise spent the next hour reviewing footage from the night before of the new roommates. It wasn't too wild of a night, probably because most of them were tired from traveling. Still, they managed to stay up past midnight and by the end of the evening, it looked as though they'd been friends for much longer.

Lauren laughed out loud more than once at some of their antics—especially Billy. It was his idea to drink shots, and he poured his famous concoction, the pineapple bomb, for everyone. Lauren wasn't much of a drinker, just the occasional glass of wine, but Billy had made her a pineapple bomb once, when they'd first started dating. He'd invited her to his apartment for dinner and she'd enjoyed the sweet and frothy mix of Southern Comfort, amaretto, and pineapple juice.

Billy had grilled steaks that night and they'd sat on his balcony and watched people walking along the busy street below. It had been a fun, dreamy night as she'd lost herself in Billy. It was intoxicating to be the recipient of his charismatic charm. That night, it was like nothing else had existed except the two of them.

Lauren smiled wistfully, remembering how perfect things had seemed—like their relationship was meant-to-be. She had never been swept off her feet like that before. And she ignored the little voice whispering in her mind that it was too good to be true.

So, when she stumbled across the video of the other woman Billy was also love bombing, she wasn't completely shocked. But it had still hurt.

"Are you dating anyone yet?" Eloise asked. Her words snapped Lauren out of her thoughts and she shook her head.

"No, it hasn't even crossed my mind. I don't think I'm ready to get back out there."

Eloise looked sympathetic. "Breakups are tough. You never know, though. I really do think it is true that when you're not looking is when you might meet someone."

Hudson walked over a moment later, carrying his laptop and a fresh coffee. "I'm heading out. I'll pop back later early afternoon to get some beach shots and before they start getting ready for the clambake." He grinned. "I think it's going to be pretty mellow until then."

Lauren nodded. "I think you're probably right."

She turned to Eloise after Hudson walked off. "Are we all set for the clambake?"

Eloise pulled up her phone calendar. "The caterers are coming at four thirty to dig the pit on the beach and cook everything. It sounds great—lobsters, clams, mussels, corn on the cob and potatoes. And butter. Lots of butter."

"I haven't had a clambake in years." Putting a clambake together was a big project—usually for a celebration or holiday weekend.

Another hour passed before the first influencer made their way downstairs. Jason, the big football player, bounced into the kitchen, looking wide awake and ready to work out in his sweatpants and tank top. He waved hello and went straight to the coffee maker. While his coffee was brewing, he rummaged around in the refrigerator and pulled out a carton of eggs, bacon, cheese and butter. He put the bacon on a cookie sheet and threw it in the oven, then found a big sauté pan and got to work beating eggs.

By the time the bacon and scrambled eggs were ready, the others made their way to the kitchen, drawn by the smell of coffee and cooking bacon. Jason smiled when he saw Katy and Anna.

"I made a big batch of eggs and bacon. Help yourself," he offered. The caterer had also dropped off a bag of egg sandwiches, bagels and an assortment of cream cheeses.

Everyone made a plate of food, except Noah, who just had a black coffee, and sat at the big oval table with the group and flipped through his phone.

"Not hungry?" Katy asked. "Jason's eggs are awesome. Or there are bagels and egg sandwiches, too."

Noah took a sip of his coffee. "Thanks. I never eat breakfast though. Just coffee." He looked around the table. "So, what's the plan for today? Are we hitting the beach? Going to a club tonight? Or what?"

"I think we're all going to the beach around noon. Melissa mentioned that she'll be dropping off coolers for us stocked with sandwiches and cold beverages at eleven thirty," Honey said.

"And I think the plan is to have a clambake here for dinner," Katy said.

Noah nodded. "Cool. I'm going to go jump in the shower then."

"OMG," Eloise whispered. "Look at Simon. What is he up to?"

Lauren and Eloise watched as Simon walked along the kitchen counter, while everyone at the table ignored him completely—they were all focused on their food. Lauren had fed him earlier, but noticed that he hadn't eaten much of his food. His tail flicked as he walked and when he reached the last cupboard, he nudged the door handle with his nose. It opened slowly and Simon climbed in and the door shut behind him.

Eloise and Lauren looked at each other, not sure what to do. "Should we say something?" Eloise whispered.

Honey paused from eating her eggs to look around the room. "Have you seen Simon?" she asked Brett.

"No. He has to be somewhere around here, though." Brett didn't seem concerned as he spread more cream cheese on his bagel.

The room fell quiet as something fell out of a kitchen cupboard and a moment later, Simon followed, then picked up the bag of rolls in his mouth and hopped off the counter.

"Simon! Drop that!" Honey scolded him. "I told you we weren't going to do that here."

Honey looked around the table. "I'm sorry. He gets into things sometimes, but he's a good boy." She got up and took the bag of rolls from the cat and put them back in the cupboard. "Simon, you still have food in your dish. Here are a few treats." She put a handful of cat treats in his dish, then sat back down.

"That's going to be great on film," Eloise said. "No one was paying attention when Simon climbed into the cupboard. I didn't realize cats could do that."

"Neither did I."

Everyone was up and eating breakfast now except for Billy. Which didn't surprise Lauren. He was not an early riser and liked to stay up late. It was almost a half hour later before he slowly made his way into the kitchen as everyone else was leaving and heading to shower and dress. Billy poured himself a cup of coffee, added three sugars and a generous amount of heavy cream. He ignored the food and headed Lauren's way. He set his mug down and held his arms out to give her a hug hello.

"So great to see you," he said. He nodded at Eloise. "Morning."

"Hi Billy." Lauren smiled. "Looks like you all had a good night. They liked your pineapple bombs?"

He grinned. "Loved them. You could have had one. I thought you'd be here."

"One of my good friends lives here. I was visiting with her." She took a sip of her coffee while Eloise kept her attention on her laptop. Lauren could tell she was curious about the two of them.

"You'll be at the clambake later?" Billy asked.

Lauren nodded. "Of course."

"Good. We'll catch up then. I'm going to head back to bed for a while, I think." He glanced toward the window. It was a warm, clear day. "That sun is hurting my eyes." He stood and grinned. "I'll see you two ladies later."

He headed upstairs, and the room was quiet.

Lauren looked around the room and addressed the production team. "I think we all can head out for a bit. Let's meet back here at noon and then we'll head out to the beach together."

They headed out, and Lauren walked back along the beach to the inn. It was a gorgeous day. She looked forward to relaxing on the beach with a stack of magazines.

CHAPTER SIXTEEN

Once Lisa cleaned up after the morning's breakfast service, she headed out for a walk along the beach. It was early, just half past ten, and perfect weather for walking. The beach was filling up already, with families settling by the water's edge and plenty of people out for their morning walks. Lisa smiled as a cute golden retriever raced by and dashed into the water. There were always dogs running on the beach and they were fun to watch.

She walked her usual fifteen minutes down and back, and noticed that the big share house was quiet and no one was out front on the beach yet. When she reached Walter's house, Kay waved her up. She and Walter were sitting on the deck that overlooked the beach. Lisa climbed the stairs and sat across from Kay and Walter at a round wooden table. Walter looked up and nodded hello, then returned his attention to the crossword puzzle he was working on.

"I was just getting ready to head out," Kay said. "I need to do some grocery shopping."

"I might take a drive out to The Whitley and sign up for that food festival." Lisa had looked online and today was the last day to register, so she wanted to make sure she got in.

"Want some company?" Kay offered.

"Sure, let's go." They said goodbye to Walter and walked next door to Lisa's driveway. They climbed into Lisa's baby-blue Mini-Cooper convertible and she put the top down and tied her hair back before heading off to The Whitley.

"I haven't ridden in a convertible in ages. This is marvelous!" Kay tipped her head back and let the sun fall on her face as the wind tossed her short curls. It didn't take them long to reach The Whitley. Nantucket was a small island, and it didn't take more than twenty minutes or so to go from one end to the other, unless of course there was heavy traffic, which was always a possibility in the summer months.

Kay gasped as they reached the end of the long driveway and pulled up to The Whitley's entrance.

"You haven't been here before?" Lisa asked.

"No. I've heard of it, of course, but haven't had the chance."

A young valet in a crisp white uniform came over to park Lisa's car and she handed him the keys. "I don't think we'll be very long."

Lisa led the way into the lobby of The Whitley. It was an impressive property. The main building sprawled along the ocean and had oversized luxurious rooms, all with stunning ocean views. There was also a group of private villas.

Kay looked around the lobby, with its high ceilings, marble everywhere, and vivid pink and blue floral arrangements throughout the room.

Lisa asked at the front desk about the food festival.

"Oh, you need to see Paula about that. Just head to her office." The receptionist, a bubbly young woman, showed them on a map exactly where to go. Lisa had met Paula, the general manager before, but had never been to her office. She'd only been to the property a few times over the years, for special dinners in the restaurant, which was one of the best on the island.

They reached Paula's office and knocked lightly on the door, which was ajar. A moment later, Paula opened it and smiled when she recognized Lisa.

"Hi Lisa, what brings you to The Whitley?"

"I hear you are including bed and breakfasts in the food festival this year. I'd like to sign up, if it's not too late?"

Paula laughed. "It's not too late, and we'd love to have you. I'm so glad you changed your mind. I was hoping you would join us."

"I only just heard of it yesterday when someone mentioned it to me. Did you send an email out? I must have missed it." It wouldn't be the first time. Lisa got so much junk in her email, it was easy to miss things.

"Yes, but no worries. You're here now. Let me get the form." Paula pulled a sheet of paper out of a folder and handed it to Lisa. "If you want to fill that out now, you'll be all set. It's just a month away now."

Lisa quickly filled out the form and also wrote a check to reserve her table and handed both to Paula.

"Perfect. Keep an eye out for an email a week or so before with info on what time to set up. We've had quite a few bed and breakfasts decide to join us this year. It should be a lot of fun. You've been before?"

Lisa nodded. "Yes, we had a wonderful time." She had thoroughly enjoyed walking around and trying all the different samples from area restaurants.

"How does it work?" Kay asked. "Maybe Walter and I would like to go."

"Oh you should," Paula said. "You taste different dishes and then vote on your favorites. There are winners for each category and the restaurants really outdo themselves."

"It's good advertising, I imagine, if they win," Lisa said.

"It really is. The winner of the chowder category had a huge banner made and put it across their restaurant. It's a good attention-getter," Paula said.

"Well, I'm looking forward to it," Lisa said. They said their goodbyes to Paula and headed back to town. As they drove, Lisa told her about Violet. Kay was suitably outraged on Lisa's behalf.

"Who does she think she is? I mean seriously, everyone knows you make the best lobster quiches. You even ship them across the country. I'm sure she doesn't do that!"

Lisa laughed. "No. I think she's just trying to get attention. If she were to win and could claim to have the best lobster quiche, she would definitely have a big banner made, I bet. And I'd never hear the end of it."

"Well, we can't let that happen. Let me know if there's anything I can do to help."

CHAPTER SEVENTEEN

Lauren slathered on sunscreen and headed to the beach a few minutes before noon to meet Eloise and the others. When she reached the share house, she saw Eloise coming down the steps along with Billy, carrying a huge cooler of food. Eloise set her chair down next to Lauren's. Billy waved hello, then ran back up to the house. He returned a few minutes later along with the others, carrying a chair and towel. He made a beeline for Lauren and plunked down next to her.

"So, how've you been? This place is great, huh?"

Lauren smiled. Billy's enthusiasm was contagious. "Is this your first time to Nantucket?"

He nodded. "I suppose it's nothing special to you, if you come here all the time?"

"I don't get here as often as I'd like. I still think it's pretty special. I'm looking forward to being here for the summer."

"Billy, do you think you might want to join the others?

We can't film you if you're sitting next to Lauren?" Hudson stood behind them, getting his camera set up.

Billy laughed. "Yeah, right? Are we going to do a volleyball shot? I could get the net set up." Lauren knew Billy was eager to do something. He wasn't the type to sit around.

"Actually, that would be a huge help, if you could do that," Lauren said.

He winked at her. "You got it."

Lauren settled into her chair and pulled a copy of *People* magazine out of her tote bag.

"Oh, I should have remembered to bring a magazine. Can I borrow that when you're done?" Eloise asked.

Lauren grinned and pulled another gossip magazine from her tote and handed it to Eloise. "I stocked up."

Eloise flipped the magazine open. "Besides volleyball, do we have anything else planned for the afternoon?"

"No. We've got the clambake later, so just volleyball. They still need to get to know each other more. The girls aren't even down yet." So far, just the guys and the production crew were on the beach. The rest of them staggered down over the next half hour. Honey and Brett came first and helped themselves to tuna sandwiches before settling near Billy's chair. Billy and Jason were just about done setting up the volleyball net, while Noah supervised.

Katy and Anna were the next to arrive. Both had their sunglasses on and cute coverups over their bikinis. They went straight for the food and grabbed iced teas and sandwiches.

Eloise stood. "I'm going to get a sandwich. Do you want one? I think there's turkey and tuna?"

"I'll take a turkey, thanks. And a bag of chips."

When Eloise returned a few minutes later with the sandwiches, Sami and Suzanne finally made their arrival. Sami was sleek and fit, toned from yoga, and looked flawless in an elegant white tank top bikini. Suzanne was tanned and in good shape too—her arms and calves were well defined and she showed off her newly acquired implants in a hot pink bikini.

"Who's ready for a margarita shot?" Suzanne asked. She held a bottle high and looked around the group, but everyone groaned.

"Maybe tonight," Katy said.

"If then. I'm still hungover," Anna added.

"Oh come on. If you're hungover, it's the best cure," Suzanne said.

But still, she had no takers. Not even Billy.

"It is a little early to be starting with the alcohol," Eloise said softly.

Lauren laughed. "Way too early. I don't know how she does it."

They ate their sandwiches and people-watched as the beach filled up. It was a perfect day for it, warm and sunny, and the air was dry with a slight breeze. Anna put a big umbrella in the sand, so she and Katy and Smith could have shade. Smith curled up by Anna's feet. His fur ruffled in the breeze and he looked happy to be with everyone.

Everyone was hungover and hungry and unusually

quiet, other than the occasional bit of idle chit chat—nothing terribly film worthy.

"Maybe they will wake up when volleyball starts," Eloise said.

For the next hour or so, everyone just relaxed in the sun, even Billy. Lauren and Eloise swapped magazines and walked to the water's edge and dipped their toes in.

"This is so much colder than the West Coast. I thought with so many people swimming that it would be warmer," Eloise said. There were lots of people in the water, kids on floats, people of all ages.

"It will warm up by the end of the summer," Lauren said as they walked back to their seats. Billy was up by then and ready to play volleyball. It took him about twenty minutes to get the rest of them to join him, but once everyone got up and into position, the energy shifted on the beach.

"Here we go," Hudson said as he swung his camera toward the volleyball net.

And he got some great coverage. Only a few of the influencers, Billy, Jason and Sami, were actually good at the game, but the rest had fun with it and laughed at themselves. They all seemed to have a good time and there were some funny shots. Katy tried to spike the ball and ended up tripping and going facedown in the sand. And then could not stop laughing.

The volleyball woke them all up and when they came back to their seats, and Billy asked if anyone wanted a beer or hard seltzer from the cooler, half of the group said yes.

"So, we talked about everyone's relationship status last night," Katy said after she'd finished her first hard seltzer. She looked at Billy. "I heard a rumor that you're dating someone. Is that true?"

Billy immediately glanced at Lauren for a split-second. Then smiled at Katy, the slow easy smile that spread across his face—the smile that had once had such an effect on Lauren.

"I'm not dating anyone now." A seagull flew by and he laughed. "I'm as free as that bird. What about you, Katy? What's your story?"

Katy giggled. "Oh, I'm free too. Totally."

They went around the group and everyone, except for Honey and Brett, was completely single. Lauren wondered who among the group was likely to pair off. It was inevitable that there would be at least one romance in the house.

Around three people started leaving the beach to go shower and rest up a bit before the clambake at six.

"Let's meet back at the house at five thirty," Lauren said to the production team. Everyone began to pack up. Hudson and the guys brought their camera equipment into the share house. They'd be eating on the massive deck.

"I wonder if this group knows their way around cracking open a lobster. That might be fun to watch," Hudson said.

Lauren smiled at the thought. She'd had to show a friend on the West Coast how to split a lobster tail and it was pretty funny, as she was totally intimidated.

"Maybe I'll suggest that one of them give a demonstration of how to do it," Lauren said.

"I've actually never had Maine lobster," Eloise said. "I can't wait—and I will need a lesson."

Lauren laughed. "It's easy, I'll show you."

It felt good to shower off the beach. Even though she'd worn plenty of sunscreen, they'd been out there for hours and Lauren's nose and cheeks were pink from the sun. She blew her hair dry and then curled up on her bed with a book for an hour or so. She felt her eyes grow heavy, and it was tempting to take a nap, but she didn't have that much time. She made herself a cup of tea instead, to wake up a bit.

She dressed in her oldest, most comfy jeans, a white t-shirt and the roomy sweatshirt she'd bought at Izzy's shop. At twenty past five, she headed back to the beach and walked over to the share house.

Eloise was already there and Hudson walked in a few minutes later. He and the other two camera guys brought their equipment out to the deck and set up in the corners, out of the way. Melissa, their catering services manager, was putting the finishing touches on the oval table on the deck. It was set for nine and had several tall citronella pillar candles to keep the bugs away. Although Lauren didn't remember that it ever seemed to get very buggy on Nantucket.

The clambake caterers were busy in the kitchen, where there were several huge pots busy steaming the lobsters and clams. They'd brought a few of their own burners too, and one of them had a vat of clam chowder simmering that smelled so good that Lauren's stomach immediately rumbled. She wouldn't be eating for a while, though. They needed to film the cast eating dinner first. Once they were done and they'd gotten all the dinner shots that they needed, the crew could enjoy a meal together.

Lauren and Eloise exchanged glances when the girls came downstairs. None of them were appropriately dressed for a clambake. They were all overdressed, as if they were going out to a nightclub. Except for Suzanne, who was the most casual with jeans and a snug white t-shirt. The guys were fine. They were all in t-shirts and jeans, too.

Lauren noticed that Melissa had put a plastic bib at each table setting. Once everyone had poured themselves a drink and settled at the table, Jason, Noah and Brett tied their bibs around their neck. Honey and Suzanne followed a minute later. The rest of them turned their noses up at the idea of wearing a bib.

"I'm not wearing that thing," Billy said. "You all look ridiculous."

"You might regret that," Suzanne said.

But Billy shook his head. "I'm good."

Katy chimed in, "I'm with Billy, no interest in a bib. What am I, five?" She and Anna laughed at the thought.

Lauren glanced at Hudson, who grinned and shook his head.

"Okay, do you all know how to crack open a lobster?" Suzanne asked the table.

A few of the guys nodded and proceeded to pick up their claws and crack them open with the iron crackers. Everyone else watched closely as Suzanne picked up her lobster and quickly snapped the tail off of the body. She set the body down and then held the tail up so they could all see.

"So there's two ways you can do this. You can grab your knife and run it down the middle of the shell and then pull the meat out. Or you can just squeeze it on both ends and give it a good twist." She demonstrated, and there was a crack when the tail split. "Now, just stick your finger in there and push the tail right out. See, easy-peasy."

Katy picked up her lobster and did a pretty good job following Suzanne's instructions and was quite pleased with herself. "I did it! And I didn't even need a bib!" She then cut a bite of lobster, dunked it in her bowl of melted butter and, on the way to her mouth, the hot butter dripped down the front of her silk shirt. She didn't realize it at first. She was too excited about the delicious lobster. But a moment later, she saw the trail of butter and made a face. "I guess I should have worn the bib."

And a few minutes later, Billy picked up a huge lobster claw, cracked it and a spray of white lobster fat splattered across his black t-shirt. He laughed it off, though. "He got me! It's all good though." He grabbed a napkin, wiped off as much of the splatter as he could, then resumed attacking his lobster.

"Suzanne, how do you know so much about lobsters?" Billy asked.

"I grew up in Maine. Home of the best lobsters in the country."

"No kidding? Do you still live there?"

Suzanne laughed. "No. I moved away years ago. I live in Brooklyn now and love it. I go home to Maine a few times a year, though. It's a beautiful place, but not much going on, if you know what I mean."

Billy nodded. "That's how I feel about LA. NYC is pretty cool, though. I haven't been there in a couple of years, but it was a good time."

Suzanne smiled flirtatiously. "Always. If you ever come to the city, let me know and I'll show you such a good time, it will make your head spin."

That got everyone's attention, and Suzanne laughed. "Get your minds out of the gutter—I just meant I'll show him all my favorite places. I love playing tourist when people come to town."

CHAPTER EIGHTEEN

Once the cast was finished, the caterers cleared the table and brought out clambake meals for the production crew. By now, Lauren and Eloise were starving. The chowder was creamy and delicious, full of clams. There were also steamers, which Lauren hadn't had in ages. She showed Eloise how to remove the neck membrane before dunking the clams first in broth and then melted butter with lemon.

"These are so good!" Eloise loved the steamers and made sure to wear a bib—they all did. She had watched Suzanne closely when she showed how to crack open the tail and didn't have any problems with it. The lobster was cooked perfectly and was so sweet.

There were also slices of linguica sausage, red bliss potatoes, corn on the cob and coleslaw. The table was quiet for a few minutes as everyone focused on their food.

Hudson sat across from Lauren and Eloise and was

the first one to finish his lobster. He took his time with the steamers and everything else.

"So, I think it's fair to say Katy may have a crush on Billy," he said.

Lauren had noticed the same. She couldn't get a read on his interest level, though, since he flirted with everyone.

"Do you think he could be interested?" she asked him.

Hudson shook his head. "You never know, but his type is usually more like Sami or even Anna, more elegant and fit.

Lauren thought about that. She'd never thought of herself as particularly elegant, but she was reasonably attractive and fit. She tried to do Pilates three or four times most weeks. It was the only workout she'd been able to stick with, and she liked the way it elongated her muscles and strengthened her back.

She'd thought that it would be hard to see Billy flirting or even dating other women, but now that she was around him again, it just felt different. She was surprised by how okay she was with it. But she realized it was because there was just no circumstance where she could imagine giving Billy another chance. The trust had been broken, and there was no way to repair it—not when it came to cheating.

And she'd learned her lesson—she'd made the mistake once before. Her college boyfriend had cheated—supposedly just once—and he apologized up and down and begged her to give him another chance. He was her first love, and she'd been devastated, but he was persuasive and she wanted to believe that it would never happen again. But she found that she could never relax again around him—she was always suspicious when she saw him around other girls. As far as she knew, he didn't cheat again, but she just couldn't get past it. It was like she was just waiting for the inevitable to happen and that wasn't a good feeling.

"I bet the overnight film will be interesting," Eloise said.

Hudson smiled. "That's often when we get our best stuff. They get comfortable and forget about all the cameras once the production crew goes home."

"It might be a quiet night, though, after last night," Lauren said.

"Maybe. But it looks like they are feeling better now," Hudson said dryly.

Lauren followed his gaze and saw that Suzanne was lining up shot glasses and Billy was mixing up a cocktail. He poured it into the glasses and they all took one and raised their shots in a toast before downing them.

"We should probably finish up and get in there," Lauren said. They were all just about done at this point. The caterers came out to clear the tables, and they headed inside. Lauren and Eloise sat in the back of the room, near Hudson and his camera. Mike and Tom were in other corners of the room, so they would catch as much as possible on film.

Lauren and Eloise stayed for two more hours, watching in amusement as the cast turned the music up and danced around the room in between more shots and cocktails. There was plenty of flirting going on. Katy tried to chat Billy up whenever she had a chance. But she had competition, as Suzanne seemed interested too. Although Suzanne flirted with all the guys, so it was unclear if she had a favorite.

Anna and Sami were more reserved and cool about it all. And the guys all seemed interested in talking to both of them.

"Playing hard to get really does work," Eloise whispered.

Lauren laughed. "It sure seems that way."

"Oh, it definitely does," Hudson confirmed. "Guys like the chase. It's more of a challenge. Katy and Suzanne are cute girls, though, so anything could happen."

By the time they decided to call it a night, around ten, the cast was still laughing and singing along to the music. Billy played a mix of songs that everyone loved and as the night went on and the drinks continued to flow, their voices grew louder and both Katy and Suzanne sang along loudly. It was almost like karaoke and the others were all cheering them on.

They said goodbye, and the cast waved and kept on singing. They all walked out together. Lauren decided to walk back to the inn along the street, which was better lit now than the beach.

"Well, enjoy your days off, everyone. I'll see you all on Wednesday," Lauren said. Their shooting schedule was five days, with Monday and Tuesday as off days.

"Lauren, if you don't have plans for dinner tomorrow night, I was thinking of going to Millie's. Someone said their Mexican is California style—supposed to be really good."

"Sure, I'd love to. I went there a few years ago. It's great."

"Hudson, do you want to join us? Unless you're busy, of course," Eloise asked.

Hudson smiled. "Sure, count me in."

"Perfect. Let's plan to meet there at six," Eloise said happily.

"See you both tomorrow." Lauren started walking toward the inn. She was suddenly exhausted after spending the day on the beach, and that delicious dinner. She was going to sleep well tonight. And she looked forward to dinner tomorrow night at Millie's.

CHAPTER NINETEEN

"I totally forgot to tell you this yesterday," Rhett began. He and Lisa and a few of the inn's guests were in the dining room Monday morning eating breakfast, and Rhett had a mischievous look. "I may have run into Violet at the post office."

Lisa set her coffee cup down. "What did you do?"

He chuckled. "I told her that I was looking forward to sampling her food at the festival."

"What did she say?"

"Nothing at first. She narrowed her eyes at me like she was trying to figure out something, like maybe how I knew she was participating. But then she recovered and smiled and said she was very excited and expected to win her category."

"Ugh. She is so full of herself."

"I don't think she knew that you were also going to be there. I told her you were excited about it too and her jaw dropped. And then she said she had to run, and she raced out of there."

Lisa laughed. "You definitely poked the bear. Now she's going to be even more determined to beat me. I wonder if her lobster quiche is good?"

Rhett reached out and took her hand. "It can't possibly be anywhere near as good as yours." He leaned over and gave her a quick kiss and Lisa smiled. She could always count on Rhett.

Lisa looked up and saw Lauren walking toward them, carrying a tray of breakfast and coffee. She waved her over to join them at their table. All the other guests were paired off and Lisa always liked to make guests feel welcome, especially when they were friends of the family.

Lauren set her tray down and said hello to both of them. Rhett took a final sip of his coffee, then headed up for a refill and to get a plate of breakfast.

"Hi honey, how was your weekend?" Lisa asked.

Lauren smiled. "Good. Busy. I am looking forward to having the next two days off."

"Do you have any special plans for your time off?"

"Mostly just to relax, maybe do some more shopping. Oh, and a few of us are having dinner tonight at Millie's."

"Oh, Rhett and I love the scallop and bacon tacos at Millie's. They are so different and have blue cheese on them. If you like scallops, you should try them."

"I do. And that does sound good," Lauren agreed.

"Tell me more about the filming. It seems like it's been pretty quiet so far, no wild parties yet," Lisa said.

Lauren laughed. "I'm not sure if Walter and Kay would agree with that. Although it hasn't been too bad yet—as you said, we haven't had any parties yet. They were a little loud last night, though." She told Lisa about the music and dancing and flirting.

"So, it's an experiment of sorts? You put all these pretty people together and then see what happens and if romance develops?" Lisa said.

"Exactly. And having them all live together amplifies everything—heightens emotions."

Lisa was intrigued. The concept of a reality show was relatively new to her. She'd tried watching one of the popular housewives reality shows, but only managed to watch a few episodes. The particular show she watched just seemed like a bunch of women fighting about silly things. She couldn't understand why they were so popular and said as much to Lauren. "Why do people love those shows so much?"

Lauren smiled. "People like to see into another world, a different lifestyle that usually includes wealth and luxury. And even though the drama does often seem petty, and annoying even, the conflict brings viewers back each week. If everyone just got along, it wouldn't make for a compelling show."

Lisa thought about that. "I suppose so. But I bet some people would enjoy a show where people are kind and get along and live in a luxurious world. I'd watch that!"

"I actually agree with you somewhat. I think sometimes these shows overdo it with the somewhat forced drama. Some of these women have interesting careers. I know I'd love to see more of that," Lauren said.

"Yes! Now that would be interesting. Maybe you can suggest it for a new show?"

Lauren laughed. "I can try. I don't have a lot of influence yet. This show is the first one that I've led. It needs to go really well." Lisa noticed a note of nervousness in Lauren's tone.

"I'm sure it will. Your concept sounds interesting. And people seem fascinated with Nantucket—it will have that aspirational quality."

"Definitely," Lauren agreed.

Lauren and Lisa both looked up as Angela walked over to the table with a cup of coffee and a jelly donut. Lisa was happy to see her, but surprised, too. "Is Mary still sick?"

Angela nodded. "She is. She called this morning and said she would like to come back on Wednesday, so you'll have me for two more days at least."

"I'm sorry she's still sick. We always like to see you, though," Lisa said.

Angela smiled. "Thanks. I always love coming back here, too." Angela had stayed at the inn when renovation work was done on her grandmother's cottage and Lisa had enjoyed her company.

"Lauren was just telling us how the show is going and what she's going to do on her days off."

"You're off Mondays and Tuesdays, right?" Angela asked.

Lauren nodded. "Yes. I'm looking forward to relaxing

and exploring the island a bit and maybe just sitting on the beach."

"Are you still up for going to see Kristen's art show? It opens on Tuesday. We could have dinner at my place first. Philippe can make us his grilled swordfish—it's so good, and then we could head into town."

"Yes, I'd love to do that. What time should I come by?"

Angela thought for a minute. "Why don't you come earlyish, say around 5:30, then we'll head to the opening at seven. I tend to fade early, so the earlier, the better." Angela hesitated for a moment and looked as though she'd said something she shouldn't have. Lisa instantly suspected what she meant.

Angela sighed. "I might as well just tell you, since your daughters already know. I spilled the beans when they were over the other night. We're pregnant."

Lisa was thrilled for her. "That's the best news, Angela. Congratulations to both of you."

"Thank you. We weren't going to say anything until I was further along, but it was kind of obvious when I was drinking water at appetizer night and everyone else had wine. Plus, I didn't want to keep the news to myself. I know there's always a risk, but I'm thinking positive."

"As you should. Just be careful not to overdo things. You'll be fine," Lisa assured her.

Angela took the last bite of her jelly donut, glanced at her watch, and then stood. "Okay, time for me to get to work. Lauren, have fun today and I will see you tomorrow night."

"Sounds good. I'll bring something for dessert, if that works."

"Perfect."

After Angela left, Lauren got herself a second cup of coffee. She wasn't in any hurry, and it was nice to linger and chat with Lisa and Rhett. She'd also been thinking about when would be a good time for the cast to have dinner at Rhett's place. They would have several evenings out at restaurants and nightclubs.

"Rhett, are you still interested in having our group come in for dinner? And with it being filmed and shown on the network?"

Rhett nodded. "Of course. I'd be crazy to turn down that kind of publicity. When were you thinking?"

"Well, I'm assuming the weekends are too busy, so what about a Wednesday or Thursday night, possibly?" If he said Wednesday was the better day, she'd probably aim for the following week.

"Wednesday and Thursday nights are about the same, so whatever works best for you. We do have a side room that might be a little quieter and out of the way."

That sounded perfect. "Great. Could we do this Thursday or if that's too soon, next week could work?"

Rhett thought for a moment. "This Thursday should work."

"It will be nine for dinner, and then another table

nearby for the production staff. I'll be there as well," she said.

"Okay, that's fine. We'll make it work. What time were you thinking?" Rhett asked.

"We'll come early, so we don't disrupt things too much. Is five good?" Lauren knew the restaurant was probably less busy then, which would be a good thing.

"Yes, that's when we open and that would work out well. It doesn't usually get too busy that early."

"Maybe I'll see if one of my girlfriends wants to have dinner that night, too. We'll sit at the bar and watch from a distance. If you don't mind?" Lisa sounded excited at the thought of it.

"Of course! You'll see a little of the craziness." Lauren laughed. "They've actually been pretty well-behaved so far, so it might not be all that exciting."

"Doesn't matter. It will still be fun to watch," Lisa said.

Lauren finished her coffee and said goodbye to Lisa and Rhett. She was ready to take a walk on the beach and then head downtown to do some more exploring.

CHAPTER TWENTY

Lauren had a relaxing day. She poked around in the shops downtown for a bit and found another book to read, one of Angela's husband, Philippe's latest suspense thrillers. She stocked up at Stop and Shop on a few things, and made herself a turkey sandwich for lunch before heading to the beach for the afternoon. It was a perfect beach day, mid-seventies, so plenty warm enough without being too hot and there was a nice breeze. She stayed there until almost four, then reluctantly went in to shower and get ready for dinner.

She decided to wear her new dress that she'd gotten at Izzy's shop. It was casual and flowy and felt nice and light on her slightly sunburned skin. She was careful with sunscreen but had missed a few spots on her shoulders and they were pink. She drove out to Millie's, which was on the opposite side of the island, tucked away in a residential neighborhood and set just behind the dunes. It was a gorgeous spot.

Eloise was already there, waiting outside by the front door. As Lauren parked, she saw a Jeep pull in, with Hudson behind the wheel.

"I love that dress. Is it Free People?" Eloise asked as Lauren walked over.

"I think it might be. I got it at a cute boutique downtown—Nantucket Threads. It's on the wharf." Hudson joined them a minute later, and they headed inside and were seated at a hightop table in the bar area. There was a stunning view of the ocean and waves rolling in. So far, Lauren had only seen Hudson in t-shirts and shorts. Tonight he was wearing a Nantucket Red, that unique faded pinkish red shade that originated from Murray's Toggery, a shop downtown. The color made his dark hair seem even darker and his brown eyes drew her attention. She forced herself to look away and focus on the menu.

They all ordered margaritas and guacamole and chips to share as an appetizer while they decided what else to order.

"My friend Angela said that the scallop and bacon tacos are amazing. Though the shrimp sound really good, too," Lauren said.

"I was looking at both of those, too. Do you want to split them so we'll have one of each?" Eloise suggested.

"Perfect, I'd love to."

"Hudson, what are you going to get?" Eloise asked.

"The steak tacos sound pretty good to me."

Their server returned with their guacamole and chips, and they placed their order.

"This may be the best guac I've ever had," Eloise said

happily as she reached for another chip.

Lauren and Hudson both agreed. Eloise asked Hudson what it was like to grow up on Nantucket. "It's just so beautiful here. Is it very different when summer is over?"

Hudson nodded. "It was great growing up here. My parents moved to Nantucket when I was in elementary school. We'd lived in a suburb of Boston before that. But an opportunity came up for them to take over a veterinary practice here." Hudson paused to have another chip with guacamole.

"It is very different in the off-season. The population triples, or maybe even quadruples, in the summer months. It's still busy, but not as crazy in September and October, and dies out fast after that. Although there is one last hurrah the first weekend in December for the Christmas Stroll. That's the last weekend for a lot of the seasonal restaurants and shops. Everything shuts down after that."

"Is it too quiet? Or kind of nice?" Lauren asked. She imagined that like Cape Cod, the lack of people and traffic might be peaceful in the cooler months.

Hudson grinned. "It's awesome. People always assume that the island must be boring when the tourists go home, but as much as we appreciate them—I mean many of the island businesses depend on the tourism—most of us just don't mind when they go away. They take the traffic with them and we start to see our neighbors out and about again. A lot of them avoid going downtown much during the summer because it's so crazy."

"What do you do in the off-season, though?" Eloise didn't sound convinced. Lauren understood, since Eloise was used to the hustle and bustle of Los Angeles.

"All the things we do in summer—except go swimming. I still walk on the beach and fish and go out to dinner with friends. Oh, and I'm in a men's hockey league—and that's something that doesn't happen during the summer. So, I keep pretty busy."

Eloise looked intrigued. "You lived in LA for a while, though? Is that how you know Billy?"

Their server arrived with their food and set the plates down. Lauren and Eloise took a moment to swap one of their tacos. Everything looked delicious.

Hudson picked up a taco. But before taking a bite, he answered Eloise's question. "I met Billy when I first moved out west. I answered an ad he'd placed for a roommate. We hit it off right away, and I stayed for five years before getting my own place, but we still hung out all the time. I've actually only been back on the island for a little over a year."

"How did that come about?" Lauren asked. "I think you mentioned that you knew Cami Carmichael?"

Hudson nodded. "We'd worked together on a few projects. I started out in the reality TV world, then had an opportunity to move to film and after my first project, other movies and a TV drama came my way. I loved the work but never really loved LA—especially the traffic."

"The traffic is the worst," Lauren agreed.

"So when Cami called me, it was a no-brainer," Hudson said.

"These scallop tacos really are incredible," Eloise said. "I'm so glad we decided to share."

"I'll thank Angela for the recommendation when I see her tomorrow. We're going to an art show opening for one of her friends," Lauren said.

Hudson looked interested. "Is it Kristen Hodges by any chance? I'm friends with the owner of the art gallery and with Kristen's boyfriend, Tyler—he plays hockey with me. I'd told them I'd try to stop by tomorrow too, as it's unlikely I can get there over the weekend because of filming."

"It is Kristen. What a small world. I haven't met her boyfriend, but I know he's a mystery author. I think he had a movie made of one of his books?"

"It was a limited series on Netflix, actually. I worked on it. My only TV drama so far. That was a very cool project," Hudson said.

"We might run into you then. I think we're going on the early side, around seven or so," Lauren said.

"I'll look for you there," Hudson said.

"Did any of you look at the film from last night after the clambake?" Eloise asked.

Lauren nodded. "I took a peek this afternoon, right before I came here. Lots of flirting going on, but no specific romances brewing yet."

"That's what I thought too. Are most of them sticking around today and tomorrow? Or are they heading off-island?" Eloise asked.

"I think most of them are staying put," Hudson said. "As far as I know."

"Jason, Noah and Billy were going to head to Boston tonight to catch a Red Sox game. I think they are coming back tomorrow at some point. As far as I know, that's it," Lauren said.

When they finished and their server cleared the table, they decided to have another round of margaritas as dessert. It was still early, and no one was ready to go home just yet.

Eloise took a big sip of her new margarita and then casually asked. "So, Hudson, what's the social life like here on the island? Do you have a girlfriend?"

He laughed. "Social life is fine. At the moment, I'm fairly newly single. I ended a relationship a little over a month ago." He paused for a moment and then continued, "I'd met Meghan soon after I moved home. She was a year behind me in school, so I sort of knew her and met her one night when I was out with friends. We hit it off right away. Incredible chemistry. She's a beautiful girl." He paused for a moment to take a sip of his margarita.

"Ultimately we just wanted different things. She knew I'd lived in LA and worked in entertainment and I think that excited her. She's bored with life here and was hoping I'd want to move back to the West Coast and take her with me. I let her know that was highly unlikely. She didn't believe me at first and kept bringing it up over the winter. I guess she thought after spending a winter here I'd be eager to get back to LA. But it was the opposite. It just made me appreciate being here even more. So we had another conversation and decided to go our separate ways."

"I'm sorry." Eloise looked sympathetic.

"It's fine. It's for the best. Better to find out early, right? What about you two?" Hudson asked.

"I've been with my boyfriend, Jim, for just over two years. He's actually coming here in two weeks to spend a week. We're pretty serious."

"I think you know my status," Lauren said wryly.

Hudson smiled. "It's been a few months since you and Billy broke up. No one new yet?"

Lauren shook her head. "I haven't gone on a single date since we broke up. Just wasn't ready, and it has been easier to not think about it and focus on work. Maybe after the summer, when I'm back home."

"Home? You mean in LA?" Hudson asked.

"Yes. Unfortunately, that's where the work is."

"You don't love it there either?"

"I don't hate it. But it's not really home, you know? When I fly into Boston and then drive over the Cape Cod Canal, that's when I feel that sense of peace, of being home. I haven't really found that anywhere else, yet."

"I understand, completely. I am so grateful that Cami thought of me for this opportunity."

"Are you busy enough with work?" Eloise asked.

"We've been pretty booked since we started up. Most of it has been projects with Cami. She likes to adapt books that she falls in love with and so far, that's worked out well. She's expanding into other projects where she's just producing and not starring, which means even more work."

"That sounds so interesting, having a mix of things

like that," Lauren said. As much as she enjoyed producing the reality shows, she did sometimes wonder what it would be like to work on a movie or a dramatic TV series.

"I like the reality stuff, but it's nice to have the variety. I think it's good for my resume too. In case things get slow with Cami, I'll have more opportunities to pick up other projects. But it doesn't look like I'm going to have to worry about that anytime soon."

When they finished their drinks, Hudson asked for the check and then insisted on paying when the server brought it. "This is on us tonight. Cami and I were grateful to get the chance to do this show. It would have been easier and less expensive to shoot on Cape Cod."

"Well, thank you," Lauren said. "As much as I love the Cape, I'm so glad they went with Nantucket, too. There's something so magical and aspirational about it. I think viewers will be excited." She grinned. "This is a huge opportunity for me too, and I don't hate the thought of being here for the summer."

"I'm loving it too," Eloise said. "I'd never really been to the East Coast before. I had no idea how beautiful it was. Or how good lobster could be."

They all laughed as they stood to leave and then said their goodbyes outside.

"I'll look for you tomorrow," Hudson said as they reached their cars.

"Thanks again for dinner. This was a fun night," Lauren said.

Hudson smiled. "It really was."

CHAPTER TWENTY-ONE

"So you have cameras watching them when you guys aren't there, right? What is that like? Do you get better footage, then?" Philippe asked.

Lauren was sitting on Angela and Philippe's huge deck, that overlooked the ocean. Philippe had just put several marinated swordfish filets onto the grill for dinner and was keeping an eye on it while they enjoyed a glass of wine. Angela was having a non-alcoholic spritzer.

"Sometimes we do. After the first day or two, the cast typically gets more comfortable in front of all the cameras, but once the big cameras and production team leaves they are less guarded. Especially if alcohol is involved."

"Are they heavy drinkers?" Angela asked.

"Some of them are enthusiastic drinkers. It's mostly social, but with an extra drink or two for most of them, especially if it's a party night or some kind of event going on."

"Any romances happening yet?" Angela asked.

Lauren shook her head. "Not yet. But last night's footage was pretty uneventful as the guys were all in Boston for the evening."

"Do you think it might become a regular series? Then you'd be back every summer." Angela looked hopeful and Lauren felt the same.

"It's possible. It would be amazing to come back again next summer. I don't want to get my hopes up, though. We really never know how a show will be received," Lauren said.

"I have a good feeling about it. I mean, it's Nantucket. Everyone has heard of this island, but very few have actually spent time here. This show will let them experience the wonder of it." Philippe grinned. "As long as there is some messy drama, of course."

Lauren laughed. "Yes, a show where everyone gets along and just goes to the beach on a pretty island might not satisfy the viewers. Hopefully, the drama will come. It always has before."

When the swordfish was ready, Philippe plated it up, along with grilled asparagus and crispy buttered new potatoes. Lauren took a bite of the fish and swooned.

"This is so good. I've never tried to cook swordfish myself. This is as good as any I've had in a restaurant."

Philippe looked pleased to hear it. "The secret is cooking it on the grill and letting it soak in Italian salad dressing for an hour or so."

When they finished eating, Angela got up to clear the

table, but Philippe motioned for her to stay seated. "I've got this. Be right back."

He returned a few minutes later with a raspberry pie and three plates. "Angela made this. She's been craving pie."

Angela laughed. "It's true. And I've discovered pie makes an excellent breakfast."

"Not every day though," Philippe said sternly, and they all laughed.

"Seriously though. This is my new favorite. Have you ever had raspberry pie?" Angela asked.

"No, I can't say that I have." It looked incredible though, with a light, flaky crust and gooey raspberries oozing everywhere as Angela cut slices for everyone and handed one to her.

Lauren took a bite and there was a flavor explosion in her mouth. "It's like eating a giant raspberry square!"

Angela smiled. "Exactly." She turned to Philippe. "Have you had any luck getting interest for Kate's book?"

He shook his head. "Unfortunately, no. I just mentioned it to a few people I've worked with. The timing isn't right for any of them at the moment. But they all said they'd keep it mind."

"I know that happens a lot, deals falling apart. I just feel so bad for Kate. She was so excited, and it seemed like such a solid, sure thing with that brother and sister team involved," Angela said.

"In this business, there are very few sure things. I think the brother is going through a bitter divorce and that kind of put a halt on most of what they are working on," Philippe explained.

"That makes sense," Angela agreed.

After they'd had enough pie—Angela went back for a second slice—they headed into town to the art gallery. They decided to take separate cars, so Lauren could just head home afterward, as they lived in opposite directions.

The art gallery was downtown, near the wharf. Lauren found a spot in the lot by the smaller Stop and Shop on the wharf. She got lucky as someone pulled out as she driving by. Philippe and Angela had to loop around a few more times before they found a spot nearby. Lauren walked to the art gallery and waited outside for them to arrive.

Angela had explained that the event was like an open house and that it would go from six to eight. There was a good crowd gathered—Lauren guessed there were close to a hundred people in the art gallery. Kristen waved when she saw them and walked over to say hello. She looked elegant in a sleeveless burnt orange silk dress that showed off her toned and tanned arms. She gave them welcome hugs all around.

"Thank you so much for coming." She glanced at a man about her age that passed by and called him over. "Andrew, have you met my friends Angela and Philippe?" She looked at Lauren. "And this is Lauren. She's a producer on the reality show that is filming here. Andrew owns the gallery."

Andrew smiled. "Yes, I remember Angela and Philippe. It's nice to see you both again. And Lauren, a pleasure to meet you. I hope the filming is going well?"

Lauren nodded. "Very well, thanks. It's a fun project."

"Help yourselves to the Champagne. And there should be some good appetizers coming around," Andrew said.

"Thanks, Andrew. I'll lead them to the champagne," Kristen said. They followed her to the back of the gallery, where there was a bar with glasses and champagne on ice. "Champagne for everyone? Angela, I think there's some sparkling water here, too."

Once they all had a glass of bubbly, Kristen walked them around and talked about her different paintings. There were seascapes with classic Nantucket elements, like lighthouses and ferries coming into the harbor. There were also gorgeous floral paintings—knockout roses on white picket fences, with the ocean in the distance and vivid blue hydrangeas. The images were familiar, but the artistry was really special. Lauren wasn't experienced in evaluating art, but she could appreciate something beautiful and Kristen had a way of capturing light and colors.

"These are really stunning," Lauren said. She was tempted to buy something but decided to hold off until she headed home. She assumed the gallery would be able to ship it better than she could.

Angela fell in love with a painting of a flower garden

with bright yellows, pinks and purples and a soft pink and orange sunset.

"Philippe, do you like this? I can see it on the wall in the nursery. What do you think?"

"I love it. Let's do it." He leaned in and gave Angela a quick kiss.

"That's one of my personal favorites," Kristen said. "I'm so glad it's going to a good home. I'll let Tony, Andrew's assistant, know."

"Is Tyler here?" Philippe asked.

"He should be here any minute. Oh, would you all excuse me? Andrew wants me to meet someone." Kristen headed off to mingle while Lauren, Angela, and Philippe slowly made their way around the rest of the gallery. Twenty minutes later, Angela tried to hold back a yawn, but failed miserably.

"I'm so sorry. I know it's ridiculous that I'm so tired already," she said.

"It's not at all. I think it's normal, especially in your first trimester," Lauren said.

Philippe looked concerned. "We can head home anytime. Are you ready to go now?"

Angela nodded. "Not just yet, but soon. Maybe ten minutes or so? We still need to pay for that painting."

"Right. I'll go take care of that now," Philippe said. He wandered off to find Andrew's assistant.

"Someone's waving at you," Angela said.

Lauren turned and saw Hudson at the champagne bar. She smiled and he headed their way. Lauren introduced him to Angela. "Hudson is helping us with equipment and camera work for the show."

"Nice to meet you. You're Bella's partner, right?"

Hudson nodded. "I am. She was hoping to come tonight, but the restaurant is short-handed, so Nick is working late. They'll probably come tomorrow."

Angela smiled. "Kristen will be thrilled, no matter when they come."

"Did you see Kristen?" Lauren asked him.

"She was by the door when I walked in and I did a quick tour of her new stuff. I'm tempted. I already have a great seascape of hers. I might sleep on it and come back."

"The one you are eyeing might be gone," Lauren teased him.

He grinned. "True. We'll see what happens."

They all chatted for a few more minutes until Philippe returned.

"We're all set with the painting. I'm going to swing by over the weekend to pick it up. It will have a sold sticker on it until then."

"Perfect. I'm ready to go, then."

Hudson glanced at Lauren. "You're leaving already? Did you all come together?"

Lauren nodded, as Angela smiled widely. "We did, but we took separate cars. I suspected I might want to leave earlier. But Lauren, you should stay."

Lauren hesitated as Kristen walked toward them.

"Oh good. I was going to come and find you to say goodbye. We're leaving, but I was just telling Lauren she should stay. No need to rush home because I'm exhausted."

Kristen laughed. "You should stay. A few of us are going for a drink in about a half hour when this winds down. You should come. Hudson is coming, right?"

He looked her way. "Right. You should come. We're just walking a few doors down to the Club Car."

"Okay, sure. I'd love to." The Club Car was modeled like a railroad car and had the cutest flower boxes along the windows. Lauren had driven by a few times when she was downtown, but she hadn't been there yet.

"Good, that's settled then. Angela, I'll walk you guys out. I need to make the rounds again," Kristen said.

"Thanks so much for dinner," Lauren said to Angela and Philippe as she gave them both a hug goodnight. "I'll call you later this week."

Once they walked off, Lauren turned to Hudson. "Show me the painting you have your eye on."

He led her to a collection of seascapes, all beautiful, but one was darker than the others. The sky looked ready to storm, and the sea was eerily flat and glasslike, as it often was before the winds kicked in. A house sat on a bluff overlooking the ocean with a single light on. The mood of the piece was in anticipation of what was ahead.

It didn't surprise her when Hudson took a step toward that painting. "This is the one. What do you think?"

"I think it's stunning." She grinned. "If you don't buy it, I might have to and I don't have anywhere to put a painting right now."

Hudson laughed. "Okay, sold. It tugged on me when I

first saw it." His eyes met hers for a brief moment. "And now I really don't want to let it go."

Lauren felt a flash of sadness that she couldn't get the painting, but it was gone in an instant and she was glad it was going to Hudson. "Do you know where you'll put it?"

He nodded. "I have a small den/office that has a distant view of the ocean. There's a big spot on the wall that should work."

"You can sit there working and be inspired."

"Exactly. I look at that painting and I see the possibilities of what's ahead."

Lauren took a sip of champagne and glanced around the room. It was starting to clear out a bit. "What is next for you, after our show wraps?" she asked.

"A rom-com, actually. It's based on a book Bella acquired about six months ago." He told her a bit about the story and Lauren remembered seeing it everywhere for a while. "I think I heard about that one on TikTok."

"That's how everyone heard about it. It totally blew up on BookTok. Bella is a huge reader and keeps an eye on things like that—what people are responding to. The screenplay is done and we should start shooting by the end of the summer. What's next for you?"

"I'm not exactly sure. The last reality show I was on before this one isn't being renewed. But there are other things coming. Possibly a new show set in LA. I should know more next month."

"So you'll be heading back to the West Coast." Hudson's tone when he said the West Coast almost made Lauren laugh. He clearly didn't miss living there.

"Well, yes. LA is where most of the work is…and my apartment. How long did you live there?"

"Too long," he said quickly, and they both laughed. He smiled as a dark-haired man walked up to them. "Tyler, have you met Lauren?"

Tyler smiled. "Not yet. You're Angela's friend? Kristen said you're coming for a drink with us. And you work with this guy?"

"I do. I'm a producer for the reality show that is filming here."

"I love that more film stuff is happening on Nantucket. We've had the film festival for a number of years now, but that's more about celebrating film in general. Now that Bella and Hudson opened their production company, it's bringing new work to the island. And I'm all for it."

"Thanks. It's exciting to be a part of it. If I can avoid needing to go back to the West Coast to find work, I'll be a happy man." He glanced at Lauren. "No offense meant."

She laughed. "None taken."

"I'm going to go check with Kristen to see if she needs any help to close down. We should be ready to go in about five minutes or so," Tyler said.

Five minutes later, as the last customer walked out, they followed and Kristen led the way to the Club Car. Tyler mentioned that he'd stopped in on the way to the gallery and made a reservation for a table.

Which was a good thing, as the restaurant was still busy even though it was a quarter past eight. They were seated by a window overlooking Main Street, with its cobblestones and people streaming by. Their server handed them menus and took their drink order.

"I know you all probably ate already, but I'm starving," Kristen said.

"She can never eat before a show," Tyler explained.

Kristen nodded. "Nerves. Now that it's over, I need something."

When their drinks arrived, champagne for Kristen and Lauren and a Cisco IPA for the Hudson and non-alcoholic beer for Tyler, Kristen put an order in for a crab cake appetizer.

"Is that enough?" Tyler asked. "You could get the halibut, it's great here."

Kristen handed the server her menu. "I don't want a big dinner, this will be perfect."

"How did you two meet?" Lauren asked. She always loved hearing those stories.

Kristen smiled. "He moved into the cottage next door. And that was pretty much it."

Tyler nodded in agreement. "We were both interested right away. But we started slow, got to know each other as neighbors first and it grew from there."

"We have a lot in common," Kristen added. "Tyler's an artist, like me. Well, not exactly like me, he writes books, but you know what I mean. We both work from home and need a lot of quiet to focus."

"We mostly live in my cottage now, but Kristen kept hers, too."

"My studio is there, so that is where I work, while Tyler is holed up in his office solving crimes." She grinned at him and he pulled her close and dropped a kiss on the top of her head.

Lauren thought about what Angela had told her about Kristen, how she hadn't had great relationships before Tyler. Her last one had been with a real estate developer who was separated but hadn't seemed in any hurry to finalize his divorce. Lauren was glad that she'd found happiness with Tyler. They seemed well suited.

She glanced at Tyler. "Hudson mentioned that you play on a men's hockey league together. Did you play as a kid, too?"

"Yeah. I think we all did. I loved playing hockey. I thought I'd be terrible as it had been forever since I'd stepped on the ice. But it comes back to you. And it's good exercise," Tyler said.

"He's being modest," Hudson said. "Tyler is our center, and he's fast."

Tyler chuckled. "It is fun. And you're just as good, probably better." He looked Lauren's way. "Hudson plays goalie and almost no one can get by him. He was a star player in high school."

"High school was a long time ago," Hudson said.

"Did you guys know each other in high school?" Lauren was surprised.

Tyler shook his head. "No. But we lived a few towns away and played against each other once or twice a year. His team always crushed it."

Hudson grinned and lifted his beer. "Those were my glory days. It sure was fun, though." Lauren tried to picture Hudson as a star hockey player. She wouldn't have thought of it, but she could see it now. He was average height at maybe five-ten or so and lean and wiry. Hudson was in excellent shape and he had an intensity about him, a focus when he worked that she could see him bringing to the ice. She had to admit, the image was an attractive one—Hudson in his hockey gear, slapping the puck away as he prevented the other team from scoring.

Kristen's crab cakes arrived along with a basket of fries that they all snacked on, just because they were there.

The conversation turned to the show. Kristen asked them how it was going and after they said things were great, Tyler mentioned that he'd heard some grumbling.

"I was at the post office the other day, mailing a package and stood in line for a while. There were two women in front of me who were pretty incensed about the show and felt it was a bad thing for the island. They seemed like the type that might do more than just complain to each other."

"What was their issue?" Hudson asked.

"It was kind of ridiculous. They were mostly complaining about what could happen. Like it might be noisy or they might make a mess on the beach. A bunch of nothing, but still it's good to be aware of it."

"We haven't had any issues brought to our attention yet," Lauren said. "But I expect that we probably will at some point. The realtor that handles the lease for the rental warned me that some people are not happy that we are filming here. But we got all the necessary permits."

Tyler grinned. "Good, then there's nothing those old biddies can do about it."

"No. But we do need to try to keep the noise level down. I'm very aware of that. We haven't had any big parties yet, but they are coming and I'll try to head off any issues by inviting all the neighbors to attend."

"We'll need extra bodies at the parties anyway," Hudson chimed in.

"That's very true. In fact, if you two are interested, it would be fun to have you attend."

Kristen looked unsure. "I don't know if I'd want to be on camera."

But Tyler looked intrigued. "That could be interesting, actually. And we could just stay in the background. It's not like anyone would want to hear what we say."

"It might be good to be a fly on the wall...you could pick up material for one of your books," Hudson said.

"That's what I'm thinking," Tyler agreed.

Kristen laughed. "Okay, as long as I can hide in the background and just observe, I'm in."

When they finished their drinks, Tyler insisted on picking up the tab and they headed out. It was almost ten and both Lauren and Hudson needed to be up early as they were filming again the next day.

They all said their goodbyes outside the Club Car.

Hudson was parked near Lauren, so they headed off in the same direction.

"I'm glad you came out with us. That was fun," he said as they reached her car.

"It was nice to get to know Kristen better. Tyler too. It was a fun night," Lauren agreed.

"See you at the house tomorrow." Hudson turned to go and Lauren slid into her car and turned on the engine. She was tired, but happy. It really had been a fun night.

CHAPTER TWENTY-TWO

For their first non-filming days, Anna and the other girls decided to stay on the island and just relax and explore without cameras following them. The guys, except for Brett, all headed to Boston on Monday afternoon to catch a Red Sox game that night.

Katy and Anna spent most of Monday at the beach in front of the house and, after showering and changing, they headed downtown in the late afternoon to do a little shopping and grab dinner somewhere. They roamed around all the cobblestone streets and popped in and out of shops. Anna picked up a thick sweatshirt at Murray's Toggery in the unique Nantucket Red shade that was like a faded pinkish red. They had a delicious dinner at the Straight Wharf, which was a short walk to where the ferries came in.

On Tuesday, Katy suggested going to a spa, and Suzanne and Sami thought that sounded like a great idea. They booked massages and facials at the spa at The

Whitley Hotel and it was one of the most luxurious spas that Anna had ever been to. When they checked in, they all got lockers and thick, soft, white robes. They undressed, put on their robes and headed into the relaxing waiting room where soft music surrounded them and there were lounge chairs around a wading pool. There was also an assortment of hot teas and infused iced waters, cucumber-lemon and raspberry-mint.

They sipped the cool waters and dipped their toes in the wading pool. One by one, they were called in for their treatments and it was an afternoon of pure, relaxing bliss. Anna had a stone massage followed by a signature facial, which included a neck and shoulder massage. By the time she was done, her skin was glowing, and she was so relaxed.

When they were all finished, they kept their robes on and went upstairs to the spa restaurant, where most people dined in their robes. They got a kick out of that. It seemed funny to sit in an elegant restaurant with a very fancy menu and be in their bathrobes. They ordered a bottle of prosecco and decided to share a bunch of different appetizers—Oysters Rockefeller, truffle fries, shrimp cocktail, a charcuterie platter of assorted meats and cheeses and some lightly fried calamari. There was plenty of food and it was all delicious.

As they ate, they talked about their impressions of everyone in the house so far. They all agreed that everyone seemed nice enough, but that Billy and Noah were not good romantic prospects, given their reputations.

"I'm not sure Jason is much better," Sami said. "He's getting a ton of attention from women. He's even more popular now that he's moved into influencing. I think it might be hard to trust any of them."

"Well, we don't have to marry them," Suzanne said. "They might be fun to date. As long as you don't expect anything serious out of it."

"That's true," Katy agreed. "A summer fling might be kind of fun."

Suzanne set her drink down and her eyes lit up. "Interesting. Do you have your eye on anyone?"

Katy flushed a bit at the question. "Not really. I was just thinking generally."

"I wonder what they think of us?" Sami lifted her glass of prosecco and took a sip.

"They all seemed interested in Anna," Katy said. "But that's nothing unusual." She looked at the others. "You've heard of pretty privilege? Anna has it, for sure."

Sami looked intrigued. "What is pretty privilege?"

Katy leaned forward and looked around the table. "So, I know I can clean up good when I do my makeup and hair and wear a cute outfit. But I'll never have pretty privilege. That's when you literally turn heads wherever you go. When people are nice to you because of how you look. Guys just give you things—buy you drinks, open doors for you, bring you flowers, send a car for you on dates. It's just another level."

Anna felt herself flush. These things did happen to her at times, but she didn't think she was alone in that.

"I'm sure that happens to all of you. You're all gorgeous," she said.

Suzanne laughed. "It does not. Not like that. I do get recognized more now though, and that's pretty cool."

"Same here," Sami said. "I'm surprised how often I am recognized. But when I'm not, honestly, nothing special happens. Not like that."

Katy nodded. "People know me now too and it surprises me every time, but it is kind of fun. I just can't imagine having real pretty privilege, like Anna does. What is that like?" she asked.

Anna felt uncomfortable talking about it. "It's not that big of a deal, really. I think it's kind of silly, actually. It's not like I deserve any special treatment. I'm sure it's mostly just that they recognize me, too." She wasn't comfortable with special treatment because of how she looked. It wasn't something she thought she would ever get used to, and she really did think it was ridiculous. No one had given her a second glance until she was around fifteen. She'd been a late bloomer, skinny and gawky and awkwardly shy. She'd always been more of an observer, content to sit back and watch others shine.

But the summer before her sophomore year, everything changed. She grew more than an inch—everywhere. She filled out in all the right places and her face lost its softness and her high cheekbones stood out. Her nose was small and straight, and her eyes were just like her mother's, a pretty shade of blue-gray. Her hair was naturally a sandy blonde, and it had lightened from spending the summer at the beach. When she went back to school that year, people looked at her differently, especially the boys. And over the years, as she grew more comfortable with herself, she developed her own sense of style—sort of a classic elegance—she liked lots of clean lines, blacks and whites and soft neutrals. She knew that she turned heads and had reluctantly accepted it.

The other three girls exchanged glances and then Suzanne changed the subject, thankfully.

"Did anyone save room for dessert? The chocolate mousse cake sounds amazing."

CHAPTER TWENTY-THREE

When they returned to the house, with full stomachs and glowing skin, the guys were all on the deck, having a beer and watching the sunset.

Katy went right up to Billy. "How was Boston? Did the Red Sox win?"

He smiled, a slow smile that lit up his whole face. "They sure did. We had a blast. Did you miss us? I have to say you're looking especially pretty tonight. All of you are glowing."

Katy laughed. "We just spent the afternoon at the spa."

"Ah, that explains it then."

Jason stood and walked over to where Anna was leaning against the deck railing. The sunset was gorgeous, with rich shades of pink and orange hovering over the water.

"You had a fun spa day, I hear?"

Anna smiled. "Yeah, it was nice. Good food too. What else did you guys do in Boston?"

"We had dinner in the North End before the game and then, after the Red Sox won, we went to a bar in Fenway for a celebratory beer. Then we walked back to The Lenox Hotel in the Back Bay. There's an Irish Bar in the hotel, so we stopped in for one or maybe it was two there," Jason said. "There was a guy on the guitar who was pretty good and the crowd was lively. It was a fun time."

"That does sound fun. I miss Boston sometimes. I haven't been to a Red Sox game in ages," Anna said.

"We should go sometime then, before the summer is over. Maybe get a group of us to go," Jason suggested.

"I'd like that."

"Oh, we had the best coffee this morning. I might try to recreate it tomorrow. It's had a thick foam and chocolate."

"Mmm a mocha. That sounds great."

Jason grinned. "If I can find chocolate syrup, and it comes out good, I'll make you one."

Anna laughed. "I will hold you to that."

They didn't stay up late. The guys were tired from a late night in Boston and the girls were ready for a good night's sleep after the relaxing massages. They were all aware that filming started up the next day and everyone wanted to look as good as possible on camera.

Anna woke the next day around eight thirty to the sound of a gentle tapping on their bedroom door. She glanced over at Katy, who was awake, but laying in bed scrolling on her phone.

"Come in," she called out, curious to who would be knocking so early.

Jason stepped inside, holding two steaming mugs of coffee and wearing a big grin.

"Remember, I mentioned trying a good coffee drink in Boston?"

Anna nodded. He handed her a mug and delivered one to Katy. "So, my experiment this morning was a success. I used the Nespresso machine, so it makes that foamy layer on top and just added a good squirt of chocolate syrup. I didn't add milk, in case you didn't want that. Try it and let me know what you think."

"Thank you. It smells fantastic," Anna said.

"This is so nice of you, Jason. We could get used to this." Katy was all smiles as she took a sip of the coffee and then gave him the thumbs up.

Anna took a tentative small sip as there was still steam coming off the coffee.

"Oh, this is really good. I can taste the chocolate."

"If you like it with milk, you can add that," Jason suggested.

"I think it's perfect. I usually drink my coffee black," Anna said.

Katy nodded. "I do too. I stopped using milk in

college to try to lose weight and just because it was easier."

Jason looked pleased that the coffee was a hit. He took a step toward the door. "I'll leave you to it, then. See you on the beach later. We don't have anything else going on today, do we?"

"Nothing until dinner. Honey is cooking for us," Anna said.

Jason raised his eyebrows. "She is? Is that a good thing?" He sounded skeptical.

Anna laughed. "I think it will be. I love her cooking videos and even tried one of her recipes and I'm not a cook and it still came out good."

"Cool. Sounds good then. See you all in a bit."

Jason left, and Anna and Katy exchanged glances as soon as the door shut behind him.

"Well, that was very interesting," Katy said. Her look suggested that there was a deeper meaning to the coffee in bed, but Anna just laughed.

"I think it was sweet of him. I don't think it means anything beyond that. He was telling me last night about wanting to try to recreate a coffee drink. I think he was just excited for us to try it."

"Well, I meant what I said. I could get used to this." Katy grinned and took another sip of her coffee.

CHAPTER TWENTY-FOUR

Anna had to admit that so far, the Nantucket summer was both more relaxing and more fun than she'd expected. They'd had a great day on the beach. She even swam for a bit. They took a break for lunch and catering had left an assortment of sandwiches and creamy potato salad that was out of this world. She went back to the beach for an hour or so and then had enough by around two and called it a day. She spent the rest of the afternoon resting in her room, reading a book, with Smith curled up by her feet. She also spent an hour or so editing content that she'd filmed on the beach and broke it into several short videos to post on social media. It was just fun shots of everyone on the beach and playing volleyball.

Katy stayed longer on the beach and was yawning as she walked into the room.

"You were smart to come up earlier. I might need a mini-nap before dinner. It was fun, though."

"Did Honey mention what she is making for dinner? I meant to ask her and forgot," Anna said.

"I think she said something about oven roasted scallops. I guess the scallops here are supposed to be really good."

"Great." Anna loved scallops and knew they were local and super fresh on Nantucket. Her stomach rumbled thinking about it and she glanced at the time. She needed to get a move on and get dressed and downstairs in time for dinner.

CHAPTER TWENTY-FIVE

The scallops that Honey was roasting smelled amazing. Almost as if she could read Lauren's mind, Honey turned and addressed the production team.

"I hope you all like scallops. I'm making plenty for everyone," she said.

Lauren was thrilled to hear it. She'd assumed they'd be eating the leftover sandwiches that catering had made earlier.

"Thank you, Honey. Let us know if you need help with anything," Lauren said.

Honey smiled and wiped her hands on her flowered apron. "I'm good, thanks. This is actually a pretty simple recipe. There's tons of potato salad left from lunch, so I figured we'd have that along with some grilled asparagus.

"Sounds perfect," Lauren agreed.

It had been an uneventful day so far. They'd been on the beach filming the cast as they chatted, swam and played a little volleyball. They all took a break for a few hours in the late afternoon, and now at a quarter to six, everyone was back and ready to film Honey cooking and serving dinner.

Everyone gathered around the big dining room table and the girls helped Honey bring all the food to the table and everyone helped themselves. Honey had set a separate batch of scallops aside and the production team all made their plates as well and resumed their positions as the cast sat down to eat.

Lauren took a bite of a scallop and sighed. It was so sweet and cooked perfectly with a little crunch from the panko coating and the lemony garlic mayo was the perfect dipping sauce. Lauren laughed when she saw Honey's cat Simon, even had his own plate of scallops. He'd looked ready to jump up on the counter twice, but each time, she'd sent him a 'don't you dare' look.

Everyone in the cast raved about the food too and thanked Honey for cooking. The conversation slowed at first as everyone focused on their food. When it started up again, Suzanne teased Jason for bringing coffee in bed for Anna and Katy.

"What about us? Sami and I like fancy coffee, too."

Jason laughed. "Okay, you got it. Tomorrow is your turn."

"If you like chocolate, you will love it," Katy said. "I told Jason we could get used to having our morning coffee served to us."

Anna laughed. "It was a nice treat."

"Jeez, Jason, you're making the rest of us look bad," Billy teased.

"Hey, I've gotta give myself an edge here. Competition is stiff with two of you."

Noah and Billy both laughed.

"So, what are we doing after dinner? I don't suppose anyone is up for a little skinny-dipping?" Billy asked. It was hard to tell if he was serious or just messing with them.

"There is no way I would skinny dip at night here," Katy said.

"Why not? It could be awesome." Billy flashed his most charming grin.

But Katy looked at him as if he was crazy to even suggest it. "Seriously, Billy? Haven't you seen the movie *Jaws*? This area has tons of great whites. You'd make a nice midnight snack for them."

Billy's grin disappeared. "Okay, you may have a point there. *Jaws* was Martha's Vineyard though, not Nantucket."

This time, everyone laughed at him. "It's basically the same thing, Billy," Jason said. "Katy's right. There have always been great whites in this area, but in recent years there have been even more, all up and down the Cape and both islands. I don't swim way out like I used to."

"Fine, Plan B then—how about strip poker?"

Suzanne made a face. "You just want to see us all naked. We're not that stupid. And I don't know about anyone else, but I am terrible at poker."

"I think I may have stayed on the beach a little too long today," Katy admitted. "I don't think I'm up for a late night tonight."

"I am feeling a little stir-crazy, though," Suzanne said. "And I had a nap this afternoon. Would anyone want to head into town and go to the Chicken Box? I hear they have good live music and it's supposed to be a fun, casual place. Have any of you been there?"

"Never been there, but I'm up for anything," Billy said. He glanced Lauren's way. "Lauren, Hudson, you guys know the island. What do you think?"

"The Chicken Box is a fun place. I think you guys would like it," Lauren said. She'd only been there once, but it had been a fun night.

Hudson agreed. "Billy, Suzanne, I think it's right up your alley. Super casual place, jeans or shorts are fine and the music is usually good."

"Okay, Chicken Box it is, let's do it. Who else is coming?"

Everyone seemed enthused about the idea.

Katy yawned, but agreed to go, since everyone else was going.

Hudson turned to Lauren and Eloise and grinned. "Looks like this is going to be a late night."

"I'll call ahead and make sure they are okay with the cameras," Lauren said. She thought that they probably would be as it was a Wednesday night and not as busy as the weekends and it would be incredible free advertising for them.

Sure enough, after a quick call to the manager of the Chicken Box, they had the green light to film.

Everyone piled into a few vehicles and headed into town. The Chicken Box was pretty busy. Lauren could only imagine how packed it must get on the weekends. They were met at the door by the manager, who led them to the end of the bar, near where the band was playing. There were some empty seats at the bar and a few tables that the manager reserved for their group. The guys set up their cameras, and Lauren and Eloise sat out of the way at a smaller table in the corner. Hudson positioned himself next to them with his camera.

"I'm going to get a soda. Can I get you guys anything?" Lauren offered.

"I'll take a soda and cranberry, please," Eloise said.

"I'll have a Coke. Wait, make that a Sam Adams. I can have one beer," Hudson said. They usually didn't drink while they were filming. But now that they were out at a bar, it was tempting.

"Hmm. Maybe I'll have a glass of wine," Lauren said.

Eloise laughed. "Fine, I'll have a chardonnay."

Lauren went to the bar and returned with their drinks a few minutes later. Katy, Billy and Noah were sitting at the bar. Billy tried to catch Lauren's eye to talk to her, but she glanced at Hudson, to remind Billy that they were filming and to keep his conversations with his other cast members. He made a face and turned his attention back to Katy and Noah.

She turned to her table with their drinks and took her seat. "Where's Suzanne and Jason?" She asked Eloise. Everyone else was sitting at a table nearby.

"Suzanne just dragged Jason out to the dance floor. She said this is her favorite song," Eloise said.

Sure enough, Suzanne and Jason were in the middle of the crowded dance floor, laughing and dancing energetically to a popular country music song. They stayed out there for the next one, which was even more popular, and Honey and Brett and Sami, Anna and Noah joined them. Katy and Billy were deep in conversation at the bar. And Lauren noticed that every so often, Katy touched Billy's arm lightly, just for a second, and then laughed. Hudson moved closer so he could hear some of their conversation and get it onto film.

"Katy is flirting hard," Eloise said. "I wonder if anything will happen with her and Billy."

"Who knows?" Lauren said. Billy was hard to read. She couldn't tell if he was just enjoying the attention from Katy or if he was interested. If he started something with her, she hoped it was real. Katy seemed like a sweet girl and Lauren hated to see Katy get her hopes up and then have Billy revert to his usual cheating ways. And Lauren actually liked Billy—she hoped he'd get his act together and be a better man. But she wasn't sure that was likely to happen any time soon.

On the next song, Katy and Billy joined the others on the dance floor and Hudson came back to their table.

"So, what do you think? Is anything developing there?" Eloise asked.

"Maybe? I know Billy and can't get a read on if he's into Katy or not. He flirts like that with everyone. She's definitely up for a little romance, though."

"That band is really good." Lauren liked the mix of country and rock that they were playing. It was mostly lively songs that kept everyone dancing.

"They're here a lot," Hudson said. "We should all come back here some night when we're not working and can enjoy it."

"I'd love that," Eloise said.

The cast seemed to be having a great time. They were laughing and joking with each other and spent a good amount of time on the dance floor. Except for Honey and Brett, the rest of them switched off who they danced with, and by the end of the night, Katy was back to chatting at a table with Anna and Sami while Suzanne was doing shots at the bar with the guys.

By eleven, they were all ready to call it a night. Both Lauren and Eloise had several cast members riding with them and Honey also drove, as she wasn't drinking at all. Lauren dropped everyone off, then headed home to the inn and fell into bed. It had been a long day. And tomorrow promised to be more of the same as they had the restaurant dinner at Rhett's.

CHAPTER TWENTY-SIX

"Rhett said he was going to save us two seats at the bar," Lisa said to her friend Marley as she pulled into the restaurant's parking lot.

"I'm looking forward to this. I watch a few of those reality shows. *Southern Charm,* and some of the *Housewives.*"

Lisa laughed. "I had no idea. You've never mentioned it before."

"Well, that's why I said yes so quickly when you invited me to come tonight. I don't mention it because I know none of you watch those shows. Lots of people think they're silly."

"I've never watched any. What do you like about them?" Lisa asked as they walked in the front door. Rhett was behind the bar and waved them over. He'd saved the two seats at the end of the bar, the side closest to the dining room, where they'd have the best views.

"Ted will be back in a minute. He's changing a keg. Daou cab for you?"

Lisa nodded. "Thanks honey. Marley, are you having a cocktail or wine? We could share a bottle if you like cabernet?"

"Sure, that sounds good."

They settled themselves onto the bar stools. They were the comfortable kind that were leather padded with a solid wooden back and armrests. Rhett returned a few minutes later, opened their bottle of wine, and poured a glass for each of them. Lisa lifted hers and tapped it against Marley's. "Cheers! To our reality show adventure tonight."

Marley laughed. "So, to answer your question from before. I like reality shows for a few reasons. They're fun and kind of messy, like real life—but amplified. A lot of these people are drama queens. But it's also interesting to see inside someone else's world. To see romance develop or disappear. There are lots of ups and downs and they edit out the boring stuff, so it keeps it interesting."

"Well, I'm certainly intrigued to see what this show is like," Lisa said.

They didn't have to wait long. Lisa was on her second sip of wine when the door opened and a small crowd walked in. It was just five o'clock, and there were only two other tables taken in the entire restaurant. Which was probably a good thing because this group was loud—they were laughing and joking as Rhett went to greet them. He led them to a big table that was off to the side, but still in view from where Lisa and Marley sat.

It was easy to see who was in the cast and who was part of the production team. Lauren waved at Lisa as she walked in with another girl and sat at a smaller table near the big one.

Once the cast was all seated, Lauren walked around the table and spoke with them for a moment or two. Lisa couldn't hear what she was saying but imagined she was giving them some direction before filming started.

"What do you think she's saying?" Marley asked.

"I haven't the slightest." Lisa was curious, though.

"From what I've read about these shows, they sometimes suggest topics of conversation. Maybe she was doing that? I am pretty sure that the producers watch the overnight filming that happens when the production team goes home. If they see anything interesting, she might remind them to mention it, possibly?"

"I forgot that they have those hidden cameras. Lauren mentioned that one morning at breakfast," Lisa said.

"Ladies, do you know what you'd like to order?" Ted had returned to the bar and stood in front of them, ready to take their order.

Lisa laughed. They hadn't even opened their menus yet, they were too busy watching the filming activity.

"We might need just another minute, Ted," Lisa said.

CHAPTER TWENTY-SEVEN

Lauren and Eloise had quite the surprise when they reviewed the overnight tapes that morning. When almost everyone else went straight to bed after the night at the Chicken Box, there were a few people in the house that caught a second wind and stayed up. Suzanne, Billy and Noah listened to music in the kitchen and sat around the island enjoying another drink or two and laughing for several more hours. They didn't head up to bed until almost one. Billy and Noah's rooms were across the hall from each other and Suzanne's was on the opposite end. But Suzanne didn't spend the night in her room.

Katy woke around eight thirty and went downstairs to get a glass of water. On her way, she saw Suzanne walking down the hall to her bedroom. But Suzanne didn't see her. And Katy didn't see which bedroom Suzanne came out of. When she went back to her room with her water, Anna was awake and the two of them discussed it and both were unsure which direction

Suzanne would have gone—she'd been flirting with both Noah and Billy equally. Much like Billy, Suzanne was an equal opportunity flirt, and it was hard to tell who she was truly interested in.

Lauren waited all day for it to come up in conversation. She was sure that Katy or Anna would ask Suzanne, but it didn't happen. Suzanne slept late though and kept to herself on the beach—she wore earphones and had her eyes closed while she laid on her back in the sun. And she was quieter than usual at breakfast and lunch.

Lauren didn't notice anything unusual in the way that Noah or Billy spoke to Suzanne—it was no different from the day before. Both were friendly and chatted about nothing in particular and Suzanne teased both of them good-naturedly. It was perplexing. Lauren usually had a better read in situations like this—body language usually gave it away. But not this time. Although she had seen which room Suzanne came out of—and some of what had happened in that room—everyone today was acting as though nothing had changed.

So, when everyone was settled, Lauren walked over to the table and chatted with the cast about possible conversation topics over dinner. She walked over to where Anna and Katy were sitting and leaned over between them and spoke softly so only they could hear. "At some point, one of you might want to ask Suzanne which room she slept in last night?"

Katy and Anna both looked surprised for a second then nodded, remembering the hidden cameras. "Do you know where she was?" Katy asked.

Lauren smiled. "I do. And if you want to know, too, you should ask. You know that will make great TV."

Katy nodded. "You're right. And I am curious."

———

Lauren returned to her seat and Eloise raised her eyebrows. "Are they going to bring it up?"

Lauren nodded. "I think Katy will. She wants to know. I'm surprised she didn't ask her privately today."

"Maybe she wasn't ready to hear the answer," Eloise said.

"It will be good if she asks soon. There's really no other drama going on at the moment," Hudson said.

"I agree. I bet she will wait, though until it's just the two of them," Lauren said.

The server came to the main table and the cast all ordered drinks and dinner. The food was excellent, and the conversation was lively. They all laughed about Jason falling asleep on the deck and forgetting to put sunscreen on his nose. It was bright red and Suzanne nicknamed him Rudolph.

Over dessert, Honey mentioned that she'd slept horribly the night before.

"I swear if I have more than two drinks, I don't get a good night's sleep. I woke up at three and couldn't get back to sleep. I went and made myself a mug of warm milk and read a book for a half hour before I felt sleepy again."

Katy glanced toward Lauren and Eloise, then leaned

forward. "I woke up early and was super thirsty. I'd forgotten to have water with my drinks the night before. I think it was around eight thirty when I went downstairs to get a glass of water." She glanced dramatically around the table. "Suzanne, you didn't see me, but I was surprised to see you walking down the hall toward your room. You were right outside Noah and Billy's rooms. I wasn't sure which one you'd walked out of, though."

The whole table turned and looked Suzanne's way. Everyone looked surprised, including Noah and Billy, who glanced at each other. A range of expressions flashed across Suzanne's face from surprise to panic to annoyance.

"It's really not a big deal. If you must know, I spent the night in Noah's room." She lifted her chin. "Though it's really none of your business."

Katy looked relieved and almost as if she regretted asking the question.

"No, it's not," she agreed. "We were just surprised and curious."

Suzanne forced a smile. "Well, if it were the other way around, I suppose I would be, too. Get your minds out of the gutter, though—it was totally innocent. Noah wanted to show me a picture of his new apartment and we weren't tired yet so we decided to watch a few episodes of *Friends*. But during the second episode, I fell fast asleep."

Noah nodded. "And I didn't want to wake her. It was a fun night. We definitely need to go back to the Chicken Box again."

Suzanne smiled. "It was fun. And I'm up for going back anytime." They smiled at each other briefly, then Suzanne looked around the table and changed the subject.

"Enough about me. What is everyone getting for dessert? We should order a few things maybe and share?"

CHAPTER TWENTY-EIGHT

"This chocolate mousse cake is so good," Lisa said as she dipped her fork into the massive slice for another bite.

"I'm glad we decided to share it, though," Marley agreed.

They'd had a delicious dinner. Lisa had loved her roasted halibut and Marley enjoyed her filet with béarnaise sauce. Both of them saved half to bring home because they needed room for dessert.

"I wonder what they were talking about over there. The whole table looked shocked for a moment. I'll have to ask Lauren over breakfast tomorrow. If she's allowed to say."

"She might not be. But if she does spill the tea, call me immediately," Marley said.

"Speaking of tea, look who is coming this way," Lisa said.

The restaurant had filled up once word got out that

filming was happening at the restaurant and all the tables were filled. But there were two empty seats at the bar, next to Marley and Lisa. They'd just opened up when two people who were having a drink while waiting to be seated were notified that their table was ready.

Lisa's nemesis and neighbor, Violet, and her sister, walked over to the bar and settled into the two empty seats. Lisa nodded hello as she didn't want to be rude. Violet did not look happy to see her. Though Violet rarely looked happy about anything. The woman's face seemed to have a permanent pout.

"Hi Lisa. Of course you're here when they are filming."

Lisa smiled sweetly. "I thought it sounded like a fun thing to see. Is that why you came in tonight?"

Violet hesitated, then laughed. "Of course not. We had no idea this was happening. We just wanted a nice dinner out and didn't want to go downtown."

Lisa signaled Ted to bring the check. They were just about finished. She'd considered getting a coffee and lingering a bit, but now she just wanted to get home. And it looked like the filming was wrapping up. They were paying their bill and two of the cameramen were heading toward the door.

Lisa and Marley put their credit cards down when Ted brought them the bill. He walked off, then came back a moment later and gave them back their cards. "Rhett says your money is no good here." He grinned, and Lisa sighed. She wasn't surprised. Rhett never let her pay when she came in, but she always tried.

"How nice for you," Violet said snidely.

Lisa ignored her and fished into her purse for cash to leave Ted a good tip. Marley did the same. They put their money down and stood to leave. "Thanks so much Ted. Tell Rhett thanks too, and I'll see him at home."

"Will do. Always a pleasure, ladies."

Violet looked their way as they stood to leave. "I hear I'll be seeing you soon at the food festival."

Lisa nodded. "That's right. I'm looking forward to it. It sounds like a fun event."

"It will be great advertising for whoever wins," Violet agreed. She looked smug and overconfident. Which Lisa found incredibly annoying.

"I think it will be fun just to meet people and have them try my food. If I win, that will be a nice bonus."

Violet had no response for that. Clearly, winning was all that mattered to her. Lisa meant what she said, though. She had no control over who won. She hoped it would be her, but if not, she expected to benefit just from being there.

"Good luck to both of you," Marley said pleasantly before they walked out. Once they were outside, she turned to Lisa.

"That woman is horrid. You have to beat her. Let me know if there's anything I can do to help? I can hand out samples or do anything."

Lisa thought for a moment and then smiled. "Thanks. Maybe there is something you can do to help." She told Marley what she had in mind, and Marley nodded.

"Piece of cake. I can definitely do that."

It was after eight by the time they got back to the beach house. The sun was setting over the harbor and Anna walked out onto the deck to get a better look and to take some shots with her camera. The production staff headed home after the restaurant dinner, so they had the rest of the evening to relax.

Katy joined her a few minutes later. "Oh, I need to grab a shot of that too, before it disappears. The colors are incredible." The sky was a rich rosy pink with splashes of dark orange and it was slipping away fast. Anna guessed they had maybe ten or fifteen minutes before darkness filled the sky.

"Do you really think nothing happened with Suzanne and Noah?" Katy asked.

Anna shrugged. "It's probably mostly true. I mean, they might have kissed a little, and she just didn't need to share that. She seems pretty direct. I don't think she would have said they'd just watched *Friends* and slept if they'd actually hooked up."

Katy nodded. "I suppose you're right. I kind of wish they had hooked up, though."

That surprised Anna. "Why would you care?"

"Well, if a romance developed with her and Noah, then I wouldn't have to worry about her going after Billy."

"Ah. Got it." Anna hadn't realized Katy was that into Billy. She thought back to their initial conversation before coming to Nantucket. They were in agreement then that neither one of them wanted to start a romance on the show. It didn't feel like a solid foundation and neither wanted to let the public in that much. But now that they were here and Katy had met Billy, things seemed to have changed. Anna was curious if Billy knew Katy was interested and how he felt. It was hard to tell because he'd flirted just as much with Suzanne and even Anna. It wouldn't have surprised her if Suzanne had been coming out of his room instead of Noah's. She wanted Katy to find love—but given what she'd read about Billy, she was a little worried for her friend.

"You know, Billy and Lauren dated for a few months. You might want to talk to her and see what she thinks of him before diving into anything," Lauren suggested.

Katy looked like she was going to protest. It was clear that she didn't want to be talked out of anything. But she nodded. "That's not a bad idea. I am curious to hear what she thinks of him. You'd never know they dated."

"Well, she's a professional. I'm sure it was awkward for her at first, having to see him and produce him," Anna said.

Katy nodded. "You're probably right. I'll talk to her."

CHAPTER TWENTY-NINE

W hen Lauren went to breakfast the next morning, she noticed that the woman who'd been with Lisa the night before at the restaurant was sitting with them in the dining room, sipping a cup of coffee. Lauren helped herself to coffee, some fresh melon, and a scoop of cheesy scrambled eggs with veggies. She brought her tray to their table when Lisa waved her over. Rhett was there too, with his usual coffee and nothing else. Lisa and her friend had already eaten—their plates were empty.

"Lauren, this is my friend Marley," Lisa introduced her.

"Nice to meet you. You were at the restaurant last night?"

Marley nodded. "It was a lot of fun to watch the filming from afar. We tried to imagine what everyone was talking about."

Lisa leaned forward a little. "There was one moment

just as they'd about finished eating where the whole table looked shocked. We were dying to know what was going on? I'm not sure if you are allowed to say?"

Lauren grinned. "I'm not supposed to—but as long as you promise to keep it to yourselves?"

Lisa and Marley both nodded vigorously, while Rhett looked amused.

"So, when one of the girls, Katy, got up this morning, she saw another girl, Suzanne, walking down the hall. She'd obviously been coming from one of the guys' bedrooms."

"Oh! And they really asked her about that at dinner? How embarrassing," Lisa said.

Lauren laughed. "Welcome to reality TV. Suzanne swears that nothing happened, though. They just watched TV, and she fell asleep."

Lisa looked a bit skeptical. "Do you think that's true?"

"Mostly. We have cameras in their bedrooms, too."

"So they have no privacy at all?" Marley sounded surprised.

"There are no cameras in the bathrooms. So that's where they change usually and sometimes where other things are rumored to happen. With Suzanne and Noah, there was a little kissing before they watched TV and then Suzanne did fall asleep soon after. What's unknown is if this will be an isolated event or the beginning of a romance."

"How fun. I feel invested now," Lisa said.

Marley laughed. "And now you can see why I am so addicted to these shows."

"What's next for filming?" Lisa asked.

"Today should be fun, actually. We have an outing to the Whaling Museum, which will be great PR for the museum. The cast are all influencers, and each of them will make a thirty-second video at the museum and whichever one goes the most viral will win five thousand dollars for their favorite charity."

"What a great idea. I'd love to be a fly on the wall at the museum," Lisa said.

"Will it be open to the public while you are filming?" Marley had a gleam in her eye and Lauren knew what she was thinking.

"It won't. But….I can get the two of you in, as long as you don't mind being part of background shots. It will look like the museum is open if a few people are there. But no worries if you are busy."

"We'll be there," Lisa and Marley said at the same time.

"Great, meet us there at two. Filming will probably go from two to four as we make our way through the whole museum," Lauren said.

"Rhett, do you want to join us?" Lisa asked.

He shook his head. "I'm good. I'll be heading to the restaurant. But you girls have fun."

"Also, I don't know if this would interest you, but we're inviting all the neighbors over tomorrow night for our first big party," Lauren said. "There will be a band and a big cookout. The theme is Nantucket Red, so we're just asking that everyone wear something in that pinkish red shade."

"I'll definitely come. I think Rhett will be at the restaurant?" Rhett nodded in confirmation and looked relieved.

Lisa turned to Marley. "You should come with me?"

"I'd love to." Marley's eyes sparkled with anticipation.

CHAPTER THIRTY

"Lauren, could I talk privately with you for a minute?" Katy asked.

Lauren looked up from her laptop where she and Eloise had been going over the film from the night before. They were sitting in the living room at the share house, where the cast was half-awake and helping themselves to bagels and coffee in the kitchen.

"Sure, let's step outside for a minute." Lauren led the way onto the deck that overlooked the beach. No one else was out there yet, so it was perfectly private. Lauren had seen the conversation between Katy and Anna, so she had a good idea of what she wanted to discuss.

"There's so many people on the beach already," Katy commented as they faced the ocean. There were people settling in with their beach chairs and others out walking and, as usual, plenty of dogs running up and down the beach.

"What did you want to talk about?" Lauren asked gently.

Katy hesitated, "It's Billy. Anna suggested that I ask you about him. I know you dated for a while?"

Lauren nodded. "We did. I think he is a great guy in a lot of ways. I really liked him. Billy is a lot of fun—when his attention is on you. When that attention shifts—well, then it's not so fun. Especially if you think things are fine, if you know what I mean?"

"So he really did cheat?" Katy sounded disappointed to hear it.

"Yes. And I found out accidentally, on TikTok of all places," Lauren said.

"Oh, that sounds awful."

"It was." Lauren sighed. "Billy swore it would never happen again—and it might not have. But the trust was gone for me. In so many ways, he really is a great guy. I don't know if he's changed or if that is just who he is," Lauren said.

Katy nodded. "Okay, thank you. I don't even know if he's interested—or just being Billy, you know?"

Lauren smiled. "Yes, I know exactly what you mean."

"What was that about?" Eloise asked when Lauren returned to the table where they'd been sitting. Hudson was set up next to them and looked interested as well. Lauren filled them in on the conversation with Katy.

"Do you think she'll back off now?" Eloise asked.

"I'm not sure. She seems pretty interested," Lauren said.

"She won't back off. I'd bet money on it," Hudson

said. "She may see it as a challenge now—to be the one that Billy falls for completely."

"That is very possible," Lauren agreed.

―――――――――

Just about everyone spent the morning on the beach, except for Eloise and Lauren who went door to door and invited all the neighbors to attend their party. Some of them seemed hesitant and Lauren didn't really blame them after all, it was going to be filmed and there would be a live band, which meant it could get loud. Walter, the older gentleman that lived directly next to them, looked intrigued though when they stopped by.

"I'll have to ask my lady friend. Kay makes all of those decisions." His eyes twinkled adorably as he said her name. "I have a feeling we'll probably be stopping by. Thank you for the invite."

After lunch, they all headed to the Whaling Museum to start filming at two.

Marley and Lisa met them by the front door and they all walked in together. A crowd had gathered as part of the street in front of the museum was blocked off for filming, and people were curious to catch a glimpse of what was going on. As soon as the vans with the cast pulled up and everyone piled out, the excitement grew and a few people requested autographs from some of the influencers and many pictures and videos were taken as the group made their way inside.

Once they were in, Lauren introduced Marley and Lisa to everyone. "These are friends of mine that are going to walk with us and be in the background."

It was hot outside and calm and cool in the museum. It had been years since Lauren went to the Whaling Museum and she was looking forward to seeing it again. There was so much interesting history shown to discover —several floors of displays of ships and whales and other artifacts of the island. There was a lot to see, and they had a private tour guide from the museum who led them through the exhibits and answered questions.

Almost two hours later, at the end of the tour, they reached the top floor and a roof deck with a reception set up for them. There was a charcuterie board with meats, cheeses, crackers, fresh fruit, and a stocked bar with a bartender. Everyone had a cocktail and commented on how impressed they were with the museum.

"Honestly, I was not that enthused to go to a museum," Katy admitted. "But this was so cool and interesting. I also got some great shots and I'm pretty sure I'm going to have the winning video."

"I agree, but I wouldn't be too sure about having the best video. Mine is going to be tough to beat," Billy said confidently, and flashed his most charming grin.

Honey laughed. "We got some great shots, too. It will be interesting to see which video wins."

"This is such a great spot," Anna said as she sipped her chardonnay and leaned against the railing. She lifted her phone and took a selfie video with the whole town in the background, "Living the Nantucket dream and leaning all about history and whales at the Whaling Museum. If you come here, this is a must see."

Alfred, the museum guide, stood nearby and looked impressed. "I look forward to seeing that video," he said. "All of them, actually." He turned to Lauren. "We're just so thrilled that you decided to visit and spotlight the museum."

"We were happy to. I tell everyone to come here if they're visiting the island." Lauren sipped a smooth pinot grigio and looked around the deck. Everyone was laughing and chatting and seemed to be having a good time.

"Looks like your conversation didn't deter her," Hudson said softly. Lauren followed his gaze to where Katy and Billy were in deep conversation, slightly away from the rest of the group. Katy looked animated as she spoke and Billy's attention was fully on her. Maybe there was something real brewing there.

"It does look that way," Lauren agreed.

"And I don't think she's the only one," Hudson said.

Suzanne and Noah were also talking and laughing, and it definitely seemed like there was a vibe there.

"Good," Eloise said. "I was hoping for at least one romance. Now we might have two, which viewers will love. I was a little worried that nothing would happen."

"I wasn't worried. I knew something would develop. When you have a houseful of people living together like this, it's almost inevitable," Hudson said.

Lauren knew it was true. Forced proximity seemed to heighten emotions and move things along faster than they would go otherwise.

Lauren watched Katy and Billy for a moment. They looked completely oblivious to the rest of the world. There was another camera focused on them, so she'd be able to view that film later and listen to their conversation. She almost didn't need to, though. It was clear from the body language that they were into each other. Katy had listened to what Lauren had told her and decided to take her chances, anyway. Lauren hoped it wouldn't turn out to be a mistake.

CHAPTER THIRTY-ONE

After they left the Whaling Museum, they stopped in a few of the shops so the cast could find something to wear in the right Nantucket Red shade. When they went to Murray's Toggery, the shop that first introduced Nantucket Red, they were all excited as they had a great selection of really high-quality sweatshirts, shirts and shorts as well as pants. Hudson even picked up a pair of shorts.

"I've neglected my Nantucket Red duties—I've actually been meaning to grab something in this shade."

Eloise got a cute baseball hat and an oversized sweatshirt that was similar to the one Lauren had bought at Izzy's shop. Not that it really mattered what the production team wore, but still, they usually liked to dress up for the themed parties too. It made it more fun and, in case they were caught in background shots, they would blend in better.

The party was officially starting at five and the band arrived an hour early to set up. The deck that overlooked the beach was huge and they fit easily into a corner of it. The catering team had both the outside grill and the kitchen oven going and they were cooking up a storm—all the usual items, burgers, hot dogs and also marinated steak tips, baked potatoes, chicken and pesto shrimp and vegetables on skewers. They also had corn on the cob and assorted chips and dips and salads.

The girls in the cast helped with the decorating while the guys went out and bought a few games for the beach and also got some extra ice and beer.

The decorating consisted of mostly white and pink streamers, balloons, big pillar candles and twinkling fairy lights that they wrapped around the deck railing. Suzanne and Billy mixed up batches of their signature shots and Anna and Honey made a big punchbowl of sparkling white sangria that had lots of fresh fruit floating in it—it looked delicious.

The first guests started arriving at five and by five thirty, the back deck was totally packed and there were lots of people on the beach, too. The guys had returned with several beach games, including horseshoes, bocce and cornhole, a really popular game where players tossed small bean bags at a wooden stand with a hole in the middle. They started playing cornhole first and there was a lot of laughing whenever it was Billy's turn, as his aim was terrible.

Lauren greeted Marley and Lisa when they walked over with Kay and Walter.

"Help yourselves to a plate of food. Everything is ready," Lauren told them. "And adult beverages are inside. We have wine, beer, mixed drinks and there's a white sangria punch that is really good." She and Eloise had poured themselves a glass of the punch and Lauren had just eaten a hotdog and chips.

The band was good and not too loud, which Lauren was relieved about. A lot of the neighbors came, and she guessed most of them were just curious about the show and the people in it.

The cast had also all invited friends to come. Katy and Anna both had friends that were crashing in their room for the weekend. And so far, since they all had friends visiting, the flirting between Billy and Katy and Suzanne and Noah had slowed a bit.

They were going to announce the winner of the first influencer video contest at the party—once everyone was through with dinner and were on dessert—which was Nantucket Cranberry Pie, a moist yellow cake with a gooey cranberry and pecan topping that was sweet and tart at the same time and paired well with the creamy French vanilla ice cream.

Lauren and Eloise tracked the different videos on the social media channels. Two of them went viral, but there was a clear winner as one went super viral and racked up over two million views.

Lauren went up to the band when they'd paused between songs. They waved her over, and she stepped up to the microphone to make the announcement.

"Thanks so much for coming, everyone. I'm happy to

announce the winner of our Whaling Museum video challenge. Anna's video has already had over 2.2 million views on TikTok alone. Congrats, Anna." She paused for a moment to make sure she had everyone's attention.

"Anna's video went viral when viewers spotted a thief in the background running out of a store and the police were able to quickly locate and arrest him." The crowd clapped and cheered, while Anna blushed.

"Anna, come on up and let us know which charity will receive your $5,000 donation."

Anna was all smiles as she joined Lauren at the microphone.

"Thank you so much! I never anticipated going viral for something like that, but I'm glad there was a happy ending and the thief was caught—thanks to the viewers and the local police. My donation is going to our local humane society for their no-kill shelter. Thank you!"

Lauren helped herself to a little more punch and brought it back to the table where she and Eloise were sitting. She'd invited Lisa, Marley, Kay and Walter to join them and they seemed to be enjoying themselves. Lauren thought they would appreciate being out of the crowd of people and watching from a distance. Plus, she enjoyed their company.

"How nice that young girl is helping animals with her donation," Kay said.

Lauren smiled and told them about Anna's dog, Smith. "He's in her room now with the door shut tight to keep him safe."

"I think you said there's a cat here too?" Lisa asked.

"Yes, Simon is in his room, too. They had to lock the door because he's an escape artist and can get it open if it's not locked." They all laughed and then Lauren added, "Anna didn't even notice the thief in the background at first. But once she rewatched it before uploading online, she did, and everyone else did too. Comments came in fast and furious. It was shared like crazy."

"And that helped the police find the guy. That's impressive," Walter said.

"So that's what they mean by social media," Kay said, and looked thoughtful. "I think I get it now. It's pretty powerful how news can spread so fast."

Lauren agreed. "It's the modern version of word of mouth—traveling at light speed!"

The band was excellent, and as soon as everyone was done with dessert, many started dancing on the deck in front of the band and on the beach. The band played a good mix of popular dance songs, both pop and country-rock. Even Kay and Walter got up and danced a few songs. Lauren walked around to check in with the other camera guys, who were stationed inside and on the beach, while Hudson was on the deck, moving around to capture as many moments as possible.

The cast seemed to be having a good time. They were all dancing and chatting with their visiting friends. And everyone seemed to be getting along. As the night went on, it grew a bit louder as tended to happen when alcohol was flowing freely. But everyone was laughing and having fun.

It wasn't until the party was winding down that the

first hint of drama emerged. All the outsiders had gone home and the only people remaining were the cast and their friends that were staying at the house and the production crew.

Lauren saw the issue before she heard about it. Sami and Billy were the only castmates that didn't have any friends visiting. And they were standing close together on the deck, talking softly and intimately. It looked as though they were both into each other. Katy saw it too and immediately pulled Anna aside to complain. Hudson got their conversation on film, and Lauren and Eloise were standing nearby and heard it all. Katy was so upset that she was oblivious to the cameras.

"She knows I'm interested in Billy! How can she go after him? I didn't think she would do that." Katy sounded distraught and Anna tried to calm her.

"They're just talking. I'm sure it's harmless. But if it's not, then it's not. There's not much you can do about that, and you and Billy are not even dating yet," she reminded Katy.

Katy sighed dramatically. "Oh, I know. But I really thought it seemed to be going in that direction. Now I'm not so sure. And Sami had told me she didn't even like Billy. So it's a surprise."

Anna took another look at Billy and Sami, who were still in a deep discussion and oblivious to anyone around them.

"It could just be that it's getting late and everyone has had a lot to drink and you've been busy with your friends.

Billy is outgoing. He probably just wanted to chat with someone and Sami was there. Don't read more into it."

"You're right. I'll try not to worry yet. I think I'm going to head to bed. I'm exhausted."

"I'll go up with you. I think the others already headed upstairs. We'll relax on the beach tomorrow. It's supposed to be a beautiful day. Things will look better then, I'm sure of it."

Katy nodded. "I sure hope so."

They walked inside and Hudson turned his camera off. "I think that's a good spot to end the night. It's almost one."

Lauren agreed and yawned. Because it was a special party, it was a later filming night than usual. "Sounds good. I'm ready to call it a night, too."

Eloise stood. "My bed is calling. I'll see you both tomorrow."

Lauren glanced at the beach. It was a beautiful night, but it was too late to walk home along the beach. She would head out with Eloise and walk the short distance to the inn along the street.

Hudson caught her eye. "I'll walk you home. You shouldn't go by yourself this late."

"You don't have to do that. I can walk on the street," Lauren protested.

"Look at that moonlight and how it reflects on the water. You know you want to walk along the beach."

Lauren laughed. "I do actually. As long as you don't mind, I'll take you up on that offer."

"Great, let's go."

They headed down the steps to the beach and a slightly cool breeze ruffled Lauren's hair. She was glad she'd worn a sweatshirt, as the temperature had dropped once the sun went down. It was still a gorgeous night, and the sky was so clear, the stars vivid in the sky. The air smelled so crisp, with a hint of salt.

"It was a good night, I think," Lauren said.

"It wasn't overly dramatic, but I think viewers will have a fun time watching the guys play cornhole so poorly and Honey and Brett tore up the dance floor. Wouldn't surprise me if *Dancing With the Stars* invites one or both of them onto the next season."

"That was a surprise. None of us knew they could dance like that." Honey and Brett were so good that everyone had made a circle around them and clapped and cheered them on as Brett whirled Honey and dipped her and they danced completely in sync with each other. It was fun to watch.

"I think most of the neighbors that came had a good time," Hudson said.

"They did, and no one called the cops on us, so that was a win." Lauren laughed. On other shows, they'd had the cops called many times when cast parties were louder than the neighbors could stand.

"What's planned for tomorrow? Just an easy beach day?" Hudson asked.

"That's it. I think most of them will be sleeping in

and won't be up for much more than that. We'll film till they come off the beach, probably late afternoon and call it a night. The static cameras will pick up anything interesting tomorrow night.

"Good. Sounds like a plan. And then we're off. Are you still up for heading to the Chicken Box to hear that band? I checked and they're playing Monday night."

"Definitely, and I'll let Eloise know. She wanted to come too."

Hudson hesitated a moment before saying, "The more the merrier."

Lauren couldn't see his expression well in the dark, but he sounded enthusiastic about having Eloise and maybe others join them. Lauren looked forward to going back there and not having to worry about filming. It would be fun to relax and listen to good music, and maybe even get up and dance if the mood struck.

When they reached the inn, Hudson stopped. "Alright, I'll see you in the morning."

"Thanks for walking me back. See you tomorrow." Lauren took a few steps toward the inn, then looked back. Hudson's dark hair gleamed in the moonlight as he walked along the beach. She appreciated that he'd insisted on walking her home and she found herself looking forward to Monday night and to getting to know Hudson better outside of work.

CHAPTER THIRTY-TWO

"*D*o *you have dinner plans tonight? Philippe made lasagna and meatballs. Would love to see you if you can get away?*" Lauren smiled at the text message from Angela and quickly texted back.

"*No plans. We're stopping filming early today, so I'm available. What time? And what can I bring?*"

"*How's six? And nothing. We don't need a thing. I made choco-late chip cookies yesterday and homemade ice cream. Just come!*"

"*Okay, see you at six.*"

Lauren didn't realize she was still smiling until Hudson commented, "You look happy. Good news?"

"You could say that. My friend Angela, the one that lives here, invited me to dinner tonight and I actually get to go."

Hudson grinned. "Excellent. I told my mom I'd come by for Sunday dinner, too. So, we'll both be eating well."

"What is your mother making? Is she a good cook?" Hudson hadn't talked much about his parents.

"Probably roast beef and popovers. My dad always loved her popovers. And mashed potatoes and gravy, of course."

"Of course." It was only eleven and Lauren was suddenly starving. She'd just had a little fruit with her coffee at breakfast. The cast had slept in and half were still in their rooms while the others were lounging around the kitchen and living room. There was a platter of bagels and cream cheese on the kitchen island. Lauren helped herself to an onion bagel and slathered low-fat chive cream cheese on it.

By noon, the entire cast was on the beach. All the friends who stayed over for the party headed home earlier that morning. It had been a late night and everyone seemed tired. The volleyball net was up, but no one moved to play. Eventually, Jason suggested bocce, and he and Billy and Anna and Katy played for a bit. Billy and Katy played as a team, and the flirtatious vibe was in full force for both of them. Interestingly, though, Lauren also noticed a similar vibe with Jason and Anna, not quite as flirty, but definitely more friendly than she'd seen before. It wasn't clear, though, if it was just a budding friendship or something more.

"Do you see what I think I'm seeing?" Hudson asked softly.

"With Jason and Anna?" Eloise asked.

Lauren nodded. "I see it. I'm not sure what it is yet, though."

"Yeah, might be nothing. I didn't think Anna would

pair up with anyone. She always seems a little detached, more of an observer," Hudson said.

"I thought the same. So, this surprises me a bit," Lauren said.

"And it looks like Suzanne and Noah are still a possibility," Eloise said. Lauren followed her gaze to where Suzanne was rubbing suntan oil on Noah's well-muscled back.

"Well, tonight could be interesting....and a good thing that we won't be there with the cameras. They're just getting pizza and staying in," Lauren said.

"Netflix and cuddling on the sofa, perhaps?" Eloise had a mischievous gleam in her eye and they all laughed.

"And over the next few days, with just the static cameras...will be fun to see if anything develops," Lauren said.

Clouds rolled in around three and the air cooled a bit, and the cast decided to head inside. Before they did, Billy walked over.

"Lauren, can we chat for a minute?"

"Sure." They went a little way down the beach. Lauren wondered what Billy needed to talk to her about. "What's up?" she asked.

"I just wanted to double-check something with you," he began. "Before I start anything with Katy, well, I just want to see if there's any possibility that you'll give me another chance? I didn't want to pressure you and wanted to give you a little time to think about it." He sounded so sincere as he pleaded with her to take him back. Lauren looked into his blue-gray eyes, with their ridiculously long

PAMELA M. KELLEY

lashes, and she shook her head. "I don't think so, Billy. I can't go back there. I just don't think I could fully trust you again." She sighed. "Even if I wanted to."

He looked away, then met her eyes with a sad smile. "Okay, I get it. But I had to ask. I know I really messed things up for us."

Lauren just nodded slightly. There was nothing more she could say.

They walked back to where Hudson was packing up his camera. Eloise put her laptop into her tote bag and smiled when she saw them.

"So, what time did you guys want to meet at the Chicken Box tomorrow night?" Eloise asked.

"How's seven thirty? I think the band comes on at eight," Hudson suggested.

"That works for me," Lauren said.

Billy looked intrigued. "You guys are going to the Chicken Box tomorrow night? Maybe we'll meet you there? I liked that place."

Hudson nodded. "Sure, everyone is welcome."

"Great, I'll see who's up for it and we'll meet you there," Billy wandered off and Eloise raised her eyebrows. "What was that about?"

Lauren told her about their conversation. "Are you sure it's a good idea for Billy to come out with us? Maybe he's just trying to see if he can change your mind?" Eloise asked.

Lauren laughed. "Well, he did say he's interested in Katy, so I don't think so."

"I wonder who else will join him? Maybe I should

bring my camera," Hudson said. He didn't look enthused about the idea, though.

"No, it's our night off. Leave the camera at home," Lauren said. She didn't want Hudson to feel like he had to work on his day off. They all deserved a night where they could just relax and enjoy being out without worrying about catching every conversation among the cast members.

He grinned. "All right. See you both tomorrow night."

CHAPTER THIRTY-THREE

"Philippe, I am so impressed that you made this. I didn't realize you were such a good cook." Lauren took another bite of the cheesy lasagna and tender meatballs. The sky was dark and the air damp and cool. Thunderstorms were predicted, so they sat inside at Angela and Philippe's round dining room table that faced floor-to-ceiling glass windows overlooking the ocean.

"Thanks. It's one of the few things I know how to make and as a single guy, I'd often make and eat it all week."

"His comes out much better than mine," Angela added.

Philippe smiled at her gratefully. "Yes, but you make the best cookies and now ice cream."

"You made homemade ice cream?" Lauren remembered she'd mentioned it when she invited her to dinner.

Angela nodded. "It's my newest addiction. I ordered

an ice cream maker recently and I've been experimenting with all the different flavors. I kept it simple this time, though, just a rich vanilla to go with the chocolate chip cookies."

"That sounds wonderful. Have you started getting any cravings yet?" Lauren asked.

Angela nodded. "So far, just ice cream and chocolate. I've been having a little of both every night. I've never done that before."

They chatted easily as they ate, and Philippe told them about the new book he was working on.

"I'm over the worst of it now. I always slow down in the middle, then usually once I get over the halfway point, it comes out in a rush. I'm feeling better than usual about this one," he admitted.

"His agent already has some film interest," Angela said proudly.

"They want to read it when I have a solid draft done. So I'm not counting on anything just yet."

Angela leaned forward. "There's some possible good news coming for Kate, too. I can't share any specifics, Kate swore me to secrecy, but she's in the middle of negotiating a new deal and it might be way better than the deal that fell apart. We should know more soon."

"Oh, that is great news. I hope it happens." Lauren knew too well how even the most sure things often didn't happen when it came to show business.

After dinner, once everything was put away, they relaxed over coffee and watched the storm over the water. The sky was dark, and the wind whipped the water into big white-topped waves. A loud crack of thunder startled them and the lights flickered for just a moment as a flash of lightning lit up the sky. It continued for twenty minutes or so before settling down.

"Okay, who's ready for cookies and ice cream?" Angela asked.

Lauren helped her bring dishes and spoons to the table while Angela grabbed the freshly made ice cream and a plate of cookies.

The ice cream was decadent, so deliciously vanilla, and the cookies were just as good—simple chocolate chip but with big chunks of dark chocolate and a dusting of flaky sea salt on top.

The storm raged on for hours, with no sign of stopping. The lights flickered a few more times, but Angela told her not to worry.

"We have a generator. So if the power goes out, it will kick on automatically." The rain was still coming down hard, and Lauren hadn't seen lightning like this in a long time. It seemed so close and lit up the whole ocean every time it flashed.

"You should stay over. I don't want to worry about you driving home in this," Angela said.

"Definitely stay. The guest bedroom is right around the corner," Philippe added.

"I have some pajamas you can borrow. We can get comfortable and watch movies. There's a new rom-com I've been wanting to check out."

Lauren hesitated, but only for a moment. She wasn't keen to head home in the storm.

PAMELA M. KELLEY

"Sounds good. I'm always up for a good rom-com."

Angela didn't think twice about getting a ladder out and climbing up to change a lightbulb in the kitchen. The ceilings were vaulted, and Philippe was already at work in his office. She and Lauren had just eaten breakfast and Lauren was in the guest bedroom room, getting changed and ready to head home.

The non-working light had been bugging her since she woke and when she turned it on, there was a cracking sound, before it flashed once and then went dark. It was daytime, so she didn't really need the lights on until later, but she wanted to get it done.

She'd climbed the ladder and changed this lightbulb before, several times actually. So she didn't think twice about doing it. She got a replacement bulb from the cupboard, secured the ladder and climbed up. It took less than a minute to remove the old bulb and screw in the new one. As she was finishing, her watch buzzed with a text message from her first client, asking if she could reschedule. That would open Angela's morning up so she didn't have to rush out the door.

She stepped back to climb down the ladder, but was distracted by the text message and lost her footing. She slipped and fell off the ladder and went down hard on her left hip. The drop was almost five feet and the impact when she hit the hardwood floor took her breath away.

212

Philippe heard the commotion, burst out of his office, and ran into the kitchen.

"What happened? Are you okay?" He glanced at the ladder in consternation. "What were you doing on the ladder?"

Angela handed him the bad lightbulb as she struggled to sit up. Her hip hurt and she felt a bit light-headed, probably from the shock of the fall. Philippe held out his hand and helped her up and into his arms for a hug.

"Promise me you won't use that ladder again until after the baby comes. Let me do it." He kept his arms wrapped around her and she leaned into him.

Angela nodded in agreement and felt her eyes well up. She wasn't a crier normally, but pregnancy hormones were making her more emotional than usual.

She grabbed a paper towel and dabbed at her eyes. "I'm fine. And I'll gladly turn ladder climbing over to you." She put her hand on her hip, which was sore now, and she knew it would likely feel worse later.

Lauren walked out of the guest bedroom and stopped short when she saw the ladder and Angela and Philippe in the kitchen.

"Is everything okay?"

Angela smiled. "All good. I lost my footing on the ladder and had a little fall. It won't happen again."

Philippe put the ladder away and Angela excused herself to use the bathroom. Once Lauren left, she'd get in the shower and get on with her day.

She felt a sudden cramp as she was about to flush the toilet and saw drops of blood in the water. Her stomach tightened with fear. Angela knew that in the first trimester, a fall wasn't as worrisome as it would be further on in the pregnancy. And she also knew it was normal to have some spotting. But she hadn't had any yet and now, moments after a fall, she was suddenly seeing blood. She chewed her lower lip, debating what to do. She decided to wait a bit and see if the spotting continued.

She didn't say anything to Philippe or Lauren and walked Lauren out to her car. The sun was shining now, and it looked like it was going to be a beautiful day. There was no sign of the storm from the evening before.

"Have fun at the Chicken Box tonight." Lauren had told her about her plans to head there on her night off with some of the people from the show. It sounded like it would be a good time and something she would have enjoyed when she was single and not pregnant. Now her idea of a fun night was watching TV with Philippe, maybe reading for a bit, and going to bed early.

"Thanks. I'll call you in a day or two with a full report. And don't forget, this weekend is the food festival."

Angela grinned. "I'm looking forward to that. I want to support Lisa, and an afternoon of sampling food is right up my alley.

Lauren laughed. "I'll talk to you soon."

Angela watched her friend drive off before heading back into the house. Philippe was back in his office with his door closed and her morning was free now until noon. She still had administrative work she could do though and settled at the kitchen island, with her laptop and a fresh cup of decaf coffee. She loved coffee but was limiting her caffeine consumption to one cup of regular.

She'd had some eggs and toast with Lauren earlier, but the plate of remaining chocolate chip cookies called to her and she helped herself to two. She nibbled a cookie and sipped her coffee as she checked her email. She called the client back that asked to reschedule and put her on the calendar for the following week. And she checked the website for her cleaning business and updated it, removing notice of a sales promotion she'd run for the past week for new clients. She'd shared it on social media and also emailed her current clients, asking for referrals and offering them a discount on their next cleaning for every new person that they referred.

The promotion had worked well, and the calendar was full of new client bookings for the next month. They were already busy with existing clients too, so Angela didn't want to take on more work than they could comfortably handle. She opened a new email and felt an intense cramp rip through her abdomen. She took a deep breath, and the pain disappeared just as quickly. But a few minutes later, another cramp came, and she went to the bathroom. There was more bleeding, heavier than before. This time, she didn't ignore it.

She knocked on Philippe's office door and went in a moment later and told him about the cramps and the bleeding.

"It's probably nothing," she said. But he looked worried.

"You had a pretty hard fall. It wouldn't hurt to get checked out. Let's go, I'll drive."

Angela called her doctor as Philippe drove and they confirmed that it was best to go to the emergency room since she was bleeding.

The Nantucket Hospital was busy, but they were triaged and Angela's vitals were taken and as soon as a doctor was available, she was brought to a room. Angela explained about the fall and the bleeding, while the doctor, a forty-something-year-old woman, listened carefully and then examined Angela. She used ultrasound to check the baby's heartbeat and also checked Angela's vital signs again. When she was done, she smiled kindly as she gave them the news.

"You're okay, and the baby is fine. It's normal to have some spotting and the fall may have brought it on. It's just your body's way of dealing with it. If it continues and gets worse, come back. But I think you'll find it will slow and probably stop completely." Her voice was calming, and Angela glanced at Philippe. He squeezed her hand and looked as relieved as she felt.

"Thank you," she said.

"You're very welcome." The doctor stepped toward the door, then smiled and added, "Oh, one other thing, I'd probably stay off ladders for a while."

Soon after, the nurse brought in Angela's discharge papers and they headed home. Angela felt relieved and much more relaxed now that the doctor had said she was fine. The cramping seemed to have stopped, and she suddenly felt exhausted. The bone-tired feeling often surprised her, but she knew that was normal too for the first trimester.

Hopefully, in a few more weeks, she'd have more energy. Now, though, all she wanted to do was crawl into her bed and nap. And as soon as she got home, that was exactly what she was going to do. She had several hours before she had to be anywhere.

CHAPTER THIRTY-FOUR

"Why don't you come with us tonight?" Katy asked. Anna and Katy were having a lazy day off from filming and had spent most of the day on and off the beach. They'd slept late and headed to the beach mid-morning. It was a perfect sunny day, and they both swam a few times and soaked up the sun. After lunch, they took a long walk on the beach and were now lounging on the deck under big umbrellas and flipping through a stack of fashion and gossip magazines. Smith was snuggled up next to Anna's hip. Every now and then she petted his head softly.

"Who else is going?" Anna asked. She liked the idea of going back to the Chicken Box, but not if it meant being a third wheel with Katy and Billy.

"A bunch of people. Some of the production crew—Lauren, Eloise, and I think Hudson and Billy mentioned that Jason might go."

The house was quiet at the moment. Billy and Jason had gone into town to run some errands. Sami, Honey, and Brett were all off-island for a few days. Anna wasn't sure where Suzanne and Noah were, but she hadn't seen them since before lunch.

"Oh, I think Suzanne and Noah are coming too. Noah mentioned it before he and Suzanne took off earlier."

"Okay, I'll go." She felt better now that she knew there was a group going. "Where did they go?"

"They were heading to Millie's for lunch. I only saw them because I happened to be picking up a package on the front step when they both walked out. I think it might be their first official date."

"Oh, that's cute. I wonder if production will have them recreate it?" Anna didn't think they'd want to miss that opportunity.

"Probably. It's nice that they get to do it without the cameras first, though."

"And you'll have the same thing tonight," Anna said.

Katy smiled. "It's not an official date, though."

"In a way that's better, don't you think? Less pressure." Anna tolerated the cameras, but for actual dating, especially a first date, she wouldn't be comfortable with it unfolding publicly. She was more private than the others, in that way. Although Katy didn't seem too keen on the idea, either. She hoped that the night out would go the way that her friend wanted it to. She liked Billy. It was impossible not to, but she couldn't imagine dating him.

Not after the recent cheating incident that Lauren had gone through.

———

"What do you think of Katy and Billy?" Lauren asked Hudson. They were sitting at their table at the Chicken Box Monday night, watching the rest of their group on the dance floor. The band was playing a popular country-rock song and Suzanne and Noah were the first ones on the dance floor, followed moments later by the others.

Lauren smiled as a text message flashed through on her phone from Eloise, who'd cancelled at the last minute due to a stomach bug. *"Am I missing anything good?"*

Lauren texted her back, *"Not yet. Stay tuned…"* She turned her attention to Hudson, who was watching Katy and Billy. He looked thoughtful.

"I really don't know," he said. "She's not exactly his type, but maybe that's a good thing."

That intrigued Lauren. "His type?"

"I mean physically. He seems to prefer blondes—model types."

Lauren laughed. "That's not me, at all."

Hudson met her gaze. "Don't underestimate yourself, Lauren. You're very pretty. You have that California blonde girl-next-door that does yoga look."

Lauren laughed, a bit stunned at the compliments. She'd never had any idea that Hudson viewed her that way. She certainly didn't. She'd been doing yoga for years, because she liked it, found it relaxing and it helped to keep her toned and lean.

"Katy's cute, but she just has a different look, if you know what I mean?" Hudson said.

She did. Katy was adorable, but she was the opposite of Anna, Sami, Lauren, and the actress he'd cheated with on TikTok. Katy was short, curvy and brunette. But Billy did look very into her and Katy seemed like she was falling hard. They had their arms around each other and were swaying to the music as the band shifted to a slower song. Suzanne and Noah were still dancing, but Anna and Jason returned to their table.

As they sat down, the band switched to a new song, one that Lauren loved, and she automatically started tapping her foot to the beat. Hudson noticed and nodded toward the dance floor. "Want to join them?"

"Sure." She followed him through the crowd to where the rest of their group was dancing.

Lauren hadn't gone dancing in ages. It was fun to move to the music and enjoy the energy of the crowd. For a Monday night, the Chicken Box was busy. The band played several fun, lively songs before slowing it down. Lauren expected to head back to their table, but Hudson smiled and held out his hand and she didn't think. She just moved toward him. When their hands touched, she felt a buzz of electricity that surprised her. Hudson pulled her close, and she wrapped her arms around his neck. As they swayed to the slow song, Lauren breathed in Hudson's scent—there was a hint of woodsy cologne that she'd never noticed before. She'd never been this close to him. It was exciting and a little unnerving.

Lauren recognized that she was attracted to Hudson. She liked him as a work colleague, but it was more than that. And it felt forbidden, which amped the excitement a bit, but was also a reminder that for several reasons, acting on this attraction wouldn't be wise. Hudson was a good friend of Billy's, for one thing. But more importantly, since they were working together, it seemed like a bad idea. And she reminded herself that these feelings could be completely one-sided. Hudson hadn't given her any reason to think otherwise. As a co-owner of the production company they worked with, he'd been completely professional. Even if he did have an attraction, she doubted that he would act on it.

When the song finished, they headed back to the table.

"Are you ready for another wine?" Hudson asked. Her glass was empty.

"Sure, thanks." Lauren noticed that Billy and Katy were still on the dance floor with Anna and Jason. They were all laughing and having a good time. Suzanne and Noah were off by themselves at the bar, sitting close together and in their own world.

Hudson returned a few minutes later with their drinks. Lauren took a sip of her chardonnay and smiled at Hudson.

"I'm glad we did this. It's fun to get out and not have to worry about filming," she said.

He grinned. "Yeah, I feel a little guilty though—as

this is all the stuff people want to see. The beginnings of romance."

Hudson was right. "Well, we don't have anything planned for Wednesday. We could come back here and assuming there are no big changes in the wrong direction, we could recreate tonight. You know what I mean." They never told the cast what to say, but they did sometimes suggest topics of conversation or to recreate something that had already happened.

Hudson nodded. "We'll see what the film shows us over tonight and tomorrow. But I agree, probably a good idea to come back. And Wednesday makes sense."

"Do you ever get out to LA anymore?" Lauren wondered if she'd ever see him again once the show finished filming.

He took a sip of his draft beer. "Not really." He grinned. "I try to avoid it if at all possible and so far I've been able to do all meetings by phone or Zoom. I don't miss LA."

"Yeah, I wouldn't either if I was back on the East Coast, especially here."

Hudson looked sympathetic. "Are you sick of it?"

"It's ok. But I'd rather be here, anywhere on the East Coast actually, except for New York. There are some reality shows that film there, but it's too much of a big city for me, and much too expensive. LA feels different, not as crowded, though the traffic is horrendous."

Hudson nodded in agreement. "Billy tried to get me to move back to LA. For at least a year, every time I talked to him, he'd mention it. I don't think he thought I'd stay here permanently. He finally gave up."

Lauren smiled. She could picture Billy trying to talk Hudson into moving back to LA. "He missed you."

"Yeah, he did. Even when I got my own place in LA, we still hung out all the time. Billy's a good friend."

Lauren was more aware of Hudson now. Her senses were heightened as she caught another whiff of his cologne when he leaned in to show her a picture on his phone. He'd gone fishing at his mother's after dinner the day before and caught a giant fish. He was animated and enthusiastic as he told her about it, but she wasn't getting any kind of vibe from Hudson, so she was pretty sure that the attraction she felt was one-sided. She was disappointed but a little relieved at the same time. She would just enjoy his friendship and their professional work relationship.

They stayed at the Chicken Box until almost midnight. As they were walking out, before Lauren headed to her car, Hudson stopped her. "Have you ever had grilled fresh striped bass?"

The question took her by surprise. "I'm not sure. I don't think so."

"You know that fish I told you about? The one I caught yesterday? I put it right in the freezer and was going to cook it up tomorrow. It's a huge fish. I could use some help eating it if you want to come by for dinner?"

Lauren hesitated for a moment. Was this a date? Was Hudson interested in that way, after all?

"My mother will be there, so you can meet her, too. If you have plans, though, no worries."

Lauren relaxed a little. If his mother was going to be there, then it definitely wasn't a date.

"Sure, that sounds fun. Let me know what time to come by and if I can bring anything."

"I'll text you, but I'm thinking about six. You don't need to bring anything, though."

"All right. See you then."

CHAPTER THIRTY-FIVE

Anna drove their little group home from the Chicken Box. Well, except for Suzanne and Noah, who took their own car. The drive back to the share house was only about fifteen minutes, and they laughed almost the whole way. She'd never realized how funny Billy was before. She knew he was an influencer, but she hadn't looked him up social media as she'd recently seen him in a movie. He'd actually played a charming drug dealer that was killed early on. He'd played the role well, but there hadn't been anything funny about it.

Katy seemed totally smitten. And Anna understood it. Billy had a certain charisma about him. When he was in the room, he seemed to command attention and Katy had told her earlier that being on the receiving end of Billy's attention was intoxicating.

"He makes me feel so seen, like he's really into me and no one else matters," she'd gushed as they were getting ready to go out earlier.

Anna was happy for her friend, but wary, too. She'd dated guys like Billy. The flame burned bright when their attention was new, but it faded fast when something else caught their attention. She didn't want to assume that Billy was like that, but his track record, especially the recent issue with Lauren, didn't bode well. Katy said they'd discussed it though.

"I asked him about it. And he was honest that he'd messed up. He swore it was a onetime thing. And he seemed so sincere."

Anna's advice was to take things slow and to always remember that they were being filmed.

"I know you're caught up in the moment, but I'd keep it as light as possible. Don't sleep with him until filming stops. You'll know him better then. And you'll know if it's real."

"It sure feels real. But that's good advice." Katy grinned. "Especially as I was so sure that I wouldn't get into anything romantic."

Anna had smiled. "You did say that."

When they came into the house, Billy went straight into the kitchen. "Is anyone else hungry? I'm going to make nachos."

"I love nachos." Katy followed him and helped by finding the big bag of tortilla chips. Billy opened the refrigerator and pulled out shredded cheddar cheese, sour cream, salsa, and a leftover cooked burger. He crumbled the burger and assembled everything except the sour cream on a plate and put it in the microwave for ninety seconds.

And Anna had to admit it smelled fantastic. She didn't think she was hungry, but when Billy set the platter of steaming nachos on the kitchen island, she dove in with the others.

"That was a fun night," Jason said as he scooped up a loaded tortilla chip and popped it into his mouth.

"It was," Anna agreed. She'd been pleasantly surprised by how much fun she'd had with Jason. Like Katy, she hadn't planned on finding romance in the house, and she wasn't exactly sure if that's what was happening with Jason, but she was enjoying his company. He was turning into a good friend, and maybe more, but she wasn't sure just yet. She'd told Katy to go slow, and she intended to follow her own advice.

"What do you two have planned for tomorrow?" Jason asked.

"We're heading to Boston in the morning," Anna said. "We have massages booked at the Four Seasons tomorrow afternoon and we're going to do some shopping on Newbury Street and have a nice dinner somewhere."

"Nice. Are you staying the night?" he asked.

"We are. We'll be back Wednesday morning in time for filming," Anna said.

"Maybe we could come back tomorrow night," Katy said wistfully. Anna knew that look—she didn't want to be away from Billy for even one night.

Anna smiled. "It's too late to cancel now. And we should probably head to bed. We have to be up early."

Katy didn't look like she was ready to leave Billy yet, but after a moment, she nodded. "You're probably right. We should go up to bed."

"You guys will have a blast in Boston. You'll have to tell us all about it when you get back," Billy said. He leaned over and kissed Katy. It was a quick kiss, but it took her breath away. "Goodnight, Katy." He grinned and flashed her his most charming grin and Anna knew Katy was totally hooked.

"Have fun, Anna. See you on Wednesday." Jason pulled her in for a hug. He didn't go for a kiss and she was grateful. They hadn't done that yet. She sensed it was coming, but the time wasn't right yet.

"Goodnight. Thanks for the nachos, Billy. They were great."

He looked pleased. "Anytime."

Anna and Katy headed upstairs and Anna was glad they were heading to Boston the next day and getting out of the house for a night. She thought it was a good idea for both of them to push pause. Everything seemed more intense in the house since they were around each other twenty-four seven. She didn't want either of them to get too attached too soon and do anything they might regret later.

CHAPTER THIRTY-SIX

"It was a fun time. It looks like we'll be heading back there on Wednesday night to try to recreate what we saw last night." Lauren updated Lisa over breakfast Tuesday morning. Lauren and Lisa were both eating a ham and cheese quiche, while Rhett sipped his usual black coffee and looked amused by the conversation.

"That's so interesting. So it's reality, but with a little help?" Lisa asked.

Lauren nodded. "Exactly. It's not scripted by any means, but we'll sometimes ask them to recreate moments or give suggestions on topics of discussion that will move the story forward." She grinned. "We didn't expect that the cast would want to join us on everyone's day off, but it worked out well that they did. Even if we didn't have the cameras with us."

And Lauren was looking forward to going back to the Chicken Box. She'd enjoyed spending time with Hudson and was looking forward to dinner with him and his mother tonight, but was a little nervous about it, too. She told Lisa about the invitation.

"You like him?" Lisa looked thoughtful.

Lauren nodded. "I do. I'm definitely attracted to him, but I'm also happy to just be friends. That is probably smarter, considering we work together. Plus, I'll be heading back to LA when filming ends and he's staying here. So it doesn't make sense to start something."

Lisa nodded. "Love doesn't always make sense, though. But you are wise to keep it professional—at least until filming ends. When does it end?"

"We have another month."

"A lot can happen in a month. It's interesting that his mother is joining you for dinner. That sends a bit of a mixed message to me. If he meant for it to be a romantic date, I don't think he would do that." Lisa took a sip of her coffee, then continued talking.

"But he likes you well enough to have you over, and he wants his mother to meet you. Maybe that's to put you at ease, so you don't worry that it's a date, yet? Does he live with her?"

"No. They're close, though. She's a widow. He lives in a guesthouse on her property."

"Oh, that's nice for both of them. I was a widow, too. Until I turned this place into an inn and Rhett was my first guest." She patted his hand, and he winked at her. They were very cute together. "I'm going to want a full report tomorrow about this dinner," Lisa said.

Lauren laughed. "Of course," she agreed.

So, even though Lauren agreed with Lisa's thoughts on her non-date, she still felt nervous, especially about meeting Hudson's mother. What if his mother didn't like her? All Hudson had said was that they were close. She didn't know anything else about his mother. It was a little intimidating.

And she didn't want to show up empty-handed. She called Angela to update her and to ask for a suggestion of what to bring. First, she asked how she was feeling and was shocked when Angela filled her in about her fall and trip to the ER.

"Are you sure you're okay? And the baby, too?"

"We're both fine. Falls usually aren't too much of a danger in the first trimester. I haven't had any spotting since. I feel great, actually. But enough about me. What's new with the show? How did your night out go?"

Lauren filled her in and finished her story by asking for suggestions on what to bring to dinner. Angela had a different take on the invitation than Lisa did.

"Don't kid yourself. It's definitely a date—disguised as a friendly dinner. He knows it would be inappropriate to ask you on a real date right now. I think it's cute that you'll meet his mother."

"I don't know if cute is the word I'd use. It's a little nerve-wracking," Lauren admitted.

"It will be fine. She will love you," Angela assured her. "Now for what to bring. I'd go to Stop and Shop and get some cookies from their bakery. They're not as good as mine, but they're pretty good."

"Okay, I'll do that. And I'll call you tomorrow."

Angela laughed. "Good! I'll want to hear all about it."

Lauren stopped into Stop and Shop that afternoon and checked out the bakery offerings and Angela was right. They had a good assortment. She chose a bag of chocolate chip with sea salted caramel that looked delicious. Her cookie choice was fast, but it took her forever to decide on what to wear to dinner. She didn't want to seem like she was putting in too much of an effort. She was tempted to wear the cute dress she'd gotten at Izzy's shop, but decided to go a little more casual. She ended up wearing her favorite faded jeans that were so soft and flattering. She wore a sleeveless rosy pink linen top that flattered her skin tone and showed off the slight tan she'd acquired.

Lauren showered and blew her hair out so that it was shiny and stick straight and kept her makeup minimal, just a little concealer, mascara, and lip gloss. Hudson had texted her earlier to confirm the time and give his address. She grabbed the cookies and headed out. Like just about everywhere on Nantucket, it didn't take long to get to his house. He'd mentioned that his mother's place was on the ocean and that he lived in the adjacent guesthouse.

He didn't tell her how stunning the house was or that it was on a huge lot for Nantucket. The main house was a sprawling white Cape Cod style, and there was a lush lawn out front. The guesthouse was a cute white cottage with gray shutters. It had two stories and a large deck. Hudson was on the deck, standing by a big grill. An older woman sat in a chair nearby. Hudson grinned and waved when he saw Lauren and gestured for her to pull into the driveway and park. She parked next to his work van and grabbed her purse, a sweater, and bag of cookies.

She walked up the steps and onto his deck. Hudson came over to greet her and pulled her in for a hug. She handed him the cookies.

"Oh, you didn't have to bring anything." He glanced at the bag before setting it on a table. "They do look good, though. Come meet my mother."

Lauren followed him, and he introduced her to his mother. "Mom, meet Lauren, the lead producer on *Nantucket Influence*. Lauren, my mother, Jane Winters."

"It's nice to meet you, Mrs. Winters," Lauren said politely. Hudson's mother looked to be around sixty. She had a chin length dark brown bob with soft bangs that highlighted her warm brown eyes. She was maybe five-three and petite. She was also wearing jeans and a white sweater with navy blue trim.

"Call me Jane. Have a seat. Hudson was about to get me a glass of pinot grigio. Would you like one?"

"Sure. Can I do anything to help?" Lauren offered.

Hudson smiled. "There's nothing to do. Just sit and relax. I'll be right back."

Hudson disappeared inside. Lauren looked around. Hudson's cottage was set back, but there was still a distant ocean view. The air was slightly cool, and she was glad she'd brought a lightweight sweater with her. She slipped it on.

"This is such a lovely location," Lauren said.

Jane nodded. "Thank you. I've lived here for almost forty years now. My husband and I married young and his family had a summer place here. We bought it from them and made it into a year-round home."

"It must be wonderful to live here year-round." Lauren was not looking forward to returning to Los Angeles.

"I love it, but it's very quiet in the winter." Jane smiled. "Hudson says you live in LA. I bet that is much livelier. Do you like it there?"

Hudson returned with their glasses of wine and handed one to Lauren and to his mother.

"It depends on the day," Lauren admitted. "I like the weather, but the traffic is brutal. It takes forever to go anywhere."

"Lauren is from the East Coast, too," Hudson said. He lifted the grill cover and she could see that there was fish as well as assorted vegetables. He flipped everything over and shut the cover again before joining them at the table.

His mother looked intrigued. "Where is your family from?"

"They're on the Cape. I grew up in West Yarmouth."

"How nice that you were able to come back this way for a show. How is it going?" his mother asked.

"It's been great to be back. My parents are coming to visit this weekend. They're going to come to the food festival with us. Well, I'll be working, but I'll be able to take the evening off to visit with them. Most of our shooting will be during the day."

"Sounds fun. The food festival gets bigger every year. I'm going with a few friends, and there's a wine dinner that evening at The Whitley Hotel. We're looking forward to it." His mother took a sip of her wine.

"Do you know Lisa Hodges? I'm staying at her bed-and-breakfast and she's going to be at the festival, giving out samples of her lobster quiche and something else."

"Is she? Yes, I know Lisa. Hudson and her son, Chase, played on the hockey team together. We'll have to make sure we find Lisa's booth and say hi. I haven't had lobster quiche before."

"It's so good. She's famous for it. Although she has a little competition this year." Lauren told them about Lisa's neighbor Violet and the battle of the lobster quiches. His mother laughed.

"That is too much. We'll have to try them both then and see for ourselves."

Lauren glanced at Hudson. "I didn't realize you played hockey in high school. Is Chase on the men's league now, too?" She remembered Hudson mentioning that he played in an adult men's league.

"He is actually. It has been a good way to reconnect with some of the guys I knew back then."

Hudson went back inside and returned a minute later carrying a stack of plates, silverware and a big serving bowl. He set it all down on the table and took the lid off the bowl.

"Mom made potato salad to have with dinner." He stuck a big spoon in the bowl. "I think everything is just about ready. I'll put it on a few plates and we can help ourselves."

He piled all the grilled vegetables onto one plate and the fish onto another and set them in the middle of the round table where they were sitting. They all filled their plates. The fish was incredible. He'd basted it with butter and lemon juice and it was light and flaky. His mother's potato salad was creamy and delicious.

They sat on the deck enjoying their dinner and the fresh air. The sun over the ocean was gorgeous—the sky was rosy pink. Lauren sipped her wine and enjoyed chatting with Hudson and his mother. She learned that Jane was a veterinarian and had a practice downtown that specialized in treating cats. Her husband had also been a veterinarian. They'd met in vet school and had worked together until his death a few years ago. He'd died from a complication with diabetes, which he'd had all his life.

"I don't think mom is ever going to retire," Hudson said as an oversized orange cat jumped onto the deck railing, cocked its head and watched them intently.

"What else would I do?" His mother laughed. "I like to keep busy." She motioned toward the cat. "Come say hello, Oscar."

The cat jumped down onto the deck and went over to

Hudson's mother and rubbed against her leg. She leaned over to pet him.

"How old is Oscar now?" Hudson asked.

His mother thought for a moment. "Fifteen, or maybe sixteen. He's my little old man. He hasn't slowed down too much, though."

Lauren helped Hudson carry everything inside when they were done eating.

"Just set that on the counter, thanks." He quickly put the leftover food in the refrigerator and the dirty dishes in the sink to deal with later. Lauren glanced around the room, and took in the cozy leather sofa and big screen TV and kitchen that was small but had everything he needed.

"Your place is great," she said.

He looked happy to hear it. "Thanks. I have two bedrooms upstairs and it's worked out well so far. I like being nearby if mom needs anything."

Once he had everything put away, they headed back outside.

"Did you save any room for cookies?" Lauren asked.

Hudson grinned. "There's always room for dessert."

"I would have helped, but I'm catted," his mother said. Lauren laughed when she saw what she meant. Oscar was curled up in his mother's lap, purring.

"Lauren brought cookies." Hudson opened the bag and passed it around. Lauren and his mother each took one, and Hudson took two.

After a little while, Oscar jumped off his mother's lap, and she stood. "I should be getting back. Thanks for dinner, honey." She turned to Lauren. "It was great meeting you. I hope to see you again."

"Thank you. It was great to meet you, too."

They watched his mother head off to her house and Lauren wondered if she should head home, too.

"Let's have another drink. You're not in a rush to get home, are you?" Hudson asked.

"No. I could have a little more wine." She'd only had one glass so far and she wasn't in a hurry to leave.

Hudson brought the wine bottle out and topped off her glass. He opened a new beer for himself and grabbed another cookie. She took one too. They sat in silence for a moment, just relaxing and enjoying the sound of the waves in the distance.

And then had a lively discussion about the different shows they'd both worked on. It turned out that they knew some of the same people and they both laughed about the things they'd seen happen on different reality shows.

"People often ask me if the shows are scripted. They find it hard to imagine sometimes when a show is really dramatic," Lauren said.

"If they only knew. I've told people that sometimes we can't show the craziest things that happen. Truth really is stranger than fiction." Hudson shook his head. "I enjoyed it, but I have to admit I don't miss doing it all the time."

"Was it hard to make the transition out of reality?"

"Not really. It's all about timing. Something opened up that wasn't reality, and I jumped on it. And then that led to more things. And then Cami called."

"I've only worked on reality shows so far. I might like to branch out too, at some point. Right now though, I'm just hoping this does well enough that they want a second season." Lauren grinned. "And then I'll get to come back next summer."

"That would be awesome," Hudson agreed.

It was almost nine by the time the sun fully set. The conversation with Hudson had been so easy and natural. At times, they were both rushing to talk, and she found that they liked many of the same things—some of the same bands and books. She felt like she'd known him longer and had the sense that he was someone that might be in her life for a long time, even if it was just as a friend. He didn't give her any reason to think that he wanted to be more than that. It had crossed her mind more than once as they talked. When she noticed how laugh lines danced around his eyes and mouth when he smiled—she found that very attractive. But it was more the expression in his eyes as he held her gaze and seemed so interested in what she had to say. She got the sense that he definitely liked her as a person, even if it never turned romantic. She couldn't help hoping that it would, though. Even while she knew it was unlikely and unwise, given that they worked together.

A gust of wind blew through her hair and almost knocked over her empty wine glass. "I should probably head home. Thanks again for dinner. This was fun." She stood to go.

"It was." Hudson stood and pulled her in for a quick goodbye hug. "See you tomorrow."

CHAPTER THIRTY-SEVEN

E loise was already in the kitchen spreading cream cheese on a bagel when Lauren arrived. Her eyes lit up when she saw Lauren. The room was empty except for the other two camera guys. Hudson hadn't yet arrived and except for Honey and Brett, who were toasting bagels, and Simon who had the roomies and was racing around the dining room, the rest of the cast was still in bed.

"Did you have a chance to look over any of the film yet?" Eloise asked.

Lauren nodded as she set her laptop on the table, next to Eloise. "I looked it over this morning after breakfast. I think we have a lot of good stuff we can use. Billy and Katy had their first kiss. Suzanne and Noah seem to be a thing now, and even Anna and Jason seem to be thinking about romance. And then there was Sami. I hadn't seen that side of her before."

"I know, right? She seemed so chill and cool, more

reserved. And then when Katy wasn't looking, she flirted like mad with Billy. I couldn't tell if he was into her or not, though."

"Billy flirts with everyone, but he seems to really like Katy." Lauren hoped that he wasn't going to screw things up again.

"Maybe it was just harmless flirting on her part, too. She hasn't paid much attention to Billy before now." Eloise ripped off a piece of her bagel and popped it into her mouth.

"I just hope she's not one of those girls that isn't interested in someone until someone else is," Lauren said.

"Right, then they suddenly become more attractive," Eloise agreed. "I don't know much about her dating life, actually. I might need to poke around a bit and see what I can find."

Lauren helped herself to a cup of coffee and a handful of grapes before sitting at the table with Eloise. She opened her laptop and checked her email. A few minutes later, Hudson arrived and waved to them before he set up his equipment and then came over to say a quick hello before grabbing coffee and heading back to his camera. His eyes were warm and friendly as they chatted, and Lauren could feel her crush growing. Each time she saw him, he seemed more attractive. And she'd taken a little more care with what she'd worn that day and had blown her hair out until it was smooth and shiny.

A half hour or so later, Eloise reported on what she'd found. "So, it doesn't look like Sami has had a serious relationship in a few years. She goes out a lot though, and there are pictures of her with a few different men over the past year. They all look romantic, but she never seems to be with anyone for long.

Sami also had an online dating diary for a while, where she talked about the different guys that she went out with. She never showed their faces—just pictures of the different places they went to, the cocktails they drank and sometimes the food they ate. She always looks gorgeous and seems to be having a good time."

Eloise sent Lauren a few of the links she'd found and Lauren went down a rabbit hole looking at Sami's past posts and her dating diary TikTok videos. They were addicting. There were some weeks where Sami went on four or five first dates. Lauren had seen some of Sami's social media before they started filming, but hadn't really studied it the way they were doing now.

After she finished watching the dating diary videos, she turned to Eloise, "I can't imagine dating like that. It seems exhausting." Lauren had never been able to juggle dating more than one guy at a time.

"I know. She makes it look fun, though. Sort of." Eloise smiled. "I am looking forward to going to the Chicken Box tonight."

That reminded Lauren that Eloise had been sick. "How's your stomach? Are you feeling back to normal?"

Eloise looked confused for a moment. "Oh, right. Yeah, I'm fine. Must have just been something I ate. So, what did you do yesterday? Anything fun?"

Lauren hesitated for a moment, as she didn't want Eloise to get the wrong idea. But then she told her all about dinner the night before at Hudson's. Eloise looked pleased to hear it.

"I had a feeling you two might hit it off," she said smugly.

"It wasn't a date," Lauren said. "We're just work friends."

Eloise smiled. "Right. Well, I'm glad you had fun."

CHAPTER THIRTY-EIGHT

"How was your trip off-island?" Anna asked Sami. Anna was curled up on the living room sofa, reading a magazine. Smith jumped up and snuggled next to her, like he always did. Anna reached over and petted him, scratching behind his ears the way he liked. Everyone else was still upstairs getting ready to head out to the Chicken Box. Anna had showered and changed right after dinner and headed downstairs to give Katy some space to get ready. Sami looked cute and tan in a sleeveless, cream colored top and jeans. She poured herself a glass of iced tea and took a long sip before answering.

"It was ok. I actually sort of had a breakup, I guess. I mean, we weren't serious, but I'd hoped it would go in that direction. Instead, we went out for a drink and he told me that he'd met someone special. Kind of ruined my night, if you know what I mean?" Her voice broke a little and Anna felt for her.

"I'm sorry, Sami. That stinks."

Sami smiled, but it didn't reach her eyes. "Yeah, well, his loss, right? Onward!"

"Yes, definitely his loss. We'll have fun tonight. Forget about him," Anna advised.

"That's my plan."

Forty-five minutes later, they were all on the dance floor at the Chicken Box, and Sami seemed to be having a great time. She danced up a storm with different people, Jason and Billy among them. It didn't bother Anna as she'd just sat down after dancing and Sami and Jason just danced for one fast song. She could tell that it bothered Katy, though. But Sami just danced one fast song with Billy, too, and then she found a new guy at the bar and they went off to dance.

Billy went up to get another round of drinks, and Katy immediately complained about Sami as soon as Billy walked away. "What is going on with her?"

"I wouldn't worry too much about it." Anna filled her in on what Sami had told her earlier and Katy was sympathetic.

"That's rough. I guess I'll cut her a little slack. Maybe she's just trying to have fun and get her mind off the breakup. As long as she doesn't get any ideas about Billy."

He returned to the table a few minutes later with drinks for all of them. Anna took a sip of her chardonnay and people-watched for a while. The music was loud, so it was hard to talk when they were playing. But it was fun to watch people on the dance floor and to observe the dynamics of their group.

She noticed that Suzanne and Noah seemed to be going strong. At first, she hadn't thought that Suzanne or Noah would be interested in starting a real relationship. Both of them seemed more the quick fling types. But they were really sweet with each other. And as far as Anna could tell, they were taking things slow and getting to know each other.

Anna wasn't totally sure, but she thought she picked up a vibe between two of the production team—Hudson and Lauren. They seemed interested in each other, but she also didn't think it had gone past the mild flirtation stage. And then there was whatever was going on with her and Jason. That had taken her by surprise. As she spent time in the house around Jason, she enjoyed his company more each day. They hadn't gone past the flirting stage yet either, but Anna got the strong sense that if she gave him the green light, it would go in a romantic direction. And she was tempted. Very tempted. But not just yet.

She wanted to wait as long as possible, until they were close to the end of the show's filming schedule. She didn't want to be that open with the whole world about her private dating life. But she also wasn't sure how much longer she could wait. It was hard—especially when Jason walked over and held out his hand to lead her to the dance floor for one of her all-time favorite slow songs—Eric Clapton's "Wonderful Tonight". As they swayed to the music and she felt his arms tighten around her, she shivered.

"Are you cold?" Jason asked softly and ran his hands along her bare arms to warm her. His touch only made her shiver again, but it wasn't from the cold.

She laughed. "No, I'm fine."

She glanced to her left and saw Billy and Sami slow dancing. Sami's eyes were closed and her arms were wrapped around Billy's neck. Anna looked back at their table and Katy was sitting there alone. She looked furious. When the song ended, Jason asked if she wanted to keep dancing.

"Yes, but not just yet. Maybe in a little bit." She headed back to their table. Billy and Sami were still on the dance floor and were now dancing to a fast song. Sami was laughing and tossing her hair off her face. Katy, meanwhile, looked positively murderous.

"I think I hate her. Maybe I hate him, too," she said when Anna sat down.

"How did they happen to go off for a slow dance?" Anna asked.

Katy frowned. "Billy was in the bathroom when the slow song started. Sami was nowhere around. I went off to use the bathroom and when I came back, the two of them were out there."

Anna nodded. "Ok, that's good. It's not like he asked her to dance while you were sitting right here. I wouldn't read too much into it."

Katy relaxed a little. "I won't. That's a good point."

A few minutes later, Billy and Sami returned to the

table and Billy sat next to Katy. He glanced toward the bar. "What do you say we head to the bar, just the two of us? Production can film as the sparks begin to fly." He smiled his devilishly charming smile and Katy immediately melted and seemed relieved.

"Sure, let's go."

They headed to the corner of the bar, where there were several open seats. Hudson moved closer to catch both film and audio of their conversation.

"Is that real? Or just for the show?" Sami asked. She looked as though she doubted it was real.

"They seem to be hitting it off," Anna said. "We came back here to recreate some of the moments from the other night when we were all here without cameras."

Sami nodded. "Suzanne and Noah are obviously into each other. What about you and Jason? Is anything going on there?"

"I'm not sure. We're taking it slow and getting to know each other. I'm a little hesitant to be that open too soon—I guess I'm a little more reserved when it comes to my own love life."

"You should be more spontaneous. Just go with how you're feeling instead of trying to suppress it. It's a freeing thing—and you never know where it will lead you." She glanced over at Billy and Katy. They were leaning into each other and Katy had her hand on Billy's forearm and they were both smiling and laughing.

"I'm going to take a lap around," Sami said as Jason headed back to the table.

He sat down next to Anna and glanced at his cell

phone, that had just buzzed with a text message. When he read it, he grinned and then texted right back. A moment later, his phone vibrated again, and he laughed out loud and showed Anna the image that had just come through.

"My mom just made a huge pot of homemade sauce, meatballs and sausages. She knows it's my all-time favorite meal. If I'm home, I usually try to have Sunday dinner with the family. I miss that."

"Your parents live nearby?" Anna asked.

He nodded. "Everyone is in Brooklyn, except for my younger brother. My parents have lived in the same town-house for thirty-something years. My sister is married and lives on the same block with her husband and their two kids. Tony lives in the East Village with a bunch of room-mates. But he makes it home often."

"That's nice." Anna envied Jason's closeness with his family. It sounded wonderful to gather often over a meal and catch up with everyone.

"What about you? Do you have family nearby?"

"Sort of. My parents live just outside the city, in Greenwich, CT. My dad is a hospital administrator and my mother is a litigation attorney. She's not much of a cook and they're always so busy. I mostly see them on holidays." That usually meant dinner at a fancy restau-rant, which was fine, but it was far from a cozy, Hallmark type of holiday. Anna was an only child. She loved her parents, but she didn't feel like she had much in common with them. Her visits home were usually short ones, and she was always glad to get back to her peaceful apartment in the West Village.

"Well, maybe you'll have to join me one Sunday. My mother always cooks extra. She usually sends me home with leftovers. You'll like them," he assured her.

Anna smiled. She was a little intimidated at the thought of meeting his family, but they sounded wonderful. And she took it as a good sign that he was even thinking of introducing her to them. She felt a rush of happiness as she lifted her glass of wine to take a sip. The band launched into a new song, a lively dance tune that made her start tapping her toes against the floor. She didn't even realize she was doing it, but Jason did, and he laughed.

"Looks like you like this song—shall we?" She stood and followed him to the middle of the dance floor. Suzanne and Noah were already there. Billy and Katy were still deep in conversation at the bar, and there was no sign of Sami. Anna caught Jason's eyes, and he held her gaze and smiled. "Are you having fun?"

"Yes, so much fun." She felt happy, really happy and relaxed. She wanted to bottle this feeling and make it last as long as possible.

CHAPTER THIRTY-NINE

"They all understood the assignment," Hudson said as he joined Lauren and Eloise at their table. He'd just finished filming Katy and Billy talking at the bar. Now they were on the dance floor and one of the other camera guys was filming that area. He took a sip of his beer, the first he'd had that night as he'd been so busy filming.

"They all seem pretty coupled up. Maybe even more so than the other night?" Lauren said.

Hudson nodded. "Yeah, and we have the added element of Sami and a potential love triangle with Katy and Billy. Katy's face is very expressive."

"I hope that she doesn't get hurt." Lauren still worried about Katy with Billy. She knew it would make for good TV, but she'd still rather have less drama if it meant someone going through the pain that she'd felt when Billy cheated.

"I've been watching Sami, and we read up about her

more this morning. I think she may be like a female Billy. She just likes to flirt and not get too serious," Eloise said.

"I wonder if that's how she really is, or just how she projects—making it seem like she doesn't care when she actually does. Like in her dating diaries, she often falls fast for these guys and then doesn't understand why it doesn't work out," Lauren said.

"She's a beautiful girl," Hudson said. "But if she changes her tune with these guys, saying she wants casual and then suddenly wants to be serious—there may be a disconnect there."

A good song came on and Lauren felt like dancing. They hadn't been out on the dance floor all night because they were there to work. But it was late, and she knew the band wasn't going to play for much longer. She looked at Eloise and Hudson. "Let's go dance."

Hudson stood, but Eloise didn't move. "You guys go. I'm tired."

The dance floor was crowded, but they made their way to where the rest of their group was dancing. They were all out there, even Sami, with a good-looking guy she'd met at the bar.

"Looks like she's over Billy," Hudson said.

Lauren watched as Sami danced and tossed her hair back and laughed with her dance partner, who seemed fascinated by Sami and also by the cameras that had been filming all night. Lauren hoped that Hudson was right.

They stayed until the Chicken Box closed at one. By then, everyone was exhausted and ready to head home and crash into bed. Lauren saw that everyone was there except for Sami. She finally saw her, walking toward them with the guy she'd been dancing with.

"Zach is going to give me a ride home. He lives right up the street, so he's heading in the same direction." Lauren hesitated. She didn't want to embarrass Sami, but she wasn't sure it was a good idea for her to get a ride home from a stranger. Hudson walked over to her and the guy smiled.

"Hey man, good to see you."

"Hey Zach." He whispered to Lauren. "I know him. He's a good guy."

Lauren nodded. "Okay, see you tomorrow then, Sami."

Sami and Zach turned to go, and once they were out of earshot, she looked at Hudson. "You're sure about this?"

He didn't hesitate. "Yeah. I don't know him well, he's a year younger than me, but we went to school together. He's very popular with the ladies, actually."

Lauren laughed. Zach was extremely good-looking. "I'm not surprised. I just wanted to make sure he's not a serial killer."

"I think we're safe there," Hudson said as they reached Lauren's car.

"Okay, I guess I'll see you tomorrow morning."

Hudson smiled and his eyes were warm as they met hers. "Goodnight, Lauren."

CHAPTER FORTY

Katy and Anna were up a little before nine the next morning and headed to the kitchen to make coffee. No one else was up yet and as they reached the first floor, they both heard the front door close. Katy ran to the window.

"Anna, isn't that the guy that Sami was talking to last night?" Katy asked.

Anna took a look and wasn't sure until he turned their way before getting into his car. There was no doubt.

"That's him. Looks like Sami had a very good night last night."

This seemed to please Katy. "Good. Maybe I won't need to worry about her with Billy anymore. I wonder if it will turn into anything?"

Anna had her doubts. "You never know. Might be a fun fling for the next few weeks. We'll all be heading home after that. Hudson said Zach lives here on Nantucket."

A minute later, the front door opened, and Lauren and Eloise walked in.

"Did you pass anyone on your way in?" Katy asked.

"You mean like the guy Sami was dancing with last night?" Eloise said. "I take it he spent the night?"

"Looks that way," Anna agreed. "We saw him leave. He didn't see us, though."

———

An hour later, Sami was the last person to make her way downstairs. She nodded at everyone and went to the kitchen, poured herself a cup of coffee and sliced an onion bagel and put it in the toaster. The guys were outside on the deck, and all the girls and the production staff were in the kitchen.

Once Sami's bagel was toasted, she added cream cheese, then brought everything to the big marble island where Anna, Katy and Honey were sitting. Lauren and Eloise were close by at the round kitchen table. They could still easily hear the conversation.

Lauren wasn't sure if they were going to ask Sami about Zach or not, but after a few minutes of idle chitchat about what a fun night they'd had, Katy brought it up.

"So we came downstairs this morning just as Zach was heading out the front door. He didn't see us, though. I guess you two hit it off?"

Sami's eyes widened and a flush spread across her

cheeks. "You could say that. He seems really nice. We're going out again tonight. One of his friends plays in a band and we're going to go hear them play." She smiled. "It definitely turned my mood around. I'm not expecting it to be anything serious, but it's fine and fun."

Katy looked happy to hear that Sami had plans to go out with Zach again. "That's awesome. Have fun."

"Do the guys know that Zach stayed here last night?" Sami asked.

Anna shook her head. "I don't think so. Unless they were up when you came home last night?"

"No, all the lights were off when we got home. We took a long walk on the beach and sat on the front deck for a while before we headed inside. If you don't mind, please don't say anything to the guys."

Katy smiled. "Of course. My lips are sealed."

The sun came out strong and they spent most of the day on the beach. The guys got out the games and they played horseshoes and then bocce. It was girls against guys and then they mixed up the teams. It made for a fun day and everyone got along great. They broke for lunch, and the catering team put out platters of sandwiches and watermelon slices.

Everyone was tired from going out the night before and they decided to just order pizzas, watch movies, and have an early night. Lauren noticed that once everyone ate, and they settled in the living room to watch TV, that everyone paired off and all the couples sat together. Except for Sami, who was out with Zach. The guys knew she was going out with the guy from the Chicken Box, but they didn't know that he'd spent the night.

Lauren and the production team headed home around ten. It was a long day, so she didn't feel bad about taking Friday night off to have dinner with her parents. And she'd see them the next day at the food festival, too. Lauren would be working, but she'd still be able to chat and visit with her parents. They were taking the ferry over in the afternoon and had booked a room with Lisa. Lauren was glad they'd be staying just a few doors down. She hadn't seen them since Christmas. She talked to her mother every few days, though.

CHAPTER FORTY-ONE

L auren saw Lisa at breakfast on Friday. But she was by herself. For the first time, Rhett wasn't with her drinking his black coffee.

Lisa smiled when she saw her and explained. "Rhett had to go into the restaurant early to meet with an electrician." Lisa took a bite of scrambled eggs, then added a splash of hot sauce to them.

Lauren had added a generous scoop to her plate, along with some honeydew melon and a slice of buttered sourdough toast. The eggs were mixed with diced ham, onions and peppers and they were delicious.

Lisa didn't seem as relaxed as usual. She glanced at her watch, checking the time as she attacked the mound of eggs on her plate.

"Are you excited about tomorrow?" Lauren asked.

Lisa put down her fork and sighed. "Yes, but I'm also a nervous wreck. Rhett is lending me a warming station for the quiches, so I can have a half dozen or so ready to cut and serve. He hasn't used it in ages, so checked it a few days ago to make sure it was ready to go…and it's not working at all. He thinks it might be a faulty cord. It looks like mice may have chewed through it."

"Mice?" That didn't sound good.

Lisa nodded. "He has kept it in the restaurant basement, stuffed in a corner where it collects dust. Every restaurant has mice. He gets it exterminated regularly, but still they sometimes get into things."

Lauren could tell Lisa was stressing about it. "I'm sure he'll find a way to get it working for you."

Lisa sighed. "He probably will. I've been making lobster quiches for the past week and freezing them to make sure I have enough on hand. Once I finish here, I'll be heading to the kitchen to make more."

"We're going to be heading to the festival early, before it gets too crowded. We'll make sure to stop by your booth and have the cast try the quiche," Lauren said. She was excited to give Lisa some publicity—being shown on the show could give a significant boost to both the inn and Lisa's online sales of the quiches.

"Thank you. I really do appreciate that." She chewed her lower lip for a moment. "I just hope everything goes smoothly."

"It will. I'm sure of it." Lauren tried to calm Lisa's fears and hoped that Rhett would get the warmer going. The quiches were probably delicious cold, but it wouldn't be the same.

Lisa smiled. "I'm not going to stress about it. You're right. I'm sure it will all be fine and I'm just being silly.

Enough about me. Your parents are checking in later today. I'm looking forward to meeting them."

"They are. I talk to my mother almost every day, but I haven't seen them since the holidays. That's one of the things I hate about living on opposite coasts."

Lisa looked sympathetic. "I'm lucky that my kids are all here now. They weren't always, though. Kate worked at a fashion magazine for a few years in Boston. Even though that's relatively close, we mostly saw her on holidays. When you're young, you have to go where the opportunities are."

"Is that when she shifted into writing books?" Lauren asked.

"Yes. She was laid off unexpectedly, went home early and found her photographer boyfriend—the one that was always too busy to come to Nantucket and meet us—in bed with one of his models." Lisa's tone was bitter as she spoke about Kate's ex. "She was devastated, of course. I told her to come home for as long as she needed. And I was thrilled when she decided to stay. She met her now-husband Jack and did a little freelance editing work while starting to do what she'd always dreamed of doing—writing a book."

"I'm so glad it worked out for her. And I love her mysteries."

"Things do have a way of working out if you are open to new opportunities and just follow your heart." Lisa laughed. "I know that sounds kind of woo-woo, but I've seen it with my children, and also with myself. It was a leap to turn my home into an inn. My son Chase helped me with that. He's a builder. And then to get the online business going has been quite the adventure." Her eyes lit up as she spoke, and it was obvious how much Lisa loved how her life had evolved.

"I think there is a lot of truth to that. My mother told me years ago to 'Do what you love, and the money will follow.' She worked in human resources and said the people who were most passionate about the careers were the ones that were the happiest and usually the ones that were the most successful. I don't think she was thrilled when I wanted to get into TV production, as it meant I'd need to head out to the West Coast where the work was. But she understood."

Lisa nodded. "So, what is next for you? Will you be heading back to California? Do you have a new show lined up after this one?"

Lauren hated to think of leaving Nantucket and going back to the real world—and LA. "Yes, I'll be heading back there. I'm not sure yet what will be next. My manager is feeling out a few things. And of course we are hoping that the show will do well. If it does, we'll be back next summer."

"Wouldn't that be nice? I have a feeling it will do well. People are always curious about Nantucket. And a show about young people staying at a gorgeous waterfront home with possible romance and drama. What's not to like?"

Lauren laughed. "I hope you're right."

CHAPTER FORTY-TWO

They did some filming downtown that afternoon as the cast visited some of the local shops in search of the preppiest outfits they could find to wear that evening. They were having another themed party and once again, Lauren and Eloise visited the neighbors in the morning and invited them all. It was likely to be a bit louder than the last party as they'd secured the band from the Chicken Box to play. Everyone was excited about that and Lauren suspected it might be a late night and a lively one.

They went back to Murray's Toggery, which had a great selection of clothing that fit the look they wanted. A few other shops did as well and everyone took videos of different cast members trying on pink and green shorts and shorts with whales embroidered on them, or anchors, or even sharks. Once again, they had a contest to see whose video would go most viral. It was great early promotion for the show—designed to build buzz.

Lauren had to laugh at Billy's final outfit—a white button-down shirt with a navy cotton sweater tied around his neck that said Nantucket across the front and bright pink long shorts with great white sharks all over them. The sweater lasted all of about five minutes before he yanked it off and tossed it in a corner.

The caterers were going to do a classic cookout with burgers and dogs, grilled chicken, and assorted chips and salads. Lauren headed back to the inn as soon as she had a text message from her parents that they'd arrived and were settling into their room. They were going to have a nice dinner the next night after the filming ended with the food festival. For tonight, Lauren had to be at the house for the party, so she invited them to attend. She thought it might be fun for her parents to be in the background. She'd get to see them and they'd get a behind the scenes look at what goes into filming.

Her parents were in the room next to Lauren's, and her mother pulled her in for a hug as soon as she opened the door. Her dad did as well. Lauren felt like she was looking in a mirror when she saw her mother—at least she hoped she'd look that good when she was her age. Her mother had the same color hair and build as Lauren and her skin was smooth, with just a few wrinkles around her eyes when she smiled. Her father's hair was totally white now, and he'd put on a few pounds around his middle, but he was in good health and Lauren was thrilled to see them both.

"Not a bad setup you've got here," her father said as he looked around the room. The view out the window was breathtaking—the sun was shining, and the harbor was full of boats. Lauren was used to it, but still took a moment every day to just stare out the window and enjoy the view.

She grinned. "I know. It's awesome. How was the ride over?" Her parents had taken the Hy-Line Fast Ferry out of Hyannis.

"It's the best way to come here, I think," her mother said. "It's so relaxing and the hour goes by so fast. There were so many dogs on the boat."

Lauren nodded. "I noticed that too, the last time I took the ferry here. That was ages ago, though."

"So, are you sure you want us to come to your party? We won't be in the way?" her mother asked.

"Not at all. For the last party, Lisa and the neighbors, who are in their seventies, came. Some of the other neighbors did, too. I think they were all just curious to see what was going on. Lisa can't make it tonight. She's getting ready for the festival tomorrow, but Walter and Kay are, and I'll introduce you. You'll like them. They live right next to the share house."

"Did you say there would be food there?" Her father asked.

Lauren laughed. "Yes. Are you hungry, Dad?"

"Starving. Lead the way."

They walked along the beach to the share house and by the time they reached the steps to the back deck, Lauren could smell the food cooking on the grill and her stomach rumbled. The band was setting up and a small crowd had arrived already, including Walter and Kay. Lauren introduced them to her parents. They all got some food and sat at a table in the far corner of the deck, away from the crowd. Hudson was there too and had his camera stationed on the deck where most of the cast was mingling. Lauren introduced her parents to Hudson.

"I love their outfits," Lauren's mother said as she took in all the preppy colors and clothes.

"I might need to get myself a pair of those shorts," Walter said as Billy walked by in his shark wear.

"Have you seen many sharks here?" Lauren's father asked him.

Walter shook his head. "No. I know they are out there, though. I think you see more of them on the Cape?"

"We do. Not near where we live in Yarmouth, but Chatham and the lower Cape, Nauset, Provincetown—they see most of the shark activity," her father said.

"I don't go in the water anymore," her mother admitted.

Her father laughed. "Anymore? It's not like you ever went in much."

"Well, that's true. But I took a paddle boarding class with a friend and it was so much fun. It was on a lake, but we were thinking of going in on one together and trying it in Lewis Bay. But then there was a sighting in Yarmouth and we changed our minds."

"I go in up to my knees. That's my limit," Kay said.

Lauren excused herself to go inside and check with Eloise. She hadn't seen the girls come outside yet.

She found them gathered around the kitchen island. There was a big bowl of white wine sangria and Anna was pouring glasses for everyone. They all seemed in great moods, except for Sami, who was sulking. She'd just received a text message and looked miserable.

"Is everything okay?" Anna asked her.

Sami shook her head. "I'm just disappointed. Zach says he has to work late and isn't sure if he can make it unless it's much later. I told him that's okay, but I don't know if I'll see him or not."

"That stinks. But at least he said he'll try to get here later. That's something," Katy said.

"I suppose."

The band started to play and everyone made their way out to the deck and spilled over onto the beach. Eloise and Lauren followed them and joined her parents. Lauren introduced Eloise, and they settled in to watch the crowd.

"So, this is your job, then. You throw parties and watch what unfolds?" her father asked.

Lauren nodded. "Pretty much. And then once we finish filming for the season, then we'll go back and edit it all into a story. That's actually my favorite part of the process."

Her mother especially seemed fascinated by the filming as they were able to eavesdrop as Billy and Katy had a conversation about Sami, who was more subdued than usual.

"What's wrong with Sami? She seems kind of down?" Billy asked.

Katy immediately looked annoyed by the question. "She's just mad that Zach can't get here until later, if he gets here. I'm sure he will, though."

"Ah, got it. Let's go cheer her up. Let's get a game of cornhole going. That will be fun and will get her mind off it. What do you think?"

It was clear that Billy was going to do it regardless, and that Katy didn't want to be left behind. "Sure. Sounds good."

Her mother looked thoughtful as they listened, then turned to Lauren. "So that's Billy. Your Billy?" She asked. Her mother had heard all about Billy, but had never met him as they'd only dated for a few months. A few intense months.

"Not my Billy. He's Katy's now. And she's welcome to him," Lauren said.

Hudson overheard that remark and winked at her.

Lauren's parents stayed for about an hour and a half. They enjoyed chatting with Kay and Walter and when they stood to leave, her parents said their goodbyes and walked back with them.

"I'll see you tomorrow a little before noon. I'll drive us over to the food festival," Lauren said.

The party was a success. The band was fantastic and had everyone dancing for most of the night. It wasn't until they stopped playing around eleven that the energy level dropped a bit. Sami had moped around all night waiting for Zach to show up, but he never did.

The production team called it quits at midnight. All the outside visitors had left, and it was just the cast. They were still laughing and dancing to music from a speaker in the kitchen. Billy was in rare form and had them all in stitches as he poked fun at everything, including sharks. Katy's eyes shone when she watched him and Lauren once again worried for her. It seemed like she was falling fast and hard.

It had been a good night overall, though. They'd gotten some great footage from what Lauren had observed, and she looked forward to reviewing all the film from the party in the morning. She yawned as Hudson walked over and nodded at the beach. "Are you ready to walk home? I don't mind getting away from this crowd for the quiet of the beach for a few minutes."

"Sure, I'm ready." Lauren said goodnight to Eloise and headed off with Hudson.

"So, what did your parents think?" Hudson asked as they walked along the shore. The beach was deserted, and the tide was low, the sand packed hard beneath their feet as they walked. The air was salty and fresh and Lauren breathed in deeply. She would miss this when she was back in LA.

"They got a kick out of it. They liked talking to Kay

and Walter and being flies on the wall. They find it amusing that I get paid to go to parties."

Hudson laughed. "That is a nice benefit of the job."

The walk went by too fast and just a few minutes later, they reached the steps to the inn.

"Thanks for walking me back. See you tomorrow," Lauren said.

Hudson's eyes met hers and he smiled. "See you at the festival."

CHAPTER FORTY-THREE

L isa couldn't remember the last time she'd felt so stressed. It was a good kind of stress, though. The electrician that Rhett hired was able to fix the warming station—it just needed a new cord, and it was as good as new. She was excited about the festival and knew she'd done everything she could to prepare. They had a refrigerator to hold the quiches before they went into the warming station and Lisa had made a huge batch of the dark chocolate bread pudding made with the rich challah bread that Rhett had liked so much. They had several huge serving trays of it, along with plenty of canisters of whipped cream for the final touch.

She also had Kristen and Kate, as well as Marley on hand to help with serving and handing out the samples. The festival opened at noon, but they arrived a little before eleven to set up and make sure everything was ready and the electricity was working at their booth.

Kristen, who was the artistic one in the family,

handled the decorating of the booth and she had gone with a white and Nantucket Red color scheme and gorgeous flower arrangements to help the booth stand out and draw people over. The colors of the flowers were vivid pinks and blues and creamy whites, with pretty pink knockout roses dominating the display. And Lisa also had a pile of brochures for the inn and info on how to order the quiches and other items online. She was optimistic that the festival might bring some new business her way.

She wasn't happy though to see that Violet's booth was directly across from hers. Violet seemed pleased by the placement, though, and waved a cheery hello as she arrived to set up her booth. Violet's color scheme was bright yellow and nautical blue. She had sailboats, anchors and whales decorating her booth, playing up the Nantucket theme.

She had helpers too, including her sister and her two teenage nephews, who held signs saying "Nantucket's best lobster quiche." Violet glanced at Lisa triumphantly when the boys first held up the signs.

"Can they do that?" Kate asked.

Marley glanced at the signs and frowned. "I don't think they can. That doesn't seem at all fair. I'll be right back."

She left and returned ten minutes later with Paula, The Whitley Hotel's general manager, by her side. Paula walked over to Violet's booth and had words with her. Lisa couldn't hear the conversation, but the boys put the signs down.

Paula stopped by their booth afterward to say hello. "I

told Violet that she needed to wait until all the votes were in before claiming that her quiche has been voted number one. Good luck!"

By noon, Lisa was fully ready and eager for people to arrive. She didn't have to wait long. Once the gates opened, people started streaming in and she was in constant motion, cutting squares of quiche, scooping up bread pudding and spraying whipped cream on top.

The lines formed fast and stayed steady. At a quarter past twelve, she saw the film crew and the cast arrive. Their presence drew a crowd of onlookers watching with interest as the influencers tasted the quiche and the bread pudding.

"This is heaven," Katy said as she took a bite of lobster quiche.

"I need this recipe," Honey said after sampling the chocolate bread pudding.

"I think everything is a hit," Lauren said after they'd tried everything.

"So far, thankfully, people seem to like both," Lisa said. She glanced across the way to Violet's booth, which was also busy, but Violet was watching anxiously as the production team interviewed Lisa and filmed the cast eating her food.

"Is that Violet, the one you told me about?" Lauren asked as she followed Lisa's gaze.

Lisa nodded. "That's her. I suppose you'll head there next. You'll want to compare lobster quiches."

Lauren grinned. "We'll try them, and we'll film....but just between you and me, that film won't make its way onto the show. We can only fit in so much, you know. Showing the cast eating lobster quiche once will be more than enough."

Lisa laughed. "I love it. Thank you."

She felt lighter as she watched the group head over to Violet's booth.

CHAPTER FORTY-FOUR

"Lisa's quiche was much better, so creamy and with more lobster," Lauren's mother said.

Her father nodded in agreement. "This one reminds me of scrambled eggs. Is it supposed to be like that?"

Lauren smiled. "No. It's not. Quiche gets like that when it's overcooked." She'd tried a sample of Violet's quiche and agreed with her parents. It was skimpy on the lobster and slightly overcooked. She didn't think Lisa had anything to worry about. She noticed Hudson's mother and another woman coming their way.

Hudson gave them hugs and introduced his mother and her friend, Jackie, to Lauren's parents.

"Lauren told me that you live on the Cape? I get over there every so often to do a little shopping. I like to stock up at Trader Joe's," his mother said.

"We're so close, but we don't get to the islands as often as we'd like. It took Lauren working here to get us over. We need to come back soon," her mother said.

"You should come around the holidays. The Nantucket Stroll is the first weekend in December and that's a magical time of year. You need to book ahead though. Hotels fill up fast."

"It's the last big hurrah before almost everything closes for the winter," Hudson added.

"That sounds very Hallmark-like," Lauren said.

Hudson laughed. "It is. Though with fur coats everywhere."

His mother made a face. "There is a bit of that, yes. But it's still worth checking out."

They chatted for a few more minutes, and then Hudson noticed that the cast was moving on.

"Mom, we have to keep moving," he said.

"Okay, we're off to do more sampling, too." His mother and Jackie headed toward Lisa's booth.

"Lauren, I think we're going to go off and explore on our own. We'll catch up with you in a bit," her mother said. Lauren agreed to text them both when they were done filming and ready to head back to the inn.

They spent the next ninety minutes wandering around the food festival, sampling everything from lobster bisque and clam chowder to tuna tartare, fried scallops, braised short ribs and more. The sight of the cast and cameras drew curious crowds, which made it take longer, but added to the overall excitement. The cast had fun making their own videos too, as they tried different things.

Billy won the last video challenge with a very funny video of Noah cheating at horseshoes. Lauren was pleased to see that all the videos were doing well, and that there seemed to be a growing buzz on social media about the show.

When they were all ready to leave, Lauren texted her parents, and they drove back to the inn. As they drove, Lauren asked them what their favorite things were that they'd tried.

"Definitely the scallop and bacon mini tacos from Millie's," her mother said.

Her father thought for a minute. "It's a tossup between Lisa's lobster quiche and that chocolate bread pudding. I'm hoping we might see one of them at breakfast tomorrow."

Lauren laughed. "I wouldn't count on it. I'm not sure they will have any leftovers."

When they reached the inn, her parents headed inside and they planned to go to dinner later, when Lauren returned from filming.

She walked along the beach to the share house. Everyone was in the living room debating whether to head to the beach. The weather was a little iffy—the sun was behind the clouds and the air had cooled, but it was still plenty warm enough. No one was hungry after everything they'd eaten at the food festival, so there was no talk of what to do for dinner. Ten minutes later, the sun reappeared, and everyone except Sami decided to hit the beach. Lauren noticed that she was quieter than usual and asked Eloise if she knew why.

"Zach never came by last night. Every time the front door opened, she went to see who it was, and it was never him. Seems like that fling may have been short-lived."

"Oh, that's too bad."

"Wouldn't surprise me if she stays in her room tonight. I don't think she wants to deal with any questions."

Lauren nodded. "You never know. Maybe she'll hear from him."

"True." Eloise looked around the room. "I can't believe we only have a few more weeks of filming. The time is flying by."

"I know. Hopefully, we'll have everything we need by then."

"It will be fun putting it all together. That's my favorite part," Eloise said.

Lauren smiled. "Mine too. I wish we could do that part of the job from here. I'm not looking forward to going back to LA."

"I am. I love it here. But LA is home, you know?" Eloise said.

Lauren just nodded. She understood how Eloise felt, but she'd never felt that way about the West Coast and after spending time here and seeing her parents again, she was dreading leaving. But she didn't really have a choice.

Around five or so, people started to drift off the beach and up to the house to shower and get out of the sun. There was some talk of ordering Thai takeout. Lauren said goodbye to Hudson and Eloise and headed back to the inn to go to dinner.

Lauren had made reservations at Oran Mor, a bistro downtown that her parents had been to years ago and loved. It was a cozy place, and the menu looked amazing. Her father ordered a frozen painkiller cocktail that was similar to a pina colada and Lauren and her mother each went with a glass of chardonnay. They decided to share an appetizer of roasted oysters and a kale almond Caesar salad. Her father ordered a tenderloin and short rib combo that sounded intriguing. Lauren and her mother both chose the lobster pasta in a mushroom, corn and tarragon cream sauce. It was even more delicious than it sounded.

As they ate, Lauren's parents caught her up on any Cape Cod gossip they thought she'd be interested in. Some of the kids she'd gone to school with stayed on the Cape and were married now, with kids.

"I ran into Kirsty Smith at Stop and Shop last week. She has two kids now, and her youngest is walking. She asked about you and I told her you were on Nantucket. She's never been here. She even said she hadn't been over the bridge in three years. Can you imagine?" Her mother stabbed a piece of buttery lobster with her fork.

"I'm not that surprised. She was born on the Cape. I've heard from other friends that many of them rarely go off Cape. The thought of driving to Boston terrifies them. I do kind of understand that, though. Boston traffic is almost as bad as LA's."

Her mother nodded. "Your father makes me drive

now when we go to Boston. He says people in the city drive too aggressively. I don't mind it."

"They really do," her father agreed.

"Are you dating anyone new yet?" her mother asked. The sudden change of subject took Lauren by surprise.

"No. Not since Billy and I broke up. I wasn't ready and haven't really had the opportunity."

Her mother was quiet for a moment before adding, "I noticed that Hudson's mother knew you. It made me wonder if there was something there. He seems nice."

"He is. But no, we're just friends and work colleagues. I went to his house for dinner one night and his mother was there. She lives next door."

"Hmm. So he's not heading back to California, too?"

"No, he lives here. He is the co-owner of a production company. The other owner is Cami Carmichael, the actress. She lives here, too."

Her mother looked impressed. "I didn't know that she lived here. Good for him. I'm sure his mother loves having him nearby."

Lauren smiled. "I think she does."

It was great to catch up with her parents. Lauren was blissfully full and content as they drove back to the inn. It was almost nine by then and they were all yawning and ready for bed.

When they reached their rooms, Lauren hugged her parents goodnight.

"Thanks so much for dinner. It was so good. I'll see you both at breakfast."

Lauren met her parents in the dining room at nine. They were heading back to Hyannis on the eleven o'clock boat, and Lauren was going to drop them off at the wharf downtown. Lisa was still in the dining room, sitting at a big round table with an empty plate in front of her. She was sipping coffee and chatting with Rhett while he ate. Lauren's father was happy to see that Lisa had put out lobster quiche and he helped himself to a slice. Lauren and her mother did as well before joining Lisa and Rhett. Lauren's mother asked how the rest of the afternoon went at the food festival.

"Great. We were busy all afternoon. We ran out of the bread pudding, but I made a ton of the quiches to make sure we had plenty and there were a few leftover. I think it went well. I ran out of the printed material I'd brought. And we already got a bunch of online sales last night. I didn't think we'd see sales so quickly."

"That's wonderful. I'm not surprised, though," Lauren said.

"I'm not either. This stuff is fantastic," her father said as he polished off his last bite of quiche.

"I'm glad you like it. Please have more. There's plenty."

Her father didn't hesitate. "I think I will, thanks." He went to get another slice.

"Did they announce any winners yet?" Lauren asked.

Lisa shook her head. "They said they had to go through all the votes—the paper slips that people filled out. I think they were going to do it this morning and post the results online sometime today."

"I'll keep my fingers crossed," Lauren said.

"Do you get to rest today?" Lauren's mother asked Lisa.

She nodded. "Yes. I'm not doing a thing today once breakfast is put away. We're going to my daughter Abby's house for Sunday dinner and that's about it. I might walk on the beach when we come home."

"That sounds fun," Lauren said.

"Are you off to work?" Lisa asked.

Lauren took a bite of quiche before answering. She was eating slowly to savor every bite. "I am. Once I drop my parents off at the ferry, I'll be heading to the share house."

When they finished breakfast and said goodbye to Lisa and Rhett, Lauren drove her parents downtown to catch the ferry.

"It was so good to see you honey," her mother said after she'd hugged them both goodbye.

"You too. I'm still planning to come in two weeks for a few nights." Lauren had planned to take the ferry to the Cape on her off-nights when the show was almost done. It was coming up fast.

"Good, your room is ready for you."

CHAPTER FORTY-FIVE

"Rhett, I won!" Lisa said excitedly. It was almost five, and they'd just gotten home from Sunday dinner at her daughter Abby's house. It had been a nice treat to have someone else do all the cooking and to just sit back and enjoy. Lisa normally had everyone to her house on Sundays and she loved cooking, but Abby figured that she would appreciate a day off after all the cooking she'd done that week for the food festival. Lisa checked her computer several times before they headed off to Abby's and the results weren't up yet.

Rhett joined her in the kitchen, where Lisa was sitting at the island with her laptop open.

"What did you win?" he asked.

"I won twice, actually! In the bed-and-breakfast category, I won for best entrée and best dessert."

Rhett put his arms around her from behind, leaned in, and gave her a kiss.

"Congratulations! I had no doubt that you would win."

"Thanks, honey. I hoped I'd do well, but I really just wanted to beat Violet. I heard that her quiche wasn't very good, but you never know."

"Now everyone will know. You'll have to update your website."

"Oh, you're right. I'll talk to Marley, she can help me with that." Marley had set up Lisa's website and marketing strategies as she had a background in selling products online. She opened her Shopify site where she took orders for her products and her jaw dropped. "Rhett, look at this!" She showed him the orders that had come in that day, and there were three times the normal amount.

"That's fantastic. Violet actually did you a favor, it seems."

Lisa wasn't sure what he meant. "How so?"

"Well, if she hadn't bragged about how she was going to win at the food festival, you never would have entered."

Lisa laughed. "That's so true!"

CHAPTER FORTY-SIX

The next two weeks flew by and each day, Lauren grew more aware that her time on Nantucket was coming to an end. As she waited in line to get on the Hy-Line Fast Ferry to go spend her two nights off with her parents on the Cape, she began to feel slightly anxious about going back to California. She'd be busy when she got there as they still had several months' worth of work with post-production edits. They'd also be doing additional cast filming, but individually, as they provided their insights on various scenes and events. The cast wouldn't know how the season would unfold until they saw the final cuts, too. Lauren and Eloise and the other editors had weeks of film to go through and decide what would stay and what would be cut.

She'd grown close to Eloise and Hudson and a few of the castmates, Katy and Anna in particular. She was still rooting for Katy and Billy and was glad that Katy had heeded her advice to take things slow. She knew that

Anna and Jason had grown close as friends. She saw a hint of a possible romantic connection, but so far nothing had developed. Suzanne and Noah were going strong, though they were also taking things slow. Suzanne some-times spent the night in Noah's room, but they mostly watched TV and kissed a lot. They were surprised, actu-ally, because Suzanne struck them all as being more aggressive and eager to have a fling.

Sami was the one that had surprised them the most. She'd initially come across as such a cool girl, very reserved and confident. And she'd fallen fast after her first one-night stand with Zach. He'd told her before they hooked up that he wasn't looking for a relationship and she'd assured him that she wasn't either. They'd hung out quite a bit over the past few weeks, but it was often late-night meetups and always last minute, nothing planned ahead. Lauren hadn't seen him around for a few days and Sami seemed quieter than usual, so she wondered if he'd ended things or worse, ghosted her. She'd mentioned to Anna at breakfast yesterday that Zach hadn't responded to her last text.

Lauren was going to miss Hudson the most. She'd see Eloise and all the cast in LA when they came in for their follow-up filming. But Hudson's work was done. And unless the show got picked up for a new season, she didn't know when she'd see him again. He'd made it clear that he had no intention of going to the West Coast anytime soon. And she doubted that had changed. She couldn't help but wonder if they might have had a chance if he was still in LA. She knew she would enjoy living there much more if Hudson were around.

The ride to Hyannis was smooth and relaxing. Lauren chose a seat inside by a window. She as watched the waves on the ocean and Nantucket Harbor grew smaller and smaller as they got further out to see. She read a magazine for a while and got a cup of tea and a donut. Before she knew it, they reached Hyannis and as she walked off the boat, she saw her mother waving. She was looking forward to a few days of relaxing at her childhood home, sleeping in her old bed, and visiting with her parents. Her mother had plans for them to head over to Baxter's Fish and Chips for lunch. It was right on the harbor and they both loved to sit outside and watch the boat traffic go by. Her mother had also mentioned something about taking a drive to Chatham to check out a shoe store she'd fallen in love with. Lauren smiled and waved as she walked off the boat.

CHAPTER FORTY-SEVEN

"I'm so glad you and Jason are finally going on a date," Katy said. She and Anna were lounging in their bedroom on Monday afternoon. Anna was sprawled across her bed, with Smith curled up at her feet. They'd come in from the beach a half hour earlier and Anna had jumped in the shower. Now she was in her robe with her hair still wet. She was letting it air dry and was feeling lazy. It was early, just a little before four, and they weren't going out until six.

"Where are you going? Is he taking you somewhere fancy?" Katy asked. She was still on cloud nine after Billy had taken her for a special wine dinner at The Whitley Hotel the night before. The Whitley was the most luxurious waterfront hotel—very exclusive, and the film crew had gone along. Katy hadn't minded, as all of her attention had been on Billy. And she'd said he'd been extra charming, and the food was good too. That sounded fun, but it wasn't what Anna wanted to do.

Jason had come up to her that morning, while she was sitting by herself on the deck, having her first cup of coffee. It was early and everyone else was still sleeping. They'd chatted about nothing in particular, like they usually did—just enjoying each other's company and gazing at the mostly empty beach.

"Let's go on a real date. Tonight. I know you're not eager to film that, but it could be just you and me. Then if we want, we can have a redo with the cameras. But I want our first time out to be special. What do you think?" He sounded a little nervous, and Anna smiled. She didn't need to think about it.

"I'd love that."

He grinned and looked relieved. "Great, where should we go? What's the best restaurant on Nantucket?"

Anna laughed. "I don't know. But you know where I'd love to go?"

"Where?"

"There's a small takeout place down by the Wharf, Oath Pizza, that has custom slices and supposedly really good gluten-free ones, too. I'd love to do that and just walk around. Maybe get some ice cream after and sit by the water."

"Well, that sounds good to me. As long as you're sure you don't want to be wined and dined?"

Anna smiled. "I'm sure."

"Okay, then." They made plans to go at six and Anna was nervously looking forward to it. She realized Katy was still waiting for an answer and she told her about their plans. Katy looked disappointed.

"Takeout pizza? I thought Jason could do better than that."

"It was my choice. I love the idea of a simple date, just walking around and playing tourist, having ice cream on the wharf and talking."

"Okay, have you decided what you're going to wear?"

Anna yawned, feeling sleepy from the sun. She reached over and took a sip of water that she'd mixed with an orange-flavored Vitamin C powder, hoping it would give her some energy.

"Not yet. Maybe you can help me decide."

Katy jumped up and opened their closet and started pulling out a few tops, along with Anna's favorite jeans. They decided on a baby blue dressy t-shirt with the jeans and brown leather sandals. When Anna's hair was almost dry, she finished it with the blow dryer until it was straight and shiny. At ten of six, she walked downstairs and Jason was in the kitchen, waiting for her. He turned and smiled when he saw her.

"You look gorgeous." His eyes were warm and affectionate.

Anna met his gaze and smiled back. "Thank you. You look great, too."

Jason was wearing a navy button-down shirt and jeans. The dark blue made him look even more tan and made his green eyes pop.

Jason drove, and they lucked into a parking spot by the wharf as someone was leaving. It was a warm night but there was a breeze by the water and Anna was glad she'd brought a lightweight sweater with her. She didn't

need it yet, but it was in her tote bag, just in case. They
walked along the wharf and over to the pizza place,
which had a long line, but it seemed to be moving quickly.
It didn't take long to order and receive their slices, and
they brought them to a wooden bench that overlooked the
harbor.

Anna was so comfortable with Jason now. They
chatted easily about just about anything. She was so
impressed with who he was as a person and realized she'd
unfairly judged him when they first met. She had never
dated a jock before and had assumed that they wouldn't
have much in common. But she learned that Jason had
been a business major in college and had always been
entrepreneurial. He'd sold funny t-shirts in college and
later grew that business online and expanded to other
products. He was also active in the community and volun-
teered with the local Big Brother organization. That was
something they had in common, as Anna did some volun-
teer work with a food pantry, especially around the holidays when they'd put together food baskets.

"I didn't expect that I'd meet anyone I would really
care about on this show," Jason said. They'd finished
eating and were just watching the boats go by on the
water.

"I didn't either," Anna admitted. "I thought it might
be a fun way to spend a few weeks on Nantucket. But it's
been so much more than that."

"I want to see you when we're back home. Brooklyn's
not that far from the West Village."

Anna laughed. "No, it's not. I'd like that." She felt a

warm glow as she realized she was looking forward to seeing Jason once they left Nantucket.

"So, what do you want to do now? We could walk around a little or see a movie, maybe? Or get a drink? I'm not ready yet for ice cream, are you?"

"Not yet. But definitely later. Let's walk around and maybe see what's playing at the movie theater."

They made their way down the cobblestone streets, popping into stores that intrigued them. Anna was tempted to buy a painting when they stopped at an art gallery. There were some beautiful watercolors of Nantucket harbor and the flowers—the pink roses and blue hydrangeas that were all over the island.

"That one would look so pretty in my living room." She pointed out a painting of a cottage that overlooked the ocean and that had flowers covering a white picket fence. It looked magical and so cozy.

Jason nodded. "That's nice. You should get it."

"It might be difficult to get it home," she said.

"They can probably ship it for you. I'm sure they deliver stuff all the time off-island," Jason said. A clerk standing nearby chimed in, "We can ship anywhere."

Anna wasn't ready to commit, though. "Thanks. I'll think about it."

They continued walking around until they reached the small movie theater, Dreamland Film, that had two movies playing at seven. It was five of, so their timing was perfect. And the smell of the popcorn was intoxicating, even though she'd just had a slice of pizza. They decided on a movie, got a box of buttered popcorn to share and a couple of waters, and settled in to watch the film.

It was a suspenseful drama and Anna quickly lost herself in the story and even jumped twice at unexpected, loud moments.

Jason put his arm around her and gave her shoulder a reassuring squeeze. She leaned against him and sighed. She felt so content and happy. She didn't want their time together to end.

When the movie was over, they were ready for ice cream and walked back down to the wharf, stood in line and then walked around licking their cones and looking at the boats.

"I wonder what it's like to live here year-round? It's such a cool place," Jason said.

"I love it here, but I don't think I'd want to live here all the time. It gets very quiet here in the winter, but it's not just that. We are so spoiled in the city, everything we could want is right there. Can you imagine wanting to get off-island for some reason and being stuck because the boats aren't running or the planes aren't flying? I'm sure it doesn't happen often, but I don't think I could do it," Anna said.

"Yeah, that's true. We have everything we need in the city. I don't see myself ever moving." He grinned. "But I do see myself coming back to Nantucket, at least for a few weeks in the summer."

"I'd love to do that, too."

They walked around a bit longer and then made their

way back to their Jeep. Jason opened Anna's door and then hesitated.

"I've been wanting to do this since the day we met," Jason said softly. He put his arms around Anna and pulled her in gently. She leaned toward him, anticipating the moment when his lips touched hers, softly at first, then with a bit more passion. She wrapped her arms around his neck and pulled him in closer and he kissed her again, even more thoroughly. When he stopped, they were both breathless.

"So, should we give them the green light to film our first date?" Jason teased.

Anna knew he was serious, though. "Yes, I think we should. I want to."

"Good. I'll let the producers know. So, where should we go tomorrow night?"

Anna laughed. "Anywhere is fine by me."

CHAPTER FORTY-EIGHT

Lauren had a great visit with her parents. They went to dinner Tuesday night at her favorite neighborhood restaurant, The Yarmouth House, and she had the lobster Thermidor, which was insanely delicious. She'd worked as a server there during school breaks while she was in college, and it was fun to see some of the people she'd worked with. And the food was always so good. She took the ferry back to Nantucket Wednesday morning and was well rested and ready to dive into work.

She'd gotten an email from Jason that he and Anna were now officially dating and open to filming a date night. She was thrilled to hear it—it would be great content for the show but mostly because she'd been rooting for their friendship to turn into a romance. She thought the details of their actual date were really sweet, but that it might be difficult to recreate with all the crowds downtown. She'd called Hudson on the ferry ride over and he agreed that for filming purposes, it might be better to have them go to an actual restaurant where they could chat over a nice dinner and they could go extra early before the restaurant got too busy.

They arranged to have their first date at Ships Inn, which was a historic bed-and-breakfast with an incredible small restaurant. The building itself was a whaling captain's home and dated back to 1831. It was the perfect spot, with white linens, and they arranged to have dinner an hour before the restaurant officially opened, so that they wouldn't disturb other patrons and so there would be room for the production team and equipment.

Jason and Anna were nervous at first and self-conscious with the cameras, but once they put their orders in, they relaxed and had a wonderful 'first date' conversation. Lauren knew that the viewers were going to love how their date turned out—and if the show was renewed, she suspected the two might still be together and that would add a fun dynamic to the second season, if they both agreed to return.

On Friday night they had their last party at the share house and they pulled out all the stops, with another popular local band and caterers that were grilling up an elevated surf and turf—steak tips, pesto shrimp and marinated lemon swordfish.

They had another group restaurant dinner planned for the following night, Saturday, their last night at the share house. Lauren was planning to fly back the following Tuesday and was going to enjoy two final days off before then.

The party on Friday night was fun but bittersweet. Lauren was acutely aware that time was speeding up, and she'd be back in LA in a week. She tried not to think of that, though, and to just enjoy the moment as much as possible.

This time when she and Eloise invited all the neighbors, almost all of them agreed to come—some were curious and others were just glad that it was going to be the last event. Although most were friendly and appreciated that they were given notice when the noise levels might be higher than normal. The cast had been pretty good about not getting too out-of-hand. It was the first show that Lauren had worked on where the police hadn't been called at least once for complaints during parties.

Lisa and Rhett came as well as Kay and Walter and got there early enough to get the table they liked at the back of the deck. Lauren, Eloise, and Hudson sat and ate with them before the rest of the crowd arrived and they had to work.

"We'll actually be sorry to see you go," Kay said. "Walter and I have gotten such a kick out of watching all the activity. It will be quiet when you leave."

"We'll have to go back to just watching the beach, which isn't such a bad thing," Walter said.

"What do you have planned for tomorrow night?" Lisa asked.

"It's our final group dinner. We're going to Galley Beach. I thought that might be a good spot to film as we can sit outside and there's plenty of room on the beach for the production team."

Rhett nodded. "That's a great spot. Will give a good Nantucket feel being right on the beach."

"Walter took me there a few weeks ago. The actual tables and chairs are literally on the beach. I thought it was just the restaurant overlooking it. It was fun to take my shoes off and stick them in the sand."

Walter nodded. "It's a crowded place, though. I assume they know you're coming?"

"Yes. We're going a bit early before it gets too crowded and they've reserved two tables for us. One for the cast and one for the production team."

"I've actually never been there," Hudson said. "So, I'm looking forward to it."

Lauren smiled as she looked around the table. She grabbed her cell phone and waved Anna over to take a picture of their table. She took a few shots, and Lauren showed them to everyone at the table.

"I'll email copies to you all," she promised. It was a great picture, with the rosy sunset in the background and their little group all with their Nantucket t-shirts or sweat-shirts. That was the only theme for their final night—everyone had to wear something that said Nantucket on it. They thought that visual would look great on film. There were a lot of Nantucket Red sweatshirts and t-shirts but also lots of pale blue, navy, red and even white.

Once they finished eating, Hudson left to man his camera. Lauren and Eloise poured themselves a glass of white wine sangria and slowly roamed the party, which was inside as well as outside and had also expanded onto the beach.

The band started playing once everyone was just about done eating. The music was lively and loud, but not too bad, and it didn't take long before people were up and dancing.

The whole cast was dancing and laughing, and everyone seemed to be having a great time. Lauren noticed that Jason and Anna were the first ones up dancing and the others followed. She was a little surprised to see Sami dancing with Billy. But Katy was inside talking with Honey and Brett in the kitchen.

When the music slowed, Katy stepped outside and found Billy leaning against the deck railing, chatting with Sami, Suzanne and Noah. She pulled him onto the dance floor and wrapped her arms around her neck. He looked down at Katy with the charming smile that Lauren knew so well. It looked like things were still going well for them, and she was hopeful, for Katy's sake, that it would continue.

Lisa and the others left an hour or so after dinner. Lauren promised she'd fill Lisa in over breakfast if anything interesting happened after she left.

The band stopped playing around eleven and most of the visitors left. A few of the cast members, Honey, Brett and Katy, headed to bed.

"I hate to head up so early, but the combination of the sun this afternoon and an extra glass of wine tonight and I'm so ready to go to sleep," Katy said. She and Anna and most of the cast had spent the day on the beach, but most of them were in and out all day. Katy had fallen asleep for several hours in the hot sun. She'd had plenty of sunscreen on so she wasn't burned, but Lauren understood why she was so tired. The sun could be draining.

By midnight, the only ones still up were Suzanne and Noah, Anna and Jason and Sami and Billy. When Anna headed to bed and a few minutes later, the others started moving towards the stairs, Lauren ended filming for the night.

"I'll walk you back," Hudson said.

They headed to the beach and walked in almost complete darkness to the inn. The moon was just a tiny sliver in the sky.

When they reached the steps to the inn, Hudson asked what her plans were for her final days off.

"Angela is having me over for a goodbye dinner on Sunday. But I'm totally free on Monday."

"Let's do something. Maybe Millie's?" That had been the first place she'd gone to with Hudson, so it seemed fitting that it would be her last dinner as well.

"Sure, that sounds perfect."

Hudson held her gaze for a moment and looked like he wanted to say something, but hesitated.

"What is it?"

He stepped toward her, close enough that she could smell a hint of his cologne, and she leaned in. He put his arms around her and she immediately felt goose-bumps and a shift as the energy around them grew charged.

"I just wanted to say that the show will be over by then. So, if you wanted, we could consider it a date?"

She smiled. "I would love that. But I'm leaving on Tuesday."

"I know, but there are things called phones and planes...we can keep in touch and even find ways to see each other. If you want?"

Lauren nodded and found her gaze drawn to his lips. She held her breath for a moment in anticipation as he lowered them towards hers and kissed her. It was a brief kiss, but it changed everything between them.

"See you tomorrow," he said as he turned to leave. She watched him head back to the beach and then went inside, feeling a sense of excitement that she hadn't felt since she first dated Billy. She didn't know how they'd make it work as they couldn't be further apart location wise. But she was thrilled that he wanted to try.

Katy was sound asleep when Anna went to her bedroom. She walked quietly so she wouldn't wake her, and changed into her pajamas in the bathroom. She was about to slip into bed when she remembered she'd left her big glass of water on the kitchen counter. She always slept with water by her side in case she woke up thirsty. She tiptoed toward the door, opened it slowly and stepped into the hallway, then stopped in her tracks as she watched a giggling Sami and Billy stumble into his bedroom.

Her heart sank on Katy's behalf. She would be devastated if she knew that Sami and Billy had hooked up. There was a slight chance that what she just saw was innocent, but it didn't look good. Anna continued on to the kitchen, got her water, and went to bed. She dreaded telling Katy what she'd seen and decided to chat with Lauren and Eloise first, as she knew they'd review the overnight film in the morning and they would know how long Sami stayed in Billy's room and what actually happened.

CHAPTER FORTY-NINE

Anna slept later than usual and when she finally made it downstairs, she was one of the last ones up. Most of the cast, including Billy and Katy, were sitting on the back deck drinking coffee. Eloise and Lauren were in the kitchen, sitting at the table with their laptops open. Anna took Smith for a quick walk, then fed him. She poured herself a cup of black coffee and spread peanut butter onto a toasted cinnamon raisin bagel. Instead of joining the others on the deck, she sat with Eloise and Lauren. They chatted a bit about how much fun the party was the night before and Anna put off her question until she was almost done eating her bagel.

"Did either of you have a chance to go through all the footage from last night yet?"

"We're looking at it now. We're just about at the end of the night, before everyone went to bed. Is there a reason you're asking?" Lauren looked curious.

"Yeah, there is. I wanted to have all the information

before I talk to Katy." She filled them in on what she'd seen.

Lauren and Eloise exchanged glances and Lauren shook her head and looked disappointed. "Let's find out," she said.

Anna slid her chair closer to Lauren so she could see as well. Lauren scrolled through the footage until they saw Billy and Sami head into his room. She switched to Billy's static camera, and they only needed to watch for a few minutes before it was clear what was happening. Sami pulled Billy in for a kiss and he resisted for a moment and then gave into it and kissed her back. Their clothes came off almost instantly, and wearing only their underwear, they climbed into bed and pulled the covers over them. Lauren fast-forwarded to less than an hour later, when Sami slid off the bed with a blanket wrapped around her, gathered her clothes and went into the bathroom. She emerged a few minutes later, fully dressed, and left Billy's room.

Anna sighed heavily. "Well, I'd hoped that it might be nothing, like maybe she stopped in his room for a quick minute for some reason and then went on her way. But this is bad. I have to tell her."

Lauren nodded. "Yeah, it's awful. She needs to know."

"I wonder how he'll defend this," Eloise asked.

"I have a pretty good guess. He'll say it didn't mean anything, that it was just sex and that he really cares about Katy. I hope she knows it will happen again? I think it's just who he is. He's not mature enough to resist," Lauren said.

Anna noticed a slight edge of bitterness in Lauren's voice. She sensed that it had been hard for Lauren to get over Billy, and this was a reminder of what she'd had to deal with. The only good thing was that even though Katy was emotionally attached, she hadn't gotten physical yet with Billy. Anna knew it would be that much harder if things had gotten more serious with them. But still, she knew this was going to be hard for her.

"When will you tell her?" Lauren asked.

Anna was trying to decide. Part of her wanted to pull Katy aside now and tell her, but she knew if she did that, it would ruin her last day at the house. They were planning on relaxing at the beach all day and then heading to dinner as a group later.

"I think I'll tell her later when we're getting ready for dinner. That way, she'll have one last fun day at the beach before Billy totally ruins it."

"That's a good idea. And it will be interesting to see what the dynamic is like today between Billy and Sami," Eloise said.

Anna wondered about that too.

Sami didn't come down to the beach until after lunch. She brought a tuna sandwich and a bag of chips with her and a tall thermos of water mixed with electrolytes. She had bags under her eyes and looked as though she felt miserable. Anna wasn't sure if that was just because she was hungover or if she felt bad about hooking up with Billy. She was quieter than usual and kept her distance from Billy, and also from Katy and Anna. She plopped her beach chair next to Honey and Brett and nodded now and then as Honey chatted on about her plans for some new project when she and Brett got home.

Katy, meanwhile, was well rested and in a great mood. She was looking forward to their dinner that evening.

"I looked them up on TripAdvisor and I know what I'm having." Katy was such a foodie and Anna found it amusing how excited she got whenever they went to a new restaurant.

"What are you having?" she asked.

"Miso butter-poached lobster and I want to get an order of lobster deviled eggs for the table and a lobster spring roll to start."

Anna laughed. "I didn't realize you were that into lobster."

"Well, I figure I might as well have my fill of it. We have it in New York, but not like this."

"You have a good point." Lobster was plentiful and delicious on Nantucket. Maybe she would order the same.

As the day went on, Anna noticed that Billy seemed no different in the way he joked with Katy and with Sami, too. He wasn't ignoring her and was just acting as though nothing had happened. Anna was fascinated and disturbed at the same time. If she hadn't happened to see Sami go into Billy's room, she never would have known. She knew that production would have seen it when they reviewed the film, but she didn't know how they would have handled it if Anna hadn't seen it, too. Would they have told Katy or let it play out and see what happened? Anna was glad she'd seen it and that she could tell Katy and let her decide how she wanted to deal with it.

———

They left the beach a little after four and, as usual, Anna took the first shower. Katy preferred to wait and lounge on her bed watching TV. It wasn't until they were both almost totally ready, and Katy was just putting the final touches on her makeup when Anna took a deep breath and told her what she'd seen and then what was on the film from Billy's room. Katy's hand shook as she finished applying her eye liner then turned to face Anna.

"You really saw her go into his room? And there's no doubt about what happened?" She bit her lower lip and her eyes looked watery and Anna felt like crying, too. She stood up and pulled Katy in for a hug.

"Yes, and I'm sorry. He's a jerk."

Katy pulled out of the hug and assessed her makeup and then half-laughed and half-cried. Her mascara had totally smudged and looked a mess. She grabbed a tissue and tried to clean it up and then reapplied concealer and more mascara. She took a deep breath.

"I'm furious and totally devastated. I really thought it was going well with Billy."

"It seemed like it was. Lauren put it best. It's just who he is. The scary thing is if I hadn't seen him, you wouldn't have known. I'm just glad you didn't get too serious with him."

Katy nodded. "I'm so glad. And it was hard. I've been so tempted. I thought it would happen as soon as filming ended. I was looking forward to it."

"Will you confront him?" Anna was curious about how Katy would handle the news. So far, while she was clearly upset, she wasn't as devastated as Anna had feared that she would be. At least she didn't seem to be.

"I'll definitely say something. But I'm not sure when. I'm too upset to say anything right now."

"Yeah, wait until the time seems right," Anna said.

CHAPTER FIFTY

Lauren, Eloise, and the rest of the production team arrived at the Galley Beach restaurant twenty minutes before the rest of the cast was due to arrive. Lauren was stunned by how beautiful the setting was. The restaurant was set on the beach and had seating inside overlooking the ocean and also had many tables outside, directly on the beach. The restaurant manager showed them to the two tables that were reserved for their group. There were no tables in front of them and they had a breathtaking view of the ocean. The sand was white and soft, and Lauren was tempted to take off her shoes.

She'd filled Hudson in earlier on what they'd seen in the overnight film.

He shook his head in disgust and when they arrived at the restaurant asked if Katy had said anything to Billy yet.

"Anna waited until just before they left. So, I don't know when she plans to say something.

"Okay, we'll be ready."

Lauren and Eloise had strategized earlier about seat placement for the dinner and put place cards at each seat. Once that was done, they took their seats, while Hudson, Mike, and Tom set up their cameras around the big table where the cast would be sitting. They chose the seats at the end, close enough to the main table that they'd be able to overhear most of the conversation. Lauren slipped her sandals off to dip her feet in the soft sand. It had been years since she'd spent so much time on the beach, and it was another thing she was going to miss when she was back in LA.

The cast filed in and Lauren watched as they looked for their place cards. They'd put Anna and Katy next to each other in the middle of the table, with Billy and Sami directly across from them. Lauren noticed that Sami's face whitened when she realized that she'd been placed next to Billy and across from Anna and Katy. She glanced toward Lauren and Eloise, and Lauren smiled ever so slightly. Sami knew that they knew what had happened. What she didn't know was if Katy was aware of it yet. Billy was completely oblivious. He didn't seem concerned, though it should have crossed his mind that production would have viewed the film from his room. He was being his usual charming self, joking and laughing with everyone around him.

Once everyone was seated, their servers came around and took drink orders for both tables. Lauren and Eloise both ordered chardonnay and when their servers returned with their cocktails, they put their food orders in.

Lauren and Eloise both went with the miso buttered lobster.

The dinner was relatively uneventful until they were on dessert. The chocolate mousse that was served to everyone in their party was light and decadent at the same time. Lauren had just taken her first bite when she heard Katy's voice.

"I thought it might be fun to go around the table and have everyone mention their favorite thing about this experience and something that surprised them."

Anna spoke first. "That's a great idea. My favorite thing is also what surprised me the most. I didn't expect that I would meet someone special here, but then I met Jason."

He leaned over and gave her a kiss. "Can I just say ditto?"

Everyone laughed, and they continued around the table. When they got to Sami, she looked slightly uncomfortable. "I guess my favorite thing about Nantucket is the beach, and a nice surprise has been making new friends here." She smiled all around the table and lingered on Billy for a moment before diving into her dessert. No one else at the table probably noticed it—except for Katy and Anna and, of course, Lauren, Eloise and Hudson.

Billy went next and before he spoke, he flashed that slow smile that used to melt Lauren's heart. She was immune to its effect now, though. "My favorite thing has been meeting Katy. And my biggest surprise is that I finally feel like I might be ready to settle down."

Lauren almost spit out her chocolate mousse. She

realized what Billy was doing. He'd figured out that they were onto him and he was setting the stage to do damage control with Katy. But she didn't think there was any coming back from this with Katy. At least she hoped she was smarter than that.

They continued around the table until it was Katy's turn. She took her last bite of chocolate mousse, picked up her napkin to dab at the sides of her mouth, and then she looked directly at Billy and spoke calmly. "My favorite thing was meeting you. I thought this was the beginning of something really special and I was eager to continue dating when the show wrapped. What surprised me the most?" She glanced Sami's way and narrowed her eyes, and then glared at Billy. "When I found out that Sami slept in your room last night—and I know you did more than sleep. I really liked you, Billy. How could you do that?" Her voice broke, and she reached for her glass of water and looked away.

Sami looked horrified, and Billy froze, unsure of what to say to fix the situation. Sami spoke first. "Katy, I'm so sorry. It didn't mean anything. We both just had a little too much to drink, and it just happened. It won't ever happen again, I promise."

Katy sent her a withering look. "At this point, I don't care if it does. Maybe you two should be together." She stood and grabbed her purse. "All I know is that I am ready to go home and I couldn't be happier that this is our last night." She started to walk off, and Billy got up and went after her. "Katy wait." She stopped and faced him. He tried flashing her the smile that had always gotten him out of trouble before, but she just shook her head and started to turn away. He reached out and took her hand. "Katy, please. It really didn't mean anything. You have to believe me. I mean, it's not like you and I were exclusive. Sami and I just hooked up. It happens. But, if you want, we can be exclusive. I really do want to make it work with you. Give me another chance, please?"

She hesitated for a moment and both tables were silent, waiting for her to respond. Lauren worried that she might agree to give Billy a second chance. That she might be convinced by his reasoning that they weren't exclusively dating yet.

But Katy pulled her hand from his and shook her head. She looked at him sadly. "I think this is just who you are, Billy. And this isn't what I want. I deserve better."

She walked away and Lauren was relieved. Katy definitely deserved better than what Billy was able to give her.

\#

"I'm not going to let this ruin my last night here," Katy sniffed. Anna had just handed her a glass of pinot grigio and they were on the back deck of the share house, looking out at the ocean. Everyone was back from dinner and it was just starting to get dark. "I mean, of course, it totally ruined my night, but I'm not going to go hide in my room. I'm going to stay up for a bit and visit with everyone—except Billy and Sami, and then I'll go to bed, get a good night's sleep and I am very much looking forward to going home and sleeping in my own apartment tomorrow."

"I'm looking forward to going home, too. We'll have dinner during the week if you're up for it?" Anna suggested.

"I'd love that. I'm ready for things to get back to normal. I'll get over Billy. It just hurts—I really thought it could work. I guess that was stupid, though, given his history."

Anna sipped her wine. "It's not stupid. I think we always want to see the good in people, to hope that they'd behave the way we'd expect. He's charming. I get why you fell for him."

Billy tried to talk to Katy again later that night, but she brushed him off. Anna heard her say, "Billy, I meant it. Go talk to Sami." She walked over to her.

"Are you okay?"

Katy smiled. "I'm fine. Or rather I will be fine. I just don't want to talk to Billy. There's no point to it, and it's too hard right now." She yawned and glanced at her watch.

"It's almost ten. I think I'm going to call it a night."

"Okay, I'll be up soon, too."

CHAPTER FIFTY-ONE

Lauren skipped breakfast at the inn and headed to the share house early the next morning. Most of the cast were leaving early to catch flights home, and they wanted to be there to film everyone leaving.

It was about seven thirty when she walked into the house. She helped herself to coffee and a bagel with cream cheese and settled at the table with her laptop. Eloise rushed in a moment later, followed by Hudson, Mike, and Tom with their cameras.

Most of the cast was up and getting ready to go. Simon and Smith seemed to sense that something was up. They were both sniffing the suitcases that waited by the door. Simon jumped up onto the island, tail twitching, and Honey rushed over and scooped him up and apologized.

"He saw me get his cat carrier out earlier, so he knows what's going on."

Everyone seemed half-awake as they made their way

into the kitchen and helped themselves to breakfast and coffee. Lauren noticed that Suzanne and Noah still seemed to be going strong. She overheard them making plans to see each other the following weekend. And Anna had told her that she and Jason were planning to get together soon, too.

Sami was quiet as she gathered her things together. She took her coffee and bagel outside and Billy followed her. Hudson was already out there and Eloise and Lauren followed and stood by the railing so they could overhear the conversation.

"Are you doing okay?" Billy asked her.

Sami nodded. "I'm fine. I just feel bad. We shouldn't have hooked up. It was stupid."

Billy shrugged. "It probably wasn't a good idea. But it seemed like it at the time. What are you going to do?" It sounded like he'd already moved on.

Sami shook her head. "I'm going to try to make better choices. You might want to do the same. Goodbye, Billy."

"Are you leaving already?"

"I just wanted one last look at the ocean before I head out. My flight's in an hour." She took the last bite of her bagel and headed back inside.

Billy looked up and saw Lauren and realized she'd overheard the conversation. He smiled his charming grin and stepped towards her, but Lauren didn't feel like talking to him.

"I need to get back in," she announced.

They all headed inside and left Billy on the deck.

Over the next hour, everyone finished packing up

and left for the airport. When the last of the cast members was gone, they wrapped for the day and Lauren said her goodbyes to Eloise and the rest of the production team.

"We're still on for Millie's tomorrow?" Hudson asked as they all walked out together.

"Yes, looking forward to it."

He grinned. "Great, I'll swing by and pick you up at six."

"So, I have some good news to share." Kate looked around the room and waited until she had everyone's attention. They were gathered at Angela's house on Sunday night for an impromptu appetizer party to say goodbye to Lauren. It was a small group, with Kate and Kristen, as well as Victoria, Lauren, and Angela.

"We signed the contract today for a new film deal with Cami Carmichael's production company. She's going to star and it will be filmed here on Nantucket! How amazing is that?"

"That's so awesome," Angela said. Everyone else offered their congratulations.

"Is it okay for me to announce it in the paper?" Victoria asked. As a reporter at the main newspaper on Nantucket, she loved covering any entertainment-related stories.

Kate happily agreed. "Of course. I'll shoot you an

email with more details and I'd love to see it in the paper. My mother will probably cut it out and frame it."

Kristen laughed. "She will! Or maybe I'll do it for both of you."

They had a fun night, with too much delicious food, as usual. Lauren really liked Angela's friends. It felt like she'd known them longer than just a few months. She was so happy for Angela, too. She remembered how hard her life had been in San Francisco, and how alone she was, before she inherited her grandmother's cottage on Nantucket and met Philippe and the Hodges family.

"How are you feeling, Angela?" Lauren asked. Angela looked fantastic—her skin was glowing and her hair was shiny.

Angela grinned and reached for a homemade chocolate chip cookie. "I'm feeling great. The morning sickness is pretty much gone now and my hair has never been this healthy. I think it might be the prenatal vitamins or pregnancy hormones, I'm not sure."

"Have you had any cravings yet?" Kate asked.

Angela laughed. "Yes. Ice cream still. I have to have it every night. But I've switched to making it with frozen bananas most of the time. It's healthier and still pretty good. I've also been craving Kalamata olives, in just about everything. Maybe it's the salt?"

Kate laughed. "I craved salty things too. I was big on pickles and chocolate sundaes. Sometimes one right after the other."

Lauren was so glad that Angela was feeling better. Something soft brushed against her leg and she saw that it was Sam, Angela's elderly orange cat. She'd had Sam for as long as Lauren could remember. She reached down and petted him and he began to purr loudly, then hopped into her lap and settled down.

Lauren didn't mind. She missed having a cat. She'd thought about getting one over the past few years, but her schedule was unpredictable—sometimes she'd work twelve-hour days or longer if they were on a shoot and it ran late. And she often traveled and was on location for months at a time. So the timing wasn't right, yet. But she hoped it would be at some point. For now, she enjoyed having Sam on her lap.

"I wish you were staying longer. It's been so nice having you here this summer," Angela said.

"I know. I hate to leave. I'm really not looking forward to going back to LA," Lauren admitted.

"Do you think there's a good chance you might be back to film again next summer?" Kristen asked.

Lauren nodded. "It's possible. It really depends how the show is received. We won't know that until after it airs, probably about six months or so from now."

"I'd love to interview some of the cast, and maybe do a feature article when the show releases, if you think that's possible?" Victoria asked.

Lauren thought that was a great idea. "Sure. I'll email you and maybe you can do a few Zoom calls with a few of the cast members."

"What's next when you go home?" Kate asked.

Lauren explained about the post-production editing that would happen over the next few months. "I'm not sure after that. I'd love to find a new project and I'm hoping that we get picked up so I get to come back here for season two."

"How did it turn out? Did any romance or interesting drama happen?" Angela asked.

Lauren nodded. "Yes, more romance than we expected and a bit of drama, especially near the end. I hope viewers will like it. We still have a lot of work to do to turn all the film into a season's worth of story."

"I can't wait to watch it," Kristen said. "I love those reality shows. It's fun to be a fly on the wall in other people's drama—and it helps me to appreciate my relatively boring but happily normal life."

Lauren grinned. "That's how it is for me too, and what attracted me to working in production on my first reality show. It's a lot of fun."

"It sounds fun. Do you ever think you might want to work on other kinds of things too, like scripted movies or TV shows?" Kate asked.

"I'd love to at some point. My agent knows I'm open to anything and is keeping an eye out for my next project once we finish this. There's a few things that she is waiting to hear back on."

They chatted for a few more hours until Angela started to yawn and Lauren realized it was almost nine. Kate and Kristen both stood at the same time.

"I should probably head home. It's getting late," Kate said. Everyone walked out at the same time, and Lauren was the last to say goodbye. She gave Angela a big hug.

"I didn't want to ask in front of the others, but how

did you leave things with Hudson? Did anything develop there?"

Lauren filled her in. "I'm seeing him tomorrow night. It's our first official date. I'm not sure what will happen after that, though."

"Just take it one day at a time. And call me immediately with a full report."

Lauren laughed. "I will. I'll talk to you soon. Feel free to call me anytime, too."

"I will. And I'm keeping my fingers crossed that your show is a hit and you'll be back next summer. I'll have the baby by then, which is hard to imagine." She looked happy and excited. Lauren was thrilled for her, too.

"I can't wait to meet her or him."

"Safe travels, Lauren. Love you!"

"Love you too." Angela gave her another hug and then she was on her way.

CHAPTER FIFTY-TWO

Lauren walked onto the front lawn at the inn a few minutes before six, just as Hudson pulled into the driveway in a red Jeep. She climbed into the passenger side and they drove off.

"This is the first time I've seen you drive anything other than your work van," she said. When she'd visited him, he'd only had the one vehicle, the van in his driveway.

He smiled. "The Jeep was in the shop when you came for dinner that night. The van is just for work. The Jeep is for fun. It's great for four wheeling on the beach."

Lauren had noticed that there were a lot of Jeeps on the island and other four-wheel-drive vehicles. There were also plenty of Range Rovers, BMWs and Mercedes —an unusually high number of luxury vehicles. She wasn't all that surprised though, and LA was similar, depending on the neighborhood.

Millie's was busy, but they were seated immediately at a hightop table in the bar. Lauren could see the dunes and the ocean from their table, and she knew she'd picture this image months from now when she was missing Nantucket.

They both ordered margaritas and laughed when they put their food order in because it was exactly the same as the first time they'd been there with Eloise. They shared an order of guacamole, chips and salsa to start and Lauren got the scallop and bacon tacos and Hudson the steak ones.

"Not very original of us," she said.

Hudson grinned. "If I find something I like, I prefer to stick with it."

Lauren met his eyes and smiled. "I do, too."

The night was magical and went by much too fast. They finished eating and ordered another round of margaritas and a dessert to share. Not because they were especially hungry for it, but because they needed an excuse to linger. Neither of them wanted the evening to end. They had such a good time and there was never a lull in the conversation. They sometimes found themselves finishing each other's sentences and laughing about it.

Finally, though, it was time to go. And Lauren was leaving the next morning. It would be a long day, with several flights to get back to the West Coast.

It was a perfect night, but as much as she loved the idea of dating Hudson, Lauren didn't see how they'd be able to sustain a real relationship now that she was leaving. When Hudson pulled the car into the driveway at the inn, they kissed for a while and neither of them wanted to stop, but it didn't make sense to take it any further.

"I wish I had more time here," Lauren said.

"I hate that you have to leave. But we can find a way to make it work. Maybe you can come back for the Christmas Stroll weekend? And you never know, I might actually get on a plane and go west. I haven't been to LA in a long time."

Lauren laughed. "And you swore you'd never go back."

"Yeah, well. Things change. Now I have a good reason to go back." He leaned in and kissed her again. When he kissed her like that, he made her think it might actually be possible for them to be together. But she knew it didn't really make sense if they could only see each other every few months.

"If you meet someone you want to date, you should do it," she said. "Because we really don't know if this will work or when we'll actually see each other again."

He frowned. "I don't want to see anyone else. I know I should probably tell you the same thing—to go on dates if you want to." He kissed her again, very gently, before saying, "I hate the idea of you dating anyone else. I'm not going to lie."

She met his eyes and smiled. "Well, at the moment, you are the only person I'm dating. And I'm not thinking of anyone else or eager to meet anyone else."

"Excellent! We're on the same page, then."

Lauren laughed. "I really had a great time tonight. Thank you for dinner."

He walked her to the front door, and they kissed again before she went inside.

"Text me tomorrow when you get home. I'll miss you," Hudson said softly.

"I will. I'll miss you, too."

CHAPTER FIFTY-THREE

Lauren didn't sleep well. She never did the night before a flight. Though she usually woke up easily on her own, she still set two alarms on her phone to make sure she'd get up early. She had time to grab breakfast if she went down as soon as it started, at eight. She'd packed the night before after Hudson brought her home. She was tired but wide awake and tossed and turned most of the night.

So when she woke, she was still tired. But she perked up after a shower. She changed into black yoga pants and a t-shirt and sweatshirt. She liked to dress comfortably for long flights. She brought her luggage downstairs with her and went into the dining room. Lisa was there and was pouring herself a cup of coffee. She had a plate of food already and smiled when she saw Lauren.

"Oh, good. I was hoping I'd see you before you headed out today."

Lauren quickly made herself a plate of eggs, potatoes,

and melon and poured a mug of coffee. She joined Lisa at the round table.

"Rhett's still sleeping, so I don't think he'll be down before you go." Lisa picked up her mug of coffee and took a sip. "I hope your summer went the way you'd hoped it would?"

Lauren wasn't sure if Lisa was referring to the show or her personal life. "It's been a great summer. Went by much too fast. We won't know for sure, until the editing is all done, but I think it's going to be a good show."

Lisa's eyes lit up. "Any last-minute drama that I don't know about?"

Lauren laughed and filled her on the Billy-Katy-Sami situation.

Lisa shook her head. "What was he thinking? I thought he and Katy looked so cute together."

"I was hoping it would work out, for both their sakes. I wanted to believe Billy when he said wouldn't do anything like that again." Lauren explained her history with Billy.

She looked sympathetic. "That must have been hard for you, at least at first, to have to work with him?"

"It was still kind of fresh then, so it wasn't easy to see him again. But I knew there was no way I'd ever take him back, so I just focused on work. I thought it might be possible that he'd behave and settle down with Katy. But it's either not in him or he's just not ready yet."

"Could be a little of both. He doesn't sound like anyone I'd want my girls or anyone I knew to date, though. Now, what about you and that cute guy with the camera? Hunter was it?"

"Hudson. He's a good friend. We went to dinner last night at Millie's."

Lisa raised an eyebrow. "Just a friend?"

"Well, there's definitely an attraction. And it was a date. Hudson wants to keep dating, but I don't know how that could work. The earliest that I'm likely to be back here is next year if the show is picked up. And maybe in early December for the Stroll."

"Oh, you really should try to come then. It's such a magical time here. Downtown looks straight out of a Hallmark movie—especially if we get a little snow."

Lauren smiled. "It sounds wonderful."

"Long-distance relationships can work. I'll keep my fingers crossed for you both."

"Thank you." Lauren appreciated Lisa's encouraging words. She hugged her goodbye when she was ready to head to the airport and said she hoped to see her in December.

It was depressing at first to be back in LA. Lauren missed waking up to the sound of the waves on the beach. She missed breakfast at the inn with Lisa. And she missed seeing Hudson every day. But still, the next two months flew by as she was busy with post-production editing. It was going well and she and Eloise were excited about how the season was shaping up. They had all the cast back in to do individual commentary for different scenes and it was fun to see them all again, even Billy. He was as charming as ever, but it was in a purely friendly way, and she was fine being friends with Billy, now. He'd always been likable, just not a good boyfriend. He was dating someone new now, a pretty young actress, and he was sure that she was the one.

Lauren still wasn't sure about the long-distance thing with Hudson. They texted daily and talked several times a week, but it wasn't the same as seeing him in person. She'd been home for two months now and it felt like she was never going to see him again. She knew he was busy with a new project that wasn't going to end until early December, and it was going to be hard for him to get away before then.

She was feeling a little nervous, too, as she didn't have a new project lined up for when she finished edits. She wouldn't know for at least another six months or so if they were getting a second season for *Nantucket Influence*, and she wanted to get her next job firmed up as soon as possible. She'd talked to her agent earlier that day and supposedly there was something new coming—she was waiting on a call with more details, so hopefully Lauren would hear more in a week or so.

She'd just arrived home, and was surprised that she hadn't heard from Hudson all day. He usually texted her in the morning or on his lunch break. They'd last talked a few days ago, and she'd told him she was concerned about finding something new. He knew what that was like.

"I'm sure something good will turn up. Is it slowing down much, or are you still working crazy hours?"

"Well, that's one good thing. As of this week, we're less busy and I'm out the door by five now, which is nice."

"I have a couple of long days this week, but it should be better by Thursday. Will you be around Thursday night?" They usually FaceTimed a few times a week.

"Yes, I'll talk to you then."

CHAPTER FIFTY-FOUR

They agreed to talk Thursday at six, which was nine on East Coast time. At a few minutes before six, Lauren got a text message from Hudson asking if they could push it to seven. She figured he must have had to work late and didn't think anything of it. She heated up some soup and changed into her most comfy pair of sweats and her Nantucket sweatshirt. She wore it constantly, and it reminded her of summer and made her feel closer to Hudson.

She finished her soup, put the dirty dishes in the dishwasher and settled in on her sofa to watch TV. At a few minutes before seven, she was surprised by a knock at the door. She wasn't expecting anyone, so she peeked through a side window and was shocked to see Hudson standing on her doorstep.

She swung the door open, and he grinned and handed her a bouquet of flowers. She pulled him into a hug, followed by a welcome kiss.

"What are you doing here? I thought we were doing a FaceTime call."

Hudson had an overnight bag with him and set it down by the door. He smiled mischievously. "I never said it would be a call. You just assumed. I thought it would be fun to surprise you."

"I'm definitely surprised. How long can you stay?" Lauren led him inside and they sat in the living room, next to each other, on her sofa.

"I have a return flight on Sunday. And I'm booked at a local hotel. My rental car is out front. We finished up our project yesterday and I'm starting planning on a new project on Monday." He smiled. "And I'm not just here to visit. I have a proposal to offer. Did your agent mention that something new might be coming in?"

Lauren nodded. "She said she'd know more specifics next week."

"I talked to her earlier and said I'd like to give you the details in person."

Lauren's heart raced. "What is it?"

"Would you be interested in working on a non-reality project? Cami bought the rights to develop Kate's mystery, and we are producing it as a limited series for Netflix. We'd like you to start with us in November if you're interested. It should wrap by the time filming starts for season two of *Nantucket Influence*, if there is one. If not, there will likely be other projects."

Lauren felt overwhelmed with happiness. It was an exciting opportunity and a chance to expand her experience and work with Hudson. It was pretty much a dream come true.

"I would love to do that. Thank you and please thank Cami for me. I am so excited. I'll need to find a place to stay, though." She wanted her own place. Things were too new for her to consider moving in with Hudson, not yet.

"I have a lead for you on that. A friend of my mother's goes to Florida in the winter and is leaving mid-October and she'll be back in June. What she's asking for rent seems pretty reasonable." He mentioned the amount, and Lauren's jaw dropped. It was about half what she was paying for rent in LA. If she sublet her place, she'd actually come out ahead financially. And if *Nantucket Influence* was renewed, they'd put her up at the inn again.

"That sounds too good to be true. Why is it so low?"

"Well, it's nothing fancy, just a small two-bedroom cape house, and it's inland, not on the water. But the demand for winter rentals is nothing like summer. It's always much less. My mother texted me a few pictures."

He opened his phone, found the pictures, and Lauren fell in love. The cottage was adorable. It was a typical Cape Cod-style home with weathered shingles, flower boxes and baby blue window shutters. There was also a small patio in the back with rose bushes all around it. Inside was light and bright with polished hardwood floors and soft, beachy tones of cream, blue and gray. The kitchen was small but had everything she'd need and it was fully furnished and the living room looked like the Pottery Barn catalog come to life with a cozy sofa and matching chair with white slipcovers that gave it a shabby chic vibe.

"If she'll have me, I'll happily take it," Lauren said.

Hudson grinned. "I'll let my mother know. So, do you forgive me for showing up uninvited?"

Lauren leaned over and kissed him. "Totally forgiven. I'm so excited that you're here. And I can't wait to go back to Nantucket and work with you."

CHAPTER FIFTY-FIVE

"What are you cooking again? That smells amazing?" Jason asked. He'd just walked in the door and Anna was arranging the flowers he'd brought in a vase. Smith always got so excited when Jason arrived. He jumped up and down until Jason scooped him up and hugged him.

"Lasagna with meatballs. I made it last night, and it's just heating up now." It was her best recipe, the one thing that she never had to worry about not turning out well. And it was great for company because she could make it ahead of time and it actually tasted better the next day.

Jason pulled her into his arms once she had the flowers in the vase and had set them in the middle of her kitchen island. He kissed her thoroughly and when she pulled back, her eyes met his and she saw so much love and warmth there that it took her breath away. It was almost November, and they'd been dating since they both left the show. Two weeks later, he'd invited her for Sunday

343

dinner with his family and she'd been a bit intimidated, but he'd assured her they'd welcome her and make her feel comfortable. And they did. Jason had the kind of family that Anna had always dreamed of and they welcomed her with open arms. She'd been back several times for Sunday dinner since and always looked forward to it.

She still couldn't believe that her relationship with Jason was so solid and so easy. She'd never been in a relationship like this, where she could totally be herself and where her partner was a supportive best friend as well as a romantic one. Jason's touch made her melt, and she was just happy being around him, even if they were just grocery shopping or taking Smith for a walk. She missed him when she didn't see him for a few days and they talked or texted daily.

Two weeks ago, Jason told her that he loved her for the first time. They were in Central Park with Smith and had just sat on a park bench to rest for a few minutes. It was a lazy Sunday, and they'd spent the weekend together, sleeping late, having a delicious brunch and then the walk in the park. He'd taken her hand, looked in her eyes, and told her he loved her. And she'd felt a rush of happiness and told him that she felt the same.

Anna glanced at her watch. Katy and her new boyfriend, Sean, were due in about fifteen minutes. Sean was one of Jason's best friends. He'd done several tours as a Marine until an injury sidelined him and now he was still in the Marines but working a desk job. He'd mentioned a month or so ago that he thought Sean and

Katy might be a good fit. Katy was a little hesitant at first. She hated the idea of a setup, and she was still not quite over Billy. But she agreed to meet up as a group for drinks.

And she and Sean hit it off immediately. Sean was outgoing and fun-loving, and he adored Katy. Things were going really well with them and they often went out with them. Anna was excited to have them over. They usually went out to dinner and this was fun for a change. She'd picked up a few bottles of good red wine and opened one and poured two glasses, and handed one to Jason.

"Cheers!" She lifted her glass to tap against his, as they often did, to celebrate the beginning of a fun night out. Jason had a funny look on his face, though. He lifted his glass, tapped hers, and took a sip. But then he reached into his pocket and got down on one knee.

"Anna, some people might think this is fast, but I think when you know who you want to spend the rest of your life with, there's no good reason to wait." He grinned. "I bought this the day I told you I loved you. We don't have to get married immediately, but I want you to know how I feel and I hope you feel the same. I can't imagine my life without you in it. Will you marry me?" His words came out in a rush, and while he took her by surprise with the proposal, she didn't hesitate.

"Of course I will!" Her eyes filled with happy tears as he slid the gorgeous princess cut diamond onto her finger. He pulled her into his arms and they kissed for so long that they almost didn't hear the doorbell. They broke apart and Anna went to open the door. Katy and Sean came in. Sean handed Anna a bottle of cabernet and Katy had a pan of brownies.

"They have a swirl of peanut butter in them," Katy said as she set the brownies on the counter.

"What can I help you with? It already smells amazing in here," she said.

"Nothing, help yourself to a glass of wine. We just opened the bottle. I'm just going to put the garlic bread in the oven to toast and we can eat once it's ready." Earlier, she'd sliced the loaf, slathered garlic butter on both halves, and wrapped it in tin foil so the outside would be crusty and the inside warm and buttery.

Katy hadn't noticed the ring yet, which didn't surprise Anna. Katy almost never noticed if people were wearing rings or not. It wasn't until Anna took a plate of sliced cheese out of the refrigerator and set it on the island that Sean noticed the ring and high-fived Jason. "Congratulations, man."

"Thank you!" Jason was beaming.

Katy looked confused, then followed Sean's gaze and gasped when she saw the ring.

"You're engaged! Congratulations! Let me get a closer look."

Anna lifted her hand and Katy pulled it even closer. "It's absolutely gorgeous." She turned to Jason. "Well done!"

He laughed. "Thank you."

"When do you plan to get married? Do you know?" Katy asked.

Anna smiled. "We haven't gotten that far. I don't think we're in a rush."

"I'd marry her tomorrow, but I'm okay waiting for as long as it takes, so Anna can have the wedding of her dreams," Jason said.

"The wedding of my dreams is just me marrying you and I'm fine with the town hall. I've dreamed of being happily married—not having a big, fancy wedding. I kind of hate being the center of attention like that," she admitted.

Jason looked stunned. "Really? I just assumed you'd want something big and fancy and photographable."

Anna shook her head. "I don't need to share my wedding online. It would probably be good for my business, but I'm okay with that."

Jason nodded. "Town hall it is, then. My mother will want to kill me, but we can always have a party after, just a small celebration at her house, maybe?"

Anna smiled. "That sounds perfect to me. My parents won't be thrilled either. I'm sure they'd rather have some formal affair at a Connecticut country club, but they also know that's not me."

"Well, of course we'll include them. Do you think they'll come to Brooklyn?" Jason asked.

"Probably. They'll whine a bit about not having a wedding they can brag about, but they do love me, so I'm sure they will come."

"All right then. It looks like this will be a celebratory dinner. I'll call my mother tomorrow and make her day," Jason said.

They all lifted their glasses and Anna said, "To love!" Jason pulled her in for a quick kiss.

When the food was ready, they filled their plates and gathered around her small dining room table. As Anna gazed around the table at her friends and at Jason, the love of her life, she felt so much happiness. And she was so glad that she'd decided to step out of her comfort zone and do the *Nantucket Influence* show. She and Katy had grown closer as friends and she'd met Jason and her life had changed in ways she never would have imagined were possible.

CHAPTER FIFTY-SIX

Lauren arranged for her apartment to be sublet to a traveling nurse. It was all done through an agency and it seemed like the best solution, as traveling nurses usually signed three-month contracts at a time and they preferred furnished units like Lauren's.

She couldn't wait to get back to Nantucket and to see Hudson again. They'd had a wonderful long weekend when he surprised her. But it went by much too fast and it had been almost a month since they'd seen each other.

She flew on an overnight flight and landed in Nantucket around ten in the morning. Hudson had offered to pick her up, but she told him she'd see him later that night instead. She wanted to get settled into her new place first. She picked up her rental car and, less than fifteen minutes later, pulled in the driveway for the cottage. Lauren had spoken to the woman that owned the cottage by phone and since she was already in Florida, Lauren stopped by Hudson's mother's house first to pick up the keys. His mother seemed happy to see her and gave her a warm hug.

"I'm so glad this worked out. Jamie is glad to have someone we know take care of her place for the winter and there's such a shortage of affordable housing." She handed Lauren the keys. "And I know Hudson is happy to have you back on the island."

Lauren smiled. "I'm very excited to be back and looking forward to working with him again."

She was much more excited to just see Hudson, but she didn't want to get into that with his mother. She suspected she already knew, anyway.

"Well, I'm sure I'll see you again soon. I'm off to check out a new yoga class downtown."

Lauren left and ten minutes later, pulled into the driveway for the cottage. It looked just as cute outside as it did in Hudson's photos. She'd only brought one huge suitcase and wheeled it to the door and stepped inside. And instantly felt at home.

The cottage was light-filled with lots of windows and it was so cozy. She brought her suitcase upstairs and into the master bedroom, which was spacious with a skylight and an ensuite bathroom. The other bedroom was smaller but would be fine for either a guest bedroom or office. It had a queen-sized bed and a desk.

Lauren took a hot shower, then crawled into bed to take a nap. She was exhausted and hadn't been able to really sleep well on the plane. She slept hard for a few hours and woke around one feeling well rested and hungry. There was no food in the house, so she went to

Stop and Shop and stocked up on groceries, including cold cut turkey. She made herself a sandwich when she got home, then unpacked and put everything away. She'd also stopped by the wine shop and picked up a bottle of prosecco for a glass of celebratory bubbly when Hudson arrived. He'd said he was going to bring a pizza with him, which sounded perfect to her. She didn't feel like going anywhere yet.

Hudson knocked on the front door at six sharp, holding a box of pizza and carrying a bottle of red wine. She took both and set them down on the kitchen counter and then went into Hudson's arms and welcomed him properly. He kissed her passionately. It felt so good to be wrapped in his arms. When they finally ended the kiss, he pulled back and smiled. "I'll be right back."

He went out to his car and returned a moment later, holding something that took her breath away. It was the painting she'd thought was so stunning when they went to Kristen's show—the one with the dark sky and the cottage overlooking the ocean. It seemed full of possibility and it really spoke to her. But she knew he'd wanted it too.

He handed it to her. "It's a house-warming gift."

"You got that for me? I thought you loved it, too." She was so touched.

He nodded. "I did. I went back a few days later and bought it. But every time I looked at it, I thought of you and how much you loved it, too. I bought myself a similar one from the collection. I knew that I wanted to give this to you, but wasn't sure about the timing. I figured I'd either send it out west if the deal with Kate didn't work out—but fortunately it did, and here you are."

"Here I am," Lauren said softly. "Thank you. This is such a thoughtful gift. I'm so happy to be back here. I'm grateful for the chance to work with you and Cami, but I'm mostly just happy to be able to see you again. I missed you."

"I missed you too, so much."

Lauren opened the prosecco and poured them each a glass and they toasted to being together again and to new beginnings with the film project and their relationship.

"How do you like the cottage?" Hudson asked.

"I love it. When I stepped inside, I felt like I'd come home. That probably sounds silly." It had been such a strong feeling, though. She'd never felt that way about her LA apartment.

Hudson smiled and put his glass of wine down. He wrapped his arms around her and pulled her in close, and kissed her. "I don't think it is silly at all. Nantucket is your home now."

EPILOGUE

O*ne month later, Nantucket Stroll weekend*

"I'm so glad you're not just visiting for Nantucket Stroll," Lisa said. It was Nantucket Stroll weekend and Lauren and Hudson had just arrived at Lisa Hodges' annual Christmas open house. Lisa had told her that she held the party every year and it was a tradition of sorts that people stopped in before heading downtown to participate in the Stroll activities. Lauren had heard so much about this magical Nantucket Stroll and was looking forward to walking along the cobblestone streets of downtown Nantucket and visiting the shops that were all decorated for the holiday. There were Christmas cookie decorating tables and carolers, and Santa would be making an appearance as well.

The snow had started falling as they pulled up to Lisa's house and swirled around them as they walked to her front door. There was already a good crowd gathered and there was so much food. The kitchen island was overflowing with chips and dips, shrimp cocktail, spiced nuts, stuffed mushrooms, lobster quiche of course, cheese and crackers and more. Lauren accepted a glass of a bubbly wine and sherbet punch that Kate had made. It was sweet and delicious, and Lauren sipped it slowly as they walked around and chatted with everyone.

Angela arrived and she looked great. She was showing quite a bit now, and had a cute baby bump. Lauren filled a plate and sat down with Angela to catch up while they ate. Hudson had wandered off and was talking with Kate's husband, Jack.

"How are you feeling?" Lauren asked.

"So good. My energy is back and I'm still working and I think keeping active is helping. Did I tell you we found out it's going to be a girl?"

"No! That's awesome. Do you have any names in mind yet?"

Angela nodded. "I like Charlotte and Charlie for short. Philippe likes Olivia, but he says he likes Charlotte, too."

"Both names are cute."

"How is the filming going? Is it so different after the reality shows?" Angela asked.

"It is. I'm learning a lot. It's such a great story. I'm excited for it to be on Netflix."

Kate walked over and heard what Lauren said.

"I still can't believe it's going to be on Netflix. I started to think it wasn't going to go anywhere, so it's amazing that it ended up with Cami and is filming here."

"Is it true that you are in one of the scenes? Kristen mentioned something about that to me," Angela said.

Kate laughed. "Yes. That was so fun. I attended a fancy cocktail party and got to dress up. I'm just in the background and think I'm maybe on screen for a few seconds, if that."

"That's so cool. We'll watch for you when it airs," Angela said.

Kay and Walter walked in, and Kay walked over to say hello.

"Lisa told me you were back on the island. How exciting that you're here to film a new show. Are you happy to be back?" Kay asked.

Lauren nodded. "So happy. It's great to be back here."

"How are the other folks doing from the show? Have you kept in touch with any of them?" she asked.

"Yes. I've seen all of them and keep in touch with a few of the cast, mostly Anna, who has filled me in on what's going on with some of the others. She says that Suzanne and Noah are still dating. And she and Jason are engaged!"

"Well, isn't that something? How's that Katy girl doing? The one that dated your charming ex?" Kay said it sarcastically and Lauren laughed.

"Katy is great. Anna and Jason actually set her up with his friend, Sean, and they are getting along really well. Honey and Brett are actually expecting, which is exciting for them. Oh, and Sami is going on a solo trip to India to study Buddhism and find herself. She will, of course, be documenting everything online."

Kay shook her head. "Of course she will. I'm happy for Katy though and the others, too."

Two hours later, Lauren and Hudson left to head downtown and experience the Nantucket Stroll. It was cold and Lauren was bundled up in a long ivory wool coat and matching cranberry cashmere hat and gloves. The snow fell softly as they walked. It was just enough to look pretty and add a festive dusting of white to the ground.

Lauren had to agree with everyone that told her how magical the Christmas Stroll was. All the shops were decorated, and many were giving out samples of chocolates or mulled cider and there were all kinds of holiday events happening. They stopped by the cookie decorating table and each decorated a gingerbread cookie and walked around eating it.

Later that night, back at Lauren's cottage, she and Hudson snuggled on the living room sofa as they watched a movie and enjoyed the warmth of the real wood fireplace that was glowing merrily.

Just when Lauren didn't think she could be any happier, Hudson told her he loved her for the first time.

"I'm so glad that you're here, and there's nowhere I'd rather be than with you. I love you, Lauren."

"I love you too. And I feel the same. I love Nantucket and it feels like home, but that's mostly because I'm with you."

"How would you like to stay here permanently? And make Nantucket your forever home?" His eyes shone and Lauren's heart fluttered.

He stood and then got down on one knee. "I know it hasn't been long, but you're the one, Lauren. When you left to go back to LA, I missed you so much. I missed seeing you every day. Now that you're back, I've realized how important you are and how much I love you. Will you marry me?" He held out the most delicate, beautiful ring. It had a platinum band, and the design was a vintage antique, with one big round diamond surrounded by a halo of smaller ones.

Lauren just stared at the ring, stunned into silence.

Hudson continued talking, "It was my grandmother's ring. If you don't like it, I can get something else."

"No, it's perfect. It's lovely. Yes, of course I'll marry you." She was shocked by the proposal as it was unexpected, but it also felt so right.

Hudson gently slipped the ring onto her finger and it fit perfectly. He grinned. "I borrowed one of your rings and had it sized to make sure it fit."

Lauren stared at her hand. The ring sparkled in the firelight. "I can't believe we're engaged."

"We can take our time getting married. I'm not in any hurry. I just wanted you to know how I felt and to make the commitment."

"I'm not in a hurry, either. Eventually, we'll plan something. I just want to enjoy being engaged to you, too."

She glanced at the window where the streetlight illuminated the snowflakes that were still coming down.

"Everyone was right. Christmas Stroll on Nantucket really is magical."

Thank you so much for reading! I hope you enjoyed the latest story in this series.

What's next for me?

The Christmas Inn, which releases at the end of September. I am so excited for you to read this book. If you enjoy Hallmark Christmas movies, this has that kind of a feel—so much Christmas, set on Cape Cod, in Chatham. It's a multi-generational story with three women, set at a cozy inn during the holidays.

Did you already read **Bookshop by the Bay** and **The Seaside Sisters?** Both are also set in Chatham, on Cape Cod. All three are standalone but a few characters visit in each book and the bookshop is there, too.

I also have a friendly Facebook group where we chat about my books, movies, food, pets-it's a great group. I often share early excerpts there and ask advice sometimes. Look for the Pamela Kelley Readers Facebook Group!

ACKNOWLEDGMENTS

Thank you for Jane Barbagallo and Taylor Hall for reading early, as well as Laura Horah and Amy Petrowich for editing and proofreading.

A huge thank you to the head of one of my favorite reality shows (who wished to be anonymous). Our conversation was so helpful and I appreciate the time you took with my many questions and followup questions. Any errors about running a show like this, are my own.

ABOUT THE AUTHOR

Pamela Kelley is a *USA Today* and *Wall Street Journal* best-selling author of women's fiction, family sagas, and suspense, such as *The Restaurant* and *The Hotel*. Readers often describe her books as feel-good reads with people you'd want as friends. She lives in a historic seaside town near Cape Cod. She has always been an avid reader of women's fiction, romance, mysteries, thrillers and cook books. There's also a good chance you might get hungry when you read her books as she is a foodie, and occasionally shares a recipe or two.

Made in the USA
Columbia, SC
01 September 2024

41418613R00221